Joyeux Winery was midrow on the first aisle. The winery flag, a golden fleur-de-lis on a background of royal blue and burgundy, fluttered on the roof. The booths were covered with temporary weatherproof curtains to protect the contents between now and the festival. I pushed the corner open with my shoulder and turned to enter the tent, box first. The curtain closed behind me, leaving me in the dark. With my hands full, I couldn't grab the flashlight on my keys and I crept to the tables just ahead of me. As I felt the edge of the table with my thigh, something exploded against the back of my head. The pain was blinding, and I could hear glass breaking as the world tipped away from under my feet. I dropped the box, grabbed the edge of the table and landed on my knees. Through the roar in my ears, I heard a soft laugh. I tried to concentrate, but my eyes closed. A shove into my shoulder ripped the table from my grip and I fell to the ground.

Just before the world went black I heard a soft whisper. "Just like a bad penny, always turning up in the wrong place. Bad, bad Penny."

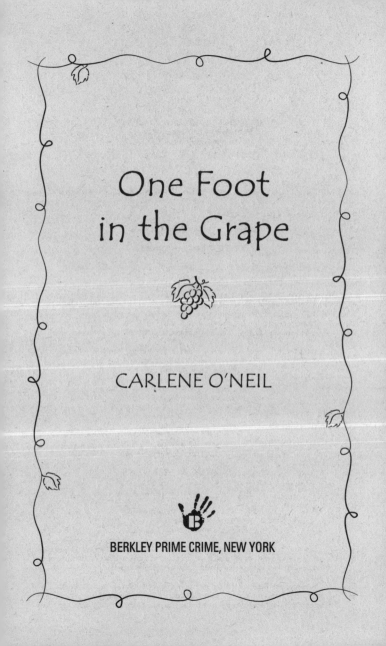

One Foot
in the Grape

CARLENE O'NEIL

BERKLEY PRIME CRIME, NEW YORK

THE BERKLEY PUBLISHING GROUP
Published by the Penguin Group
Penguin Group (USA) LLC
375 Hudson Street, New York, New York 10014

USA • Canada • UK • Ireland • Australia • New Zealand • India • South Africa • China

penguin.com

A Penguin Random House Company

ONE FOOT IN THE GRAPE

A Berkley Prime Crime Book / published by arrangement with the author

Berkley Prime Crime Books are published by The Berkley Publishing Group.
BERKLEY® PRIME CRIME and the PRIME CRIME logo are trademarks of
Penguin Group (USA) LLC.

For information, address: The Berkley Publishing Group,
a division of Penguin Group (USA) LLC,
375 Hudson Street, New York, New York 10014.

ISBN: 978-0-425-27401-9

PUBLISHING HISTORY
Berkley Prime Crime mass-market edition / May 2015

PRINTED IN THE UNITED STATES OF AMERICA

10 9 8 7 6 5 4 3 2 1

Cover illustration by Robert Crawford.
Cover design by Danielle Abbiate.
Interior text design by Kelly Lipovich.

Acknowledgments

I'd like to thank Dawn Dowdle, my agent, for your help and belief in this book. When the call came in, your excitement matched my own. Also, thank you to my editor, Robin Barletta, for taking this book and giving it such a great home.

Finally, love and thanks to my family and friends who gave me encouragement and support along the way. You knew I could do it long before I did, and I'm grateful.

One

A SIMPLE house rule, ignored once, and I end up with a dead body on my hands. Actually more than one, but I'm getting ahead of myself.

The rule is, never answer the front door. I learned growing up it was usually a tourist. The house, with its stone walls and copper roof aged to a green patina, drew visitors toting cameras. While my aunt loved guests at the winery, she protected our privacy at home, and had planted screen trees years ago. Now, I don't get many visitors, and I like it that way. The house is invisible from the street, flanked by my vineyards, rows of lush green soldiers standing tall and straight, shoulder to shoulder. Visitors have to manage the drive through my grape barricade. The occasional knock on the door first thing Saturday morning means someone has gone the distance. More often than not it's an attempt to sell me something, usually magazine subscriptions or membership to a church that doesn't let you drink.

I don't have time for magazines, and I wouldn't join a church that doesn't let me drink. After all, I own a winery. Until recently the knocking went unanswered. My niece Hayley, new to the household, didn't know the rules.

"Antonia Martinelli's here." She lifted her eyebrows and disappeared down the hall.

Terrific. I'd rather buy magazines.

Antonia's a distant relative, my aunt Monique's cousin. They'd been close and, toward the end, Antonia had made it easier for my aunt and ultimately easier for me. I was grateful to her, although, to be honest, she'd never been one of my favorite people. When I was young she'd sneak up and grab us for playing in her vineyards. Used to spook the hell out of me.

The tap of her cane down the hall announced her arrival before Antonia stepped into the room. Her silver hair was swept up. It glinted in the morning sun as she stepped over Nanook, my malamute. As she passed by the faintest scent of lavender tickled my nose. She stopped at the armchair that held my gray tabby, Petite Syrah.

"Move." Antonia pointed the cane toward the floor.

Syrah opened her green eyes, rolled to the edge of the seat and, with a surprisingly loud thump, landed on the ground and walked to the door with as much dignity as she could muster.

"Penelope, that cat is overweight, and why would you let it up on the furniture? I hope I don't get cat hair all over me."

Good. Maybe she wouldn't sit and I could get back to my quiet Saturday morning. Too bad I had on my standard weekend sweatsuit. White. Antonia's ability to reduce me to the awkward teen I'd once been wasn't helped by my resembling the Michelin tire man. I stayed seated on the couch, gathered my own dignity, and turned to face her.

"Hi, Antonia. Want coffee?"

She looked at the clock on my desk, then at her wristwatch, as if to confirm the time. "No. I had mine hours ago."

She eyed the photos on the side table and picked up the one closest to her. It was a black and white of her and my aunt as teens in the vineyards. Knee-deep in grapes, they smiled into the camera.

"I remember when this was taken. We were so young then." She set the picture down and turned to me. "I can see Monique in you. You've got the blonde hair and you've inherited your aunt's good skin, but you've aged."

Gee, thanks. "I haven't lived here for twenty years."

"What are you now, forty?"

"No. I'm still in my midthirties." Okay, late thirties.

She eyed my legs, curled up under me. "You get your height from Monique too. Enjoy it while you can. Soon you'll start to shrink."

Wow. The church folk were looking pretty good right about now.

"Your aunt would be glad you've decided to keep the winery. Glad you decided to quit the city and come home."

"Me too." Six months earlier I hadn't been so sure. Antonia didn't need to know my return to Cypress Cove was prompted by my getting fired.

Antonia was once again focused on the picture and seemed lost in thought. She'd always looked the same to me, with her silver hair and black dresses. What could she want? She'd never come by before, not since I'd been back.

Something was different. She'd always exuded confidence,

but now she sat with her foot tapping, and she twisted a ring on her finger. There was a slight tremble in her hands as she folded and pressed them to her lap.

"Antonia?"

She looked away. "You're probably wondering why I'm here. The truth is, I need a favor."

Okay, this was a switch. Antonia never needed anything from anybody.

"Someone is sabotaging the wines at Martinelli. I want you to help me find out who it is." She got up and walked to the window. "Don't suggest I talk with my children. The damage is being done by someone with access to the barrels." She reached out to hold on to the windowsill. "It could very well be one of them."

While I searched for an appropriate response, Antonia turned to face me. "First time I've ever seen you speechless. Say something, for heaven's sake."

I took a second. "What makes you think someone is sabotaging you?"

"Martinelli Winery doesn't make the kind of mistakes I'm finding. Last year there were a couple of bad barrels. This year there are dozens."

I relaxed and leaned back on the couch. "Wait a minute, Antonia. I've only been back at the winery for a short time, but I grew up in this business. Some years are just better than others."

Antonia moved over to the French doors and looked out at the grapes, full and ripe in the autumn sun. "You aren't listening. One barrel is fine, another ruined. One is excellent, the next rancid. It's random. It's deliberate."

I saw her point. Problems happened to an entire crop, not random barrels.

"You need to go to the police."

"I don't want the publicity. It's bad enough people think our standards are slipping. If my customers suspect we won't be able to deliver our orders, they'll start pulling deliveries. I want you to help me." She paused. "Monique would want it too."

It wasn't fair for her to use my aunt as leverage, although I had to agree with her. Martinelli Winery was a mainstay of the wine industry in this part of California.

"Even if I agreed, why me?"

"I can't. If my family or employees are responsible they're already watching me. No one will notice you, a neighbor and fellow vintner. Frankly, you're the best choice I had."

"I won't let that go to my head. What would you want me to do?"

"Listen. Watch. Find out who the culprit is and tell me." Antonia looked at my desk, completely free of papers or work, and even I could see the light layer of dust. My camera and closed laptop were the only items on its surface. "Actually, I'm surprised you aren't more curious. After all, didn't you do that type of thing at the paper?"

I nodded. "Investigative photojournalism."

"There. You see? You must like prying. You should be used to watching people. Asking questions."

It's true. I'd worked for the *San Francisco Press* and been paid to do what I do best: stick my nose into other people's business.

That ended six months ago, when my editor wanted to digitally add spectators to a photo I took at a riot. I refused, assuming we were in the business of accurately reporting the news. I guess I was pretty vocal about it and, in the end, my boss and I reached an agreement. He agreed I could refuse to alter my work, and I agreed I was fired.

I rode my indignation right out of there and into every other paper for miles around. It didn't take long to realize computer software had changed photojournalism forever. Selling papers was more important than accuracy. Beyond that, I'd been labeled as rigid and inflexible, somebody difficult to work with.

Antonia waited patiently for an answer, which wasn't like her. It was strange the wines were in the barrels before the problems turned up. It didn't make sense. I'd begun to pick at the puzzle, trying to make the pieces fit.

Okay, I admit it. I'm nosy, I'm intrusive and, yes, I was curious. "Before I agree to help you, is there anything else you can tell me?"

Antonia took a deep breath. "About six months ago I began to notice little items missing around the main winery. Things out of place, paperwork moved, that kind of thing. At first I didn't think much about it. Then about a month ago, someone broke into the winery office."

"Did they take anything of value?"

"A few hundred dollars and the account ledger, but that was it. Then last week a noise woke me around midnight. It came from the attic. I put on my robe and went out into the hall, but by the time I got to the stairway the house was quiet again. When I went up there the following morning, things weren't as I'd left them, but it was impossible to tell if anything was missing."

"Do you think it has something to do with the ruined wine?"

"I don't know." The hand that held the cane trembled slightly, but her voice was strong and her gaze steady.

"Martinelli Winery is the legacy of my family. If someone's trying to hurt it, or its reputation, I will stop them."

I believed her. If I didn't help her, she'd pursue it without me.

"Okay, let's see what we can find out. On our own." I stood and looked at her.

"Excellent, Penelope." Antonia breathed deeply. Her shoulders relaxed. "Where do we start?"

"Please call me Penny."

"You've been Penelope to me your entire life. I'm too old to start calling you something else."

Right. "Who has access to the house, the winery?"

"I've thought of that. You know Marvin."

"Your manager."

"Yes. He's often at the house, usually in the library and kitchen."

I was surprised. "The kitchen? He eats with the family?"

Antonia sniffed. "Of course not. He's allowed to come to the kitchen and have the cook fix him a tray to take back to his apartment. Certainly on most days he comes to the house for one reason or another."

She turned to look out the window. "I believe you know Todd. He's in charge of the tasting room. Then there are my three children. Do you remember them?"

"Not really. I went to public schools."

"True, they were gone most of the time. Francesca is a few years older than you, and then there's my son, Stephen."

"Stephen must be about my age, but I don't know if I'd recognize him. I remember Chantal, though." Chantal was Antonia's youngest, and she'd stolen a boyfriend from every girl in town, including me.

"Why would they do something to hurt the winery?"

Antonia stamped her cane. Even with a rubber tip, that was going to leave a mark. "That's what I want you to find out."

Good point. "Okay, that's five people. Does anyone else have access to both the winery office and the house?"

"Of course. Two of my children are married and I also have servants and part-time help at the winery."

"Let's start with the servants. Do they live in?"

"No." She turned to face the window and I had to strain to hear her next words. "No one but the family. And Marvin."

"So, if we assume the same person ransacked both the winery office and the attic—a big assumption, I understand— then for the moment we can focus our efforts on the people with access to the house at night." I looked at her. "Are you sure you don't want to tell the police about this?"

"Penelope, we've just established that someone intimately involved in the winery is trying to destroy it. Best case, it appears one of my employees is responsible. Going to the police, and the publicity that would ensue, is the very last thing I want."

There were steps in the hall and Hayley came through the doorway. "I'm heading to the office and wanted to say good-bye."

Antonia looked up from across the room, her brows creased. "Did you hear our conversation?"

"This is Hayley's home, Antonia. She's a grown woman and I won't allow you to speak to her that way."

I looked at Antonia and realized I was no longer intimidated by her. "I didn't ask you here. You came on your own. If you no longer want my help, then that's fine too."

Antonia raised her brow and paused. "Very well. You can

discuss the issue here, but please remember it's a private matter."

No kidding. I rolled my eyes at Hayley.

Antonia moved toward Hayley. "I'll walk to the office with you. I want to ask Connor when he plans on bringing in the rest of the harvest. Perhaps we can coordinate the temporary workers so neither of us gets behind."

Connor was the reason for any success my winery enjoyed. He'd had offers to manage other wineries, but stayed with my aunt because she gave him complete control of the vineyards, which is how it should be. He decided all of the day-to-day operations, from hiring the seasonal help to actually turning the grapes into wine. Connor came with an added bonus: he was great with tourists and visitors. I'd offered him the same arrangement when I'd returned to the winery and was grateful every day that he'd accepted.

"I can tell you when we're going to harvest," Hayley said.

"That's right. I forgot you're the assistant manager now. You can learn a lot from Connor. I want to talk to him about a couple of other things as well."

Antonia turned to me. "He's a fine man, about as good as they come."

"I know that. That's why he's my manager."

Antonia waved her hand. "I don't mean his skills as a manager. I mean as a man. He'd make a great catch for any single woman. Especially one recently back in town and not getting any younger."

Antonia playing matchmaker? "Thanks. Especially for the not-getting-any-younger comment, but I'm not interested."

"Don't take that tone with me, Penelope Lively. If you had any sense, you'd see Connor is about as good as they come. You'd do well to snatch him up and get him off the market before someone else does."

Running the winery was hectic enough without dating my manager. We got along great. That was enough.

"He's all yours, Antonia." I got a small but satisfying glimpse as the pink in her cheeks deepened.

"Don't listen to me, then. You never did." She moved toward the door. "I'll be off. We should talk again before the festival."

The Autumn Festival was two days of wine, food and judging the local wineries' best selections. For the first time, the smaller wineries were invited to participate.

"Your first year to compete. Are you ready?"

"We've been ready for weeks." I smiled.

"Your aunt would be proud."

I nodded, not trusting my voice. Hayley and Antonia walked down the back steps to the winery office.

The sun had come out early and burned away the coastal fog that settled almost every night. The day was bright and clear. I opened the window, leaned out and breathed in the morning air. Sugar in the grapes is highest in the fall, and the vineyards fill the valley with a spicy, sweet fragrance.

I ran my hand over Petite Syrah, curled once again in her armchair, silver-gray fur luxurious in the morning sun.

"She doesn't think you belong on the furniture."

Syrah pushed against my hand. I rubbed between her ears and stared out over the vineyards. If Martinelli Winery was in trouble, the entire central coast winery business would suffer, including our own humble efforts.

I picked up my camera. I'd always been fascinated with photography. If it was on film it was indisputable. At least it had been. Photo "enhancing" was done every day and without public knowledge. I was right to refuse to alter my work, but that didn't help with the loss of my career.

I was back at the winery, but I still found comfort in the same place I always found it: behind a camera lens. Now, though, the focus was landscape photography. Nobody asked me to alter my work and there was never a lack of subject matter. Grape leaves wore their autumn finery, the russets, yellows and purples as beautiful in their own way as any maple or elm. Those who believe California doesn't have seasonal color have never lived on a winery.

Syrah followed as I stepped out though the French doors and onto the back deck. She curled up and resumed her nap in the sun's warmth.

The arbor was heavy with pale yellow roses, the last of the season. I took a few shots and walked down the back steps to look out over the fields. Sunlight glimmered through the vines and warmed my face. The chaos of life in the city seemed far away. If ever there was a place free from malice, sheltered from the evils of the world, surely it was here.

Of course, I'd been wrong before.

Two

I WALKED back into the sunroom, took a seat at the desk and downloaded the photos onto my computer. When I finished, I walked down to the winery and spent the next hour taking one last look at the barrels. Weeks before, we'd rolled them outside and washed them, rinsing them with water and citric acid. Every barrel needed to be inspected for cracks and defects. Nothing scientific. You stick your head in each one and look around.

Hayley walked up beside me. "Thanks for defending me earlier, but I didn't hear the conversation. What's up with Antonia?"

"Trouble at her winery. The vintages have been bad and she thinks maybe it's being done on purpose."

Hayley nodded. "There's been talk their wines have been off lately. I've noticed it. The last time I had a Martinelli Chardonnay it was great, but the bottle before that wasn't drinkable. You think Marvin is slipping?"

"I can't believe that. He's impossible and has a mean streak, but he's extremely good at what he does."

"So if Marvin isn't losing his touch, could someone be doing it on purpose?"

"That's exactly what Antonia thinks. She asked me to help figure it out."

"Ha! A chance to be nosy. I'm sure you're dreading that." Hayley knew me too well. Busybody, meddler, snoop. I'd been called these and worse.

"If you don't have anything else to do, you can help me soak these barrels."

All the barrels, old and new, are "soaked up," which is simply filling them with water to swell the wood. This tightens the staves and ensures the barrels are leak-free.

"Let me grab the hose."

"The new ones come in tomorrow." I'd ordered some additional barrels of French oak. Like most wineries, we used both American and French oak. The American oak imparted a stronger bite to the finish of the wine. I liked it, although many people finished with just the French oak, which left the wine smoother and more buttery.

When we were finished I looked at my watch. "It's lunchtime. Want to grab a bite?"

"It's later than I thought, and I still need to load the truck. I'll grab something later. See you in a bit."

I returned to the house. The front door opened and footsteps sounded as Connor made his way down the hall. He had an apartment above the winery office but took his meals here.

"So, you talked to Antonia?"

He nodded. "She wanted to know about our inventory control."

"She didn't ask you about when you were bringing in the rest of the harvest?"

"Not a word." Connor poured a cup of coffee and sat down. "It would be a little odd for Antonia to ask about when to harvest. Now that I think about it, it's odd she's asking about inventory control. I'm sure they have a system as good as ours over there."

"I might be able to explain that." I told Connor of Antonia's suspicions.

"If she thinks something's wrong, then there is. No one is better at this business than Antonia." Connor took a sip of coffee and studied me over the rim of his cup.

"What?"

"Why would she come here to tell you something's wrong at Martinelli?"

"Antonia doesn't want to go to the police. She wanted to talk about it."

Connor lifted an eyebrow. "Really? Just wanted to talk about it? Just a couple of gals shootin' the breeze? Odd that Antonia never stopped by before, just to talk."

I shrugged. "She wants me to help her figure out the problem, but quietly, especially since it's probably someone connected to the winery."

"Did you think this through?"

"Why, because you think it might be a bad idea?"

"Pretty much."

"I owe her. She was here for Aunt Monique. I came down as much as possible, but with work it wasn't as often as I wanted."

Connor kept his eyes on his cup. "You did what you could,

and Monique knew that. Antonia was over all the time. The two of them talked nonstop for hours."

"So you understand why I want to help her. This is my chance to say thanks."

"It's just that if your snooping around doesn't go well, or she doesn't like the outcome, you might get caught in the fallout."

I shook my head. "She knows she may not like the answers, but if I don't help her she'll try to find out who's responsible on her own."

"That might be a better idea."

"I already told her I'd help. Anyway, how do you know a good idea until you try it?" Truth is, I'm not very good at picking out the good ideas from the bad. I'll pretty much try them all.

Connor rubbed his eyes.

"What?"

"Never mind. Okay, I follow you're going to help her, and I understand why. Where do you start?"

"Spending time with the logical people." I ticked off the names on my fingers. "As winery manager Marvin has plenty of opportunity, but I can't imagine his motive. It only hurts him when quality is off. Same with Todd, but since he's limited to the tasting room, I don't know how he fits." I shrugged my shoulders. "Then there are her three kids."

Connor nodded. "Rumor is Stephen's being groomed to take over the winery. We'll see if that ever happens. I can't imagine Antonia handing over the reins."

"You're probably right. He's going to be like Prince Charles—in his sixties and still not running the place. Anyway, that leaves her two daughters."

"Francesca lives in the city, but she's down here all the

time. I understand she bought some land nearby. There were stories about how she got it, but I've never heard what really happened."

"Chantal still lives at home, even though she's in her thirties. Boy, that Chantal. I remember *her*, all right. She's a real piece of work. I haven't seen her since I moved back. Does she still have that same, you know, figure?"

Connor smiled but avoided my glance. "If I remember correctly."

He stood, got more coffee and paced around the kitchen, cup in hand.

"Will you come and sit back down?" I looked at him when he didn't answer. "What?"

"Well, the thing is, if you live here and you're single, or I guess if you're a single male . . . Actually forget the single. If you're a male, sooner or later—"

"Stop, you can't be serious. You're not about to tell me you dated her."

I don't know why I was surprised or why it mattered. Chantal had rubbed every female in town the wrong way at one time or another, and if the stories were true, had rubbed up against most of the men as well. Not that they complained. Chantal was stunning. She was curvy in that classic Hollywood va-va-voom way, not to mention beautiful and rich. Man, she really ticked me off.

Connor held up his hands. "We went out a couple of times. She wanted to become an item—"

I lifted an eyebrow. "Yeah, Connor, ya think?"

"—but I let her know I just wasn't interested. She's kind of a messed-up kid, if you want to know the truth."

"Oh, please, she's in her thirties."

"She hasn't figured out who she is, apart from the Martinelli family. Then there's the winery itself. She shouldn't drink. She's been in rehab a couple of times and I don't think she's ever held a job. She just doesn't seem to know what she wants to be when she grows up."

"I guess." Although the last time I saw her, she looked pretty grown-up to me. Not sure exactly how she could grow up any more. Or where. "She'd better get it together soon." I shook myself. "Enough of Chantal. Anything else?"

"I know where you can see most of them tonight."

"Where?"

"Do you remember the Monterey County Wine Growers Association?"

"Sure. MCWGA. Wasn't Monique the president?"

Connor nodded. "Now Antonia is. They're holding annual elections tonight. All the Martinellis will be there, if only because Antonia wants to be president again. She'll want their votes. Hayley and I are driving over together. You should come too."

"Great idea."

He moved around the kitchen. The sunlight caught his dark blond hair, full and with the hint of a curl. It fell to the edge of his collar. He wore a denim shirt in a sky blue that matched his eyes. He sat back down at the table, the earthy sweetness of grapes on his skin.

I thought about what Antonia said. He was a catch; I just wasn't up for the chase.

Connor caught my eye and smiled. I looked away and caught a reflection of myself in the glass door. Right. I'm sure the reason we weren't together was because I wasn't up for the chase. My sweatsuit had wine stains from the barrels and highlighted my ten extra pounds. My hair was doing the frizz thing from the spray of the water. I tried to smooth it. Yeah, much better. I'm sure he found me irresistible.

I avoided his gaze. The invitation to the festival sat on the table and I picked it up.

The Cypress Cove Vintners Association
In Conjunction with Martinelli Winery
Invite Penelope Lively
Owner of Joyeux Winery
To Participate in the Twenty-fourth
Annual Autumn Festival

Penelope again. Antonia must have dictated the invitations.

"Antonia asked if we were ready for this." I slid the invite across the table.

"What did you tell her?"

"We've been ready for weeks."

"We've been ready for years."

Connor had been at this winery, working with my aunt, since he'd graduated from UC Davis with a degree in viniculture.

"You know this invitation belongs to you more than me," I said. "It's your victory. Not mine. Congratulations."

"This is for all of us. Hayley too."

"How's she doing?"

"Taking on more responsibility all the time. I really don't need to watch her anymore. She took care of most of the details for the festival."

Connor filled me in on the wines we were entering into

the competition until Hayley bounded up the outside steps and joined us in the kitchen.

"The last of the cases are loaded on the truck and ready to go." She ran her hands through her hair. "Marvin's going to wish he'd kept his mouth shut."

Marvin had remarked the smaller wineries shouldn't be allowed to compete in the festival tasting. Ever since, Hayley had been anxious for the time when Martinelli and Joyeux could compete taste to taste.

"I need to get over to Martinelli Winery," Hayley said.

Connor stood and stretched. "Give me ten minutes and I'll come with you." He walked down the path, back to the winery office.

Hayley came over to stand next to me. Moments later she nudged me in the ribs. "Nice view."

Three

AFTER Hayley and Connor left, I grabbed my camera and a pair of scissors. Nanook followed me outside and flopped down in the shade.

I tried to spend a part of every day in the garden. Things grew so fast in the mild climate I needed to come out most days just to keep up. I snapped shots of the garden with the winery in the background. This time of year the sunflowers managed to take over the garden, much to the delight of the birds. I cut several bunches for the house, leaving a few on the flat stones. Rabbits loved the seeds and I had more than enough.

After I finished in the garden, I went through my prints and postcards for various shots to sell at the festival. They were good publicity for Joyeux Winery and a nice reminder for visitors of their time here.

The seasons of the year were clear in the images. Early

spring leaves, freshly unfolded green against the bluest of skies; summer shots, where the terrain of golden hills shimmered like waves in the background; autumn, the perfect time on a winery, when the fiery orange and deep purple grape leaves challenged seasonal colors anywhere. The winter shots, done in black and white to heighten the starkness of the barren branches, showed none of the life that would burst forth when the cycle began anew.

The doorbell rang just as I finished. What good was living in the middle of nowhere if people still managed to show up unannounced?

I might have ignored it but Todd Ryan from Martinelli Winery stood there. He spotted me and waved through the glass. I opened the door.

"Hi there." I moved to let him in. "I thought I'd see you tonight at the Wine Growers Association, but here you are."

In his late twenties, Todd wore his usual outfit: a white, long-sleeved cotton shirt, jeans, and cowboy boots. He had his Stetson on and brown curls were tucked behind his ears. He had a nice smile. "I was driving by and thought I'd stop in. Hope you don't mind."

"No, of course not." I didn't really know Todd and couldn't imagine what he wanted. "Coffee?"

"Thanks, but no. I don't want to take up a lot of your time." He took off his hat, turning it in his hands.

"It's no problem." The curiosity was getting to me. "What's up?"

Todd smiled. "I'm getting married soon—"

"I heard that. Congratulations."

"Thanks. The thing is, Joanne, that's my fiancée, really loves your landscapes. She feels you're the best photographer in town. We know you don't do events, but if you're willing to be our photographer . . ."

I looked at him. "Are you sure? It's your big day. You don't want to take any chances."

"Believe me, we'd be honored. Um, we don't have a lot of money . . ."

I waved my hand. "I wouldn't charge you. I'm more than willing to try if you're willing to take the risk."

"That would be really great." Todd smiled. "I didn't think there was this much to getting married. Joanne and I want something small and there's still a lot going on."

"When's the date?"

"Ten weeks, December twenty-first. It's a good time of the year. Before Christmas and after all the tourists go home."

If Todd was in charge of the Martinelli tasting room, he'd have access to every area of the winery. "So, you've been in charge of the tasting room for what, a year now?"

"Not quite. I started last November."

"How do you like it?"

"I enjoy the work, and Antonia's great."

"Really?" I tilted my head as though this surprised me, which, in a way, it did.

"She's not bad. Not like the way she comes across. As long as you do your job, she leaves you alone." He studied the brim of his hat and continued. "It's more than that. She goes out of her way if she knows you're interested in learning. I have my degree and want to run my own winery someday. Still, there's so much to the actual process of making wine. If it weren't for Antonia, I don't know if I'd be learning much at all."

"Marvin isn't the best teacher?"

Todd grimaced. "He thinks if he explains something his

job's in danger. No chance of that from me. Not for a long time. And Stephen . . ."

"That's right. I forgot Antonia's son is starting to take on more responsibility. How's it going?"

"Okay, I guess. My time is spent in the tasting room, but I know he's made some changes. They upgraded some of the equipment. He tries to keep up with Marvin and Antonia when they discuss the winery. Stephen seems so easygoing and they're both such strong people. I think he's caught in the middle. Lately, there has been more pressure. I know there's been some trouble with the consistency of the wines, and Antonia is relying on Marvin more than ever."

I tried to look surprised. "What's been going on with the wines?"

He shrugged. "Could be a lot of things. The truth is, it's not a fun place to work right now." His hand tightened on his hat, crushing it.

"What makes you say that?"

"There's a lot of tension. The wines have been disappointing, and now there's something going on with . . ."

I waited. Sort of. "Todd?"

He put up his hands. "Forget it. I shouldn't have said anything."

"Todd, at least finish what you—"

"No." He started for the door. "Honestly, forget it. We can talk about the photography later, if you're still willing."

"Of course."

"That's great. See you tonight, Penny."

He walked down the path. His shoulders were hunched and he walked with his head down. He didn't look back. What was going on that had him so agitated? Todd had something on his mind, and it wasn't Marvin. Marvin was a jerk, but that wasn't anything new.

I shook my head. Antonia was here this morning about troubles on her winery and Todd was here now . . . What had Todd said? There was something going on with . . . what?

I turned from the window. Todd was getting married. Married and probably not earning much money right now. Todd struck me as a nice guy, and it seemed unlikely he'd take money from a competitor to sabotage Martinelli Winery. He also sounded like he enjoyed working for Antonia. Still, if he wanted his own winery, he needed to start a nest egg. Maybe he already had.

I spent the rest of the afternoon with the winery sales ledger, my largest responsibility. The wine business, like most everything else, was at the mercy of the economy. I would have guessed alcohol was pretty recession-proof. I figured when things were good, people liked to indulge. When things were bad, they liked to indulge even more.

However, wine is a luxury item. Our clients were cutting back on inventory. Hotels were at 50 percent occupancy and restaurants were closing. If your wine didn't sell fast enough it got struck from the wine list. It took regular calls and visits to see if customers were out of stock or if they needed anything.

Hayley came in through the back door. "I need a handkerchief for my face. There's a lot of dust from the tractor."

She tied a bandanna around her throat. This was the busiest time of the year at the winery and I wouldn't see much of her for the next couple of weeks. She looked a lot like her great-aunt and had a lot of the same traits as Aunt

Monique. The same smile, the same streaky blonde hair and the same habit of running her fingers through it.

Aunt Monique started Joyeux Winery in 1982. Joyeux means joyful in French and was my grandparents' name when they entered Ellis Island. Like so many immigrants of the time, they left the island and entered America with a different name: Lively, in their case.

I was glad my aunt revived the original family name for the winery. Joyful was how I felt every day here in the vineyards. Then I looked down at the ledger and the tension between my brows rose. Before I moved back I never paid much attention to the business end of running the winery. I assumed it did fairly well. Either Aunt Monique didn't go into this for the money, or I still had a lot to learn.

Hayley looked at me. "You don't look very happy with the accounts."

"I don't care if we get rich doing this, but I'd like to know we can keep a roof over our heads."

She walked over, her expression worried.

"It's not as bad as it sounds, but sales are down. I've called most of our clients, getting our name back out there. We just haven't been at the top of their list, probably because we haven't been in front of them. The response was good, though. Maybe soon we can start using more black than red ink in the books." I stood and walked to the window. "The reality is we're going to always remain a smaller winery, with specialty wines, because of the grapes we specialize in."

My aunt wasn't interested in producing a lot of one type of varietal, so she made a calculated move. She bought land that ran in a ribbon across the Carmel Valley, on the western side of the Santa Lucia Mountains. The three hundred acres ran west to east and benefited from a perfect soil mix of gravel and loam. The winery sat at just over one thousand feet above the Pacific Ocean, which was nine miles to the west. The result was a much wider variety of grapes than you could normally get to flourish on a winery this size. The western boundary was lower and closest to the cooler air of the Pacific. The Pinot Noir grown there would probably burst with the heat found at the eastern end of the property, while the Cabernet grown on the protected, sun-drenched hillsides to the east wouldn't ripen on the cooler western boundary.

We produced Zinfandel, Cabernet, Pinot Noir, Chardonnay, and Syrah. About twelve thousand cases per year. Certainly on the small side, but respectable.

I turned to Hayley. "Wine Growers meeting tonight."

"I know. Wouldn't miss it." She smiled and gave a small laugh.

"What? Do you know something I don't?"

"Maybe. I went online to see who was running for office this time around. I figured Antonia would be there and of course she is, but you'll never guess who's running against her. Go on, guess." She laughed and looked even younger than her twenty-seven years.

"Hayley, come on. Just tell me."

"Okay. I can't believe it. I don't know if Antonia knows yet and I want to see her face—"

"Enough already. Who is it?"

"Francesca."

"No." I looked at her. "Her daughter? What is she thinking?"

Hayley threw up her hands. "Can you believe it? It's really going to rattle Antonia."

I shook my head. "She must be planning on moving back

from the city. She isn't here often enough to be president. How would she manage this and still live in San Francisco?"

"I think she's going to try. She has a successful law practice. She can't be thinking of giving that up."

I shrugged my shoulders. "Why would she take this on? It's a lot of work and she's taking on Antonia. Why she would go to the trouble?"

"You don't know the history. Two years ago Antonia gave Stephen his promotion. Until that time Francesca was really involved in the winery's future. After that, forget it. Even though Antonia had always said she was leaving it to Stephen, Francesca was furious."

I nodded. "Antonia told Aunt Monique years ago that if she ever had a son, she'd leave him the winery."

Hayley nodded and walked toward the back door. "Ironic, isn't it? Sometimes powerful women can be the most sexist of all. It's like they break through the glass ceiling and then repair it behind them. Francesca's determined to be a part of the winery community, even without her mother's help. I don't like Francesca, but I can see why she'd be angry at Antonia."

"You don't like Francesca? Why? You like everybody."

Hayley stepped outside, talking over her shoulder. "I'll let you make up your own mind tonight."

Four

HARVEST time in wine country was always the busiest time of year, but Joyeux Winery had it easier than some. The wide selection of grapes we grew allowed us to spread out the harvest. The larger wineries that specialized in one particular type of grape kept a frenzied pace while they picked everything at once. Our grapes ripened from the west to the east, whites to reds, and over a longer period, but we still had a couple of late nights when we brought in the bulk of the harvest.

Although we're busy, this is the best part of the season, in particular after the harvest is complete. Relief sets in at having escaped a heavy rain or, our biggest fear in October, an early frost.

I glanced at the calendar. The election for the MCWGA officers was late this year. Usually they tried to get them out of the way in late summer, before harvest began. I wondered how it had slipped through the cracks. If Antonia meant to schedule it earlier and forgot, it was a symptom of something wrong. Antonia never let anything slip.

I snapped the ledger shut, headed to the kitchen and immediately was overwhelmed. I'll be the first to admit, success in the kitchen escaped me. The only thing I could reliably make was salad. I opened the fridge and got out lettuce, blue cheese, pears and candied walnuts. I put in a lot of walnuts. It tasted like dessert.

There was enough for Hayley and Connor, but this time of year they grabbed meals when they could. The tractor noise grew in the six acres of Zinfandel planted at the rear of the house. Connor stopped every few minutes to taste random grapes and gauge the color against the setting sun. The day you harvested was the day you could see and taste the wine the grape would become.

Hayley and Connor came in a while later.

"Two or three days, tops, on the Zinfandel." Connor eyed the salad.

"I made extra. Help yourself." I pushed the bowl toward him.

Hayley grabbed a serving spoon. "Move over."

As they hunted for the last of the candied walnuts I stood and moved to the door. "While you finish, I'll go and get dressed for this evening."

Connor looked up. "Dressed into what?"

I looked down at my white sweat outfit. "Pretty much anything would be an improvement."

Connor shrugged. "You look fine to me."

If I looked fine this way, then clearly I wasn't spending enough time on how I looked.

"Maybe I should just go get ready." I quickly dressed in

29

my second-favorite outfit—a long heavy-knit sweater, jeans and heeled boots.

We took Connor's truck. Hayley sat between us. She looked out the window and didn't say a word for most of the trip.

"What's on your mind?" I asked.

"Just the harvest."

I nodded. She'd taken on more responsibility and had complete control over a small portion of the vineyard. An entire year of work would be judged by what she did over the next seventy-two-hour period.

The junior college offered classes in viniculture and, in exchange for internships at the local wineries, allowed the MCWGA to use one of the lecture rooms for its monthly meetings.

We finally found a parking spot in the back. "Wow. Good turnout."

"Election night always draws a big crowd. You know." Hayley glanced at me. "You ought to run. How about vice president?"

"How about we not pursue that line of thought?"

"I'm serious." She stepped out of the truck. "It would raise exposure for the winery, and you'd be really good at it."

"We can always use more press," Connor said.

Hayley nodded. "Besides, you'd easily win. Nobody wants to be vice president with Antonia as president. She forced Stephen to do it last year."

"That's your best selling point? I'd win because nobody else wants the job? Wow, where do I sign up?"

"Just think about it. It would be good for you and the winery. Besides, it's a great way to meet men."

Connor grunted. "Penny doesn't need to meet men."

"What do you mean by that?"

"I just meant you don't need to meet any men right now." Connor stopped. "I mean, you don't need any . . ." He shook his head. "You know what? Forget it. It came out wrong."

Damn straight it did. "Hayley, go ahead and nominate me."

"Wow. That was fast. It was just a suggestion. Maybe you should think about it."

"If I think about it, I'll come up with a million reasons why it isn't a good idea."

I turned and walked away before I changed my mind, and made my way through my fellow vintners. Hayley was right. I couldn't recognize more than a few faces here and there. I needed to get out more.

I turned at the tap on my shoulder.

Todd stood behind me. "Sorry I left so abruptly today. I was rude and want to apologize."

Given our earlier conversation, I couldn't help but take a closer look at him. Tension was etched between his brows.

"Todd, if you ever just want to chat . . ."

Suddenly he smiled and his face relaxed. "I'm fine. I promise. Just with getting married and some family stuff going on and the job . . . everything is getting to me. I need to figure out a couple of things. That's all."

"Well, if you're sure . . ." I turned to go.

Antonia's eldest daughter, Francesca, walked up. "Hello, Todd."

Todd nodded, tight-lipped and with every bit of tension I'd seen earlier. He turned away. "Talk to you later, Penny." He didn't even glance at Francesca.

What was that about?

Francesca's eyes followed Todd. "Hello, Penny. You've been back, what is it, six months?" Francesca turned her pale face toward me. She wore her brown hair in a bun so tight it pulled the skin up around her eyes. She had on very little makeup and wore a tailored skirt suit. People in Cypress Cove dressed how they wanted. You didn't see many suits here, and she stood out.

"Hi, Francesca. About that long. I hear you're running for president tonight."

Francesca laughed, but it didn't quite reach her eyes. "My idea of term limits. Mother's been in charge for far too long."

"I'm surprised you're interested in the job. It's a lot of work."

She shrugged and looked around the room. "I run a suc- cessful law firm. I think I can handle this."

I didn't like her patronizing attitude. "I don't think you appreciate the amount of time Antonia puts into the associa- tion. There are a lot of afternoons during the week that Antonia meets with the tourist board, the local businesses, that kind of thing. How are you going to do all of that from the city?"

"As I said, I'll manage."

Wow. I really didn't like this woman. "So, who's going to nominate you?"

Francesca pointed to the back of the room, where a tan man with silver hair was on a cell phone. "I don't believe you've met my husband, Brice. He'll nominate me and, in spite of the objections you've raised, Penny, I just might win. My mother isn't the easiest person to get along with, you know."

She had me there.

"While I find your concern I might be taking on too much, well, touching, don't worry about me. I've decided to play a bigger role in the valley. I intend to be around for a long time, with or without my mother's support."

She flicked her hand as she turned to leave. I was dismissed.

I've been rebuffed before, by the best, and believe me, Francesca was nowhere near the best. I raised my voice. "Oh, that's right. I heard Antonia was leaving the winery to your brother, not you. What a shame. For you, that is. I'm sure, though, she knew what she was doing."

Several people stopped.

Francesca turned and moved in close. "That's right. She's leaving it to my brother. She's leaving the winery to my unqualified, uninspired brother. If you think that's going to stop me, though, you'd better think again. It isn't enough to stop me. Not nearly enough."

I wasn't sure how to respond.

"Speaking of the uninspired, here's my brother now, playing lapdog to my mother as usual."

Antonia swept into the room, cane on her arm. With that silver hair, thick and swept up, Antonia was a formidable woman. She knew it too. You could see it in the way she walked, with her head held high and shoulders back, her stride long and sure.

Stephen followed Antonia. Francesca's lapdog comments about her brother, while nasty, weren't easily dismissed. Stephen did look something like a lapdog. I would never have recognized him if Francesca hadn't pointed him out. He was easily the most forgettable person I'd ever seen. Everything about him was beige: his hair, clothes and, even from across the room, personality. He followed Antonia to the front of the room.

"We'll continue this conversation, Penny. You can count on it. Now, however, I must go pay homage. After all, isn't that what one does with royalty?"

Francesca walked over to her mother. Antonia said something and Francesca shook her head. Without another word, Antonia walked away. Francesca, with a small, amused smile, watched her go.

I turned. Someone else watched the exchange with me. Todd's hands worked at his sides and there was tension along his jawline.

If someone was trying to sabotage Martinelli Winery, Todd was in a position to know. He spent most of his time there. He could have seen something, might have stumbled across the answer. He wouldn't go to Antonia if he suspected Francesca unless he had proof. Was that the source of Todd's anger? He either knew or suspected Francesca of the sabotage but couldn't prove it? Francesca certainly had motive. She was angry with both her mother and brother. She also had access. No one would notice her out at the winery, or in the fermentation building. It wasn't that every bottle had to be ruined. Inconsistent product was enough to destroy a winery's reputation.

Antonia took a seat at the head table and people began to file into the rows of chairs. Hayley and Connor were seated near the front and I slipped in beside them.

"I saw you talking to Francesca," Hayley said.

"What a piece of work. She's going to run for office and thinks she can manage it from San Francisco. She doesn't want the job. She just wants to get under Antonia's skin."

Antonia leaned in to the microphone. "Let's begin. The first item for discussion is label standardization."

Most of the vintners that belonged to the MCWGA, including Joyeux Winery, produced sparkling wines, what is referred to as Champagne in certain parts of Europe.

Sparkling wine and Champagne are created the same way, referred to as *méthode Champenoise*. Sugar and yeast are added to wine and carbon dioxide is created, causing the bubbles.

Legally, we called our wine anything we wanted in the states and were restricted from the word "Champagne" only on bottles shipped to Europe. The Champagne region of France won this point, and I had no argument with it.

I looked around the room. This was a topic Aunt Monique fought for years. We used the "sparkling wine" label. Some wineries used both terms. The members were divided. Someone in the back said the "Champagne" label added panache. I raised my hand. Antonia nodded.

I faced the room. "Calling it Champagne only adds panache if you actually think the French product is superior, something I certainly don't believe to be true. Look, we can't call it Champagne in Europe. Fine. If we make this an issue, it appears even we feel Champagne is better. I want the world to know we make the finest sparkling wine in the world. It's fresh, it's unique and it's completely Californian."

There was a smattering of applause and when Antonia called for a vote, a majority of hands went up, Antonia's included.

"That's it, then. Going forward, members will adhere to the 'sparkling wine' moniker. Now, on to elections for the coming year."

While the secretary and treasurer were elected by a show of hands, Hayley leaned over. "If you want to participate, you can volunteer for a project or two, a little at a time. You sure you want to run for office?"

I nodded but didn't speak. Like most things, you don't really know what you're getting into when you volunteer, but I didn't stop Hayley when, a few moments later, she nominated me for the office of vice president.

Once again, Antonia raised her brow at me. I shrugged.

"As she is running unopposed, I appoint Penelope Lively as vice president for the coming year." She glanced around the room and her gaze settled behind me. I turned. Francesca sat several rows back.

"Now, are there any nominations for the office of president?"

On cue, Stephen raised his hand. "I nominate Antonia Martinelli."

Antonia nodded at her son, and I heard my voice, along with several others, second the motion. Antonia was difficult, but she was committed. She worked hard at the job.

"Any other nominations?"

There was a moment of silence before a voice came from the back of the room. "I nominate Francesca Martinelli for president."

Brice was off the phone and I got a good look. The only man in a suit, he was as out of place as his wife. His hair was slicked straight back, held there with lots of hair gel. The sparkle of his gold bracelet and cuff links was visible from across the room. Francesca was several seats behind me, that amused looked still on her face. She smirked and gave me a phony little finger wave.

I felt my arm shoot up in the air.

Hayley grabbed my other hand. "What are you doing?"
"Not a clue."
Antonia nodded at me. "Yes, Penny?"
I stood, stalling.
"Penny?"
"Um, I was wondering, when do I officially become vice president?"
Antonia thought for a moment. "I suppose as of now. I haven't been asked that before. Why?"
"I'd like to make a recommendation. I propose all officers are required to actually live in Monterey County. It is, after all, the Monterey County Wine Growers Association." I turned to face Francesca, now rigid in her chair, the amused smile gone. "It would seem to me being a resident should be an obvious prerequisite for the job."
Francesca stood. "This is ridiculous. You can't do this."
Stephen stood. "If Penny isn't the vice president, then I still am, and I second the proposal."
"I didn't think he had it in him," Hayley whispered.
Antonia looked over at her son. There was a slight nod of her head as she asked for a show of hands.
"Good job. The majority agree with you, although"—Hayley turned over her shoulder—"you're getting the evil eye from Francesca."
It was a dark look indeed that Francesca cast my way. I looked about the room. Todd gave me a smile and a nod of his head, as did several other members.
"That's it, then," Antonia said. "As I am running unopposed, I will continue as president through the coming year."
Antonia closed the meeting shortly thereafter. As she passed

by me, she stopped. "As vice president, you're now cochairing the Autumn Festival, which means I'll see you tomorrow evening at my house to review the schedule, say, around six?"

Right. Already I had regrets.

Connor and Hayley knew everyone, and I was soon alone in the back of the room.

"Well, well. I guess my mother has found another lapdog." Francesca came up next to me. She lowered her head toward mine. "I don't like being embarrassed, and I don't like you. Stay out of my way."

I'd met people like her before. Classic bully. At that moment, she reminded me of my previous editor. I moved close enough to feel her breathing. We locked eyes.

"You don't like me? Good. I must be doing something right." Anger warmed my face. I wanted to grab that little bun and give it a good twist. "I bet you get a lot of opportunities in your line of business to treat people like dirt. Don't try it here. Not on me."

"Watch yourself. I'm capable of more than you think."

Could she be responsible for the events at Martinelli Winery?

"Really? Tell me exactly what you're capable of, Francesca, because I'd really like to hear. I know you wanted to take over your mother's winery and show you're capable of running it. Guess what. You aren't going to get that chance. Too bad."

Francesca turned white. Her lipstick crept into the tight lines around her mouth. "My mother will regret her decision. Stephen is a fool." She took a breath. "My advice to you is you shouldn't get involved in something you know nothing about."

I shook my head. "I don't think I'll be taking any advice

from you. Not now or any time in the future." I paused. "So, you've made it pretty clear you hope your brother fails. What exactly would you do to make sure that happens? Tell me, Francesca, just how far are you prepared to go?"

Francesca moved back. "I don't know what the hell you're talking about. Just stay out of my way."

Five

I TOLD Hayley and Connor about Francesca's remarks on the way home. The perfect responses, far too late to be useful, filled my thoughts deep into the night. As a result I woke up late, tired and more irritated than usual.

The jeans and sweater from last night went back on and I had my first cup of coffee in hand when I walked past the front door. There was a girl I didn't recognize about to press the bell.

I should just hang a sign down at the front gate: "Solicitors Welcome! This Way!" I motioned that whatever it was, I didn't want any, and she started to knock. She had spunk. I sighed and opened the door.

"Hi, my name's Sylvia. I work for the *Monterey Centennial* and I want to write an article on your winery." She spoke around a retainer, and her enormous smile told me this was probably the first time she'd been able to say that to anyone.

She wore a yellow sundress and had long blonde hair caught back with a white headband. She held a reporter's notepad. Probably an intern. Still, we're a small winery. Free publicity wasn't to be turned down. Sylvia reached into her yellow shoulder bag and pulled out a full box of business cards, enough to last about a semester. She practically shook when she handed me one, excited as could be to give one to somebody besides her mother.

I took the card and stuck it in the back pocket of my jeans. "Sylvia, how many wineries have you written about?"

"You'll be the first."

"How many have you asked?"

She chewed on the inside of her lip. "It's kinda funny, now that you mention it. I thought everyone would want to talk to me, you know? But everybody's been too busy."

I looked at her. "When did you set out to get this interview?"

"Last week."

"Your timing needs a little work. Wineries focus on the harvest this time of year. Give me a call in a couple of weeks and I'll give you all the time you need for an article."

After Sylvia left, I ate a bagel and mulled over last night's exchange with Francesca. I was expected at Martinelli Winery that evening to discuss the festival. In the meantime, I was caught up on the ledgers and wasn't needed at the winery. Connor and Hayley would be busy and unlikely to get a break before nightfall, so I was free for the day.

Francesca had gone to Layton Law School. I decided that would be my first stop and managed to get myself out the door a short time later.

My car was already twenty years old when I discovered it under a tarp behind a neighbor's house. I don't know how the

1963 Jaguar XK-E Roadster made it to Northern California, but the owner thought I was doing her a favor when I offered her nineteen hundred dollars for it, a lot of money back when I was a teenager waiting tables. Sure, it was filthy and needed paint, new tires and a major tune-up, plus the windows wouldn't roll down. The body was mint, the leather interior was perfect, and she handled like a dream. It's the only car I've ever owned, and I still get a thrill every time I start the engine.

The drive went too quickly, as it always does when you're fortunate enough to be on this stretch of Highway 1. I left the ocean behind, parked in the Layton lot, and decided to start at the library. They'd have back issues of the yearbooks and most kept some current information on alumni. Hopefully they'd share it.

The school was busy, students everywhere, but when I tried the library door it was locked. There was a sign in the window that announced it was closed for an earthquake retrofit. Most of the public buildings over a certain age in California needed to have this done. With any luck we'd never have to find out if it actually worked.

The school administration office would be the next place to find information on a graduate. I pulled open the doors and tried to figure out what to say. I try not to lie if I can help it. If I don't, though, it's almost impossible to get people to tell you things they had no business telling you. Besides, lying comes naturally to me. I'm not proud of it, but there it is.

I walked in and looked around. The office was drab and gray, the same standard school administration office found everywhere. The linoleum, the walls, the two ladies that sat there with piles of paperwork, all gray. The one nearest me looked up from her work, peered over her bifocals and sighed. "It's Sunday. We're officially closed."

"Oh. Well, since I'm here do you mind if I ask you a quick question?"

She just looked at me.

No great burst of inspiration. I had nothing. "Ah, I was wondering how much longer the library would be closed?"

"Several weeks. They tried to get the retrofit done during the summer. Now they'll be lucky to get it done by the end of the year." She paused. "You can't be a student here, or you'd know about the library. That's all anyone's been talking about."

"No, that's right. I was just wondering where I could learn more about the school."

She leaned toward me, over her paperwork. "Why?"

Right. Why. "My name's Sylvia, and I'm from the *Monterey Centennial*."

I pulled Sylvia's card from my back pocket and slid it across the counter. This was an easy one. I even had identification.

Gray Lady sighed again and shuffled over to the counter. "Yes?" Her name tag read "Ethel." No kidding.

"The paper is starting a new column on nationally recognized institutions and businesses that have been around for at least one hundred years. We're calling it 'The Sensational Centennials.' Sort of a play on our own name, you know?"

It's shameful how I come up with this stuff. Ethel just gave me a blank look.

"Well, anyway, we decided it would be great to start the column with a story on our very own Layton Law School."

Again with the sigh. "How can I help you?"

"Would it be possible to take a peek in the library, at the school archives, just to get information on the history of the school? I'd also love to feature comments from some of the local graduates."

Ethel gestured toward a room to the rear of the administration area. The odor of mothballs floated across the counter. "You don't need the library. You'll probably find everything you want in there. Old pictures, school curriculum, yearbooks, that kind of stuff. We even have letters from Layton to his father, asking for money to establish the school."

"I'm sure I'll find everything I need there. Thanks so much for your help." I picked up my bag and walked around the end of the counter. After Ethel motioned me into the proper room and I was left on my own, I searched the shelves and found the yearbooks from the mid to late 1990s. The classes were small and Francesca's picture was in the fourth book, 1998. She was one of those people who had never been young. Her hair was pulled up in the same tight bun. She was never a pretty girl, but at least nowadays she had style; back then she was just plain. I thumbed through the rest of the book and spotted candid shots of her taken throughout the year—in the library, as a member of the debating team, with her hand raised in class. Under Francesca's picture it stated her goal: "To one day run the largest and most successful winery in Monterey County."

As I returned the book I scanned the walls and spotted class pictures with the graduates listed underneath. I found 1998 but couldn't find Francesca. I took a second look and scanned the names. No Francesca.

What was going on? I went back out to the office.

Ethel looked up. "Yes?"

"You know, it occurred to me a friend of mine graduated from here in 1998. We lost track of each other years ago, but I'd love to see her again. Does the school have any way to get in touch with its graduates?"

She looked over her glasses. "Sure they do, but it's just for graduates."

"Oh." I waited.

She sighed. "Maybe I can help you. I was here in '98 and might remember the name."

"That would be terrific. It's Francesca Martinelli."

Ethel gave a snort and pulled off her glasses. "She didn't graduate. Not from here, anyway. She was expelled."

"Really? I can hardly believe it. You don't remember what for, do you?"

"Of course I do. When a student from one of the most prominent families in the area is expelled during finals, you remember. We weren't supposed to know. Of course, we all did. She was kicked out. For cheating." Ethel turned back to her paperwork. "Never did like her."

She was finished with me, so I gathered my things and left. Maybe Francesca finished law school elsewhere. Maybe not. I know she still told people she'd gone to Layton. I'd ask Francesca if that could be considered false advertising. She'd know. After all, she was the lawyer.

AT home I was greeted by the phone ringing and checked the caller ID. Ross Sterling, one of my closest friends.

I grabbed the phone. "Hey."

"Haven't seen you. Feeling neglected."

"Me too. I just haven't been to town. How's business?"

"Oh, you know."

"You're so understated."

"That's me. The blasé gay."

Last year Ross, a chef, opened a restaurant called Sterling. He'd opened in the old city hall right in the center of Cypress Cove, a beautiful old structure owned by Antonia. Since her grandfather founded the town, it would be difficult to find real estate she doesn't own. As fate would have it, the second week he was in business, Hollywood's most illustrious leading lady, the one with the big teeth and even bigger—well, you know which one—was quoted in *Restaurant Review* saying that his salmon bisque was the nectar of the gods, or something like that. Now he was booked ahead for six months, and it was considered the best restaurant in town.

"Before I forget, Thomas says we need more of your postcards in the store."

Two years ago, I introduced him to Thomas, another friend of mine. Thomas now owned the gift store and coffeehouse adjacent to the restaurant, called Beauty and the Bean. They are perfect together. Both big and gorgeous. When they met, hopes fell and hearts shattered from here to Santa Cruz.

"Glad to hear they're selling well. I can drop them off this afternoon, before I go over to Martinelli Winery. Now that I'm vice president of the MCWGA I get to cochair the festival. Lucky me."

"Antonia came in for lunch and told me. She has most everything done, though, so don't even think you're going to have any input."

"Antonia's been running this thing for so long she doesn't need my opinions."

"Oh, I don't know. Some fresh eyes won't hurt. As for the postcards, you don't need to worry about dropping them off. We can get them tonight at Martinelli Winery."

"Why have you and Thomas been summoned?" I knew Ross had little patience for Antonia. He said she was the most ostentatious queen he'd ever met, which, coming from him, meant something.

"Well, aside from our booth, Antonia wants me to feed the judges at the festival during the wine competition, as if I didn't have enough to do already. Plus, I'm sure she expects me to bring a little something for tonight."

"Oh, please. You love showing off your culinary expertise. Plus, there are worse things than having Antonia on your side."

"I suppose you're right. Anyway I don't want her raising my rent. I promise I'll bring your favorite."

"The spinach ricotta tart?"

"None other. See you tonight."

I rang off and spent the rest of the morning with my stock of prints and postcards.

IT was early afternoon when the door slammed behind me. Connor walked in. "Do you still have the ledger in here?"

I nodded and pointed at the book on the desk. He walked over and took a seat. He skipped through the pages and added entries. Connor is very structured, and it shows in the records he keeps. Every expense as well as technique is recorded there, which proves invaluable come planting season or tax time.

In a decidedly different approach to life, I couldn't be less organized. Connor likes a game plan, while I trust my instincts. Connor looks at morning glories and thinks cutting back. I don't prune any more than necessary, and barely even then. Hayley is pretty much in between us. I couldn't imagine the winery without either one of them.

I walked to the desk, looked over his shoulder and checked how many tons of grapes we'd brought in. So far it was a good year. Hayley came through the back door.

I looked at both of them. "We have an hour before we need to leave for the Martinellis'. Care for a glass of Cabernet?"

Hayley smiled. "Sure. Just don't tell the boss." She paused and looked at her watch. "Do I really need to be there tonight? I sort of made a date."

"Okay, putting aside that I want to hear about this date, it was your idea I run for office. If I need to be there, I won't be there alone. Besides, you need to know the schedule of the festival as much as we do. Can you go out later?"

"I suppose. I just don't feel like an evening with the Martinellis."

"It's only for a couple of hours. How bad can it be?"

Hayley looked at me. "You haven't spent much time with them, have you?"

"Why, what exactly am I in for?"

"Don't even try to explain it," Connor said. "She'll just have to see it for herself."

Six

I DIDN'T ask Hayley about her date, but only because I didn't get a chance.

When we were on our way to Antonia's, Hayley looked over at me. "I know you want to ask, but I've only been out a couple of times with this guy. It's new, and I don't want to jinx it, you know? I just want to make sure it actually turns into something first."

"I understand. I'm just curious."

"I know."

Connor didn't take his eyes off the road, but I saw his smile.

The ornate gates stood open when we arrived just before six. The Martinelli logo, a blue-and-gold shield with a silver falcon caught midflight, embellished the arches above the entrance. The road through the vineyards leads upward to the circular drive of the home, known as Martinelli Manor. We passed the gardens, a formal design that showcased Antonia's roses. Built by Antonia's grandfather, the house is three stories in front. Circular turrets balance the corners of the structure. These were almost entirely concealed by ivy, now bronze and copper in the chill of an early fall. The roof, shingled in hand-chiseled slate, glowed in the setting sun. To the left of the house were the storage buildings, the fermentation building, the tasting room and the winery office. Antonia's grandfather had finished them in the same Italian renaissance style of the main house. All of the buildings featured stone and plaster exteriors topped with slate roofs. The overall effect was of a small village frozen in time.

"I never get over how beautiful this is," I said.

Connor nodded. "It's impressive all right. Our entire operation would fit in the fermentation building alone."

Hayley jumped out as soon as the truck stopped. "Marvin's in charge of the winery locations at the festival. I need to make sure he gave us the tent we were supposed to have."

The location of each winery's exhibition tent was decided on a lottery basis. We had a great spot, center and on the main row.

"I've seen the map where we're going. Marvin wouldn't move us anywhere else."

Hayley spoke over her shoulder. "I want to check anyway." She walked down the path.

"Maybe if she didn't react, he wouldn't keep trying to bait her."

Connor shook his head. "I think she's right. He's one of those people that needs to make trouble."

I turned to look over the sweep of the valley below us,

bordered on two sides by the Santa Lucia Mountains. In the distance sat the Pacific, where the sun balanced on the horizon. At the bottom of the bluff, just below us, was the area where the festival took place.

"Well, you ready to enter the lion's den?" Connor asked.

I reached into my bag and grabbed the smaller camera I usually carried. "Let me take a couple shots of the house. The setting sun is perfect."

Connor waited patiently while I snapped several of the winery and grounds. The final rays of sun tinted the slate roof a glowing bronze, while the ivy blazed in a brilliant golden hue.

"It's perfect, isn't it?" Chantal Martinelli sauntered up to where we stood, balancing both a martini glass and herself on four-inch red heels.

Chantal hadn't bothered, though, to actually glance at the sunset. She watched Connor. She looked stunning. As if long chestnut hair and enormous green eyes weren't enough, when she gets around an attractive man she seems to *swell*. She must have an air pump hidden somewhere in her demi-cups.

"Hello, Chantal," Connor glanced at me. Amusement pulled at the corners of his mouth. "It's incredible. Your mother's done a terrific job with this place."

Chantal gave an impatient shrug. Red silk rippled in the early evening breeze, and a heady whiff of Obsession perfume filled the air.

"She had a lot to begin with, you know. Most of the vineyards were established years before she inherited."

I knew some of the history. Antonia's grandfather left

the winery to both sons and they fought over it. Antonia's father eventually bought his brother out.

"What's impressive is how Antonia has continued expansion of the winery. That's not an easy thing to do," Connor said.

Chantal sniffed. "Lately it's been Stephen. My brother's dedicated to improving this place, but she'll never give him credit."

I faced her. "Todd told me Stephen had gotten involved only recently. What improvements has he made?"

Chantal didn't bother to look at me, just finished off her martini and smiled at Connor. "My brother's updated the fermentation building, if you'd care to see it."

"I'd like to take a quick look." Connor turned toward the building.

"Penny, you can go keep my mother company. We'll be right back." She tucked her hand into the curve of Connor's arm.

Connor stopped. "You should come take a look, Penny. See if there are any ideas you think we can use." He was just being polite. We both knew he made all decisions concerning improvements. Maybe he wanted to avoid being alone with Chantal. That thought cheered me and I smiled at Chantal. She rolled her eyes and dropped her hold on Connor, but went ahead and opened the large double doors.

Fermentation has its own perfume, and either you like it or you don't. I love it. It smells like yeast and, depending on the type of wine, a mix of fruits. I smelled the apples and citrus from the Chardonnay, the blackberry and plum from the Cabernet and the reds. When yeast is added to the grapes most of the sugar in the grapes is converted into alcohol. The rest turns into carbon dioxide that escapes into the air and carries the scent through the room until, in the older wooden buildings, the fragrance is captured by the walls.

The building has its own sounds too. You can put your ear to a barrel and listen to the grapes turning into wine. The juice bubbles from the center to the top, and it has always reminded me of the ocean captured in a shell.

"Stephen replaced our steel tanks and added a new destemming area." Chantal laughed and pulled Connor down a side row. "I don't really know what all of that means. As you know I tend to just stick to consuming the family wine, not necessarily worrying about how it's made."

"Yes, Chantal, we're all aware you're the happy beneficiary of your family's hard work," I said.

Connor glanced over his shoulder at me but I refused to look at him. "Antonia told me about the destemmer. It's supposed to be state-of-the-art."

Chantal glanced at the equipment. "What's it supposed to do?"

"It will keep more of the fruit whole and still destem the majority of the grapes."

He inspected the equipment then turned back down the aisle. "I thought Antonia installed this a while back, before Stephen got so involved."

Chantal stopped. "No, this was entirely Stephen's doing." Connor shook his head but didn't pursue it.

Chardonnay and Sauvignon Blanc, in sixty-gallon oak barrels, rested in a dozen rows that ran down the center of the building. To the rear of the structure were the open-top tanks. The fifteen-hundred-, three-thousand- and six-thousand-gallon tanks were now made of enclosed stainless steel, but at

Martinelli they used both steel tanks and wooden barrels. We did the same. The time spent in oak barrels gave the wine a depth and flavor you couldn't achieve any other way.

We walked down the center aisle to the rear of the building. At its most active stage, fermentation generated considerable heat, and the room was warm and humid. Fans whirled in the background to keep the heat down and clear away the carbon dioxide.

Chantal stayed close to Connor. At the rear doors, she turned her back on me and again put her hand on Connor's arm. "Would you like to see the new crushers?"

Crushing is gently squeezing the grapes to break the skins and release the juice. In traditional winemaking, the fruit was crushed by trampling it barefoot. Now, the grapes are loaded into large metal containers, where blades and hooks move them through the machinery. There were two at Martinelli, one each for red and white wines, to avoid color problems.

"I think we should get back. Your mother's expecting us." Right. Like I was going to hang around and let her ignore me any longer. Besides, Connor was too good for her. Maybe he didn't need my help, and at the moment he looked amused. It didn't matter. I'd seen the best of them act like idiots when women like Chantal set their sights on them. Better I save him from himself.

"Of course, we can't keep mother waiting, now, can we?" Chantal's face betrayed nothing as she settled in beside Connor, took his arm and led the way back out through the building. He tried to remove his arm from hers and Chantal tightened her grip. He couldn't very well pull away without it being obvious and causing a scene. As we walked up the front steps, his face reddened. I gave him a big smile.

We entered the main hall. Portraits of Martinelli ancestors lined walls plastered in cream, which glowed against polished parquet floors. Stone details framed the doors leading to separate rooms off the entry, and the entrance itself was bordered by grapevines carved in marble. Breathtaking crown molding and vaulted ceilings capped the space, with filtered light coming from the leaded windows flanking the entrance doors. Chantal entered the hall and set her empty glass on an antique Italian walnut console table. Right on the wood, without a coaster. I couldn't take it, and moved over to slide a copy of *Architectural Digest* under the dripping glass. Chantal didn't notice and walked farther into the space.

"Mother, Connor's here." Chantal glanced over at me. "Penny too."

A voice came from the room on the left. "In the library."

As we entered, Chantal headed to the bar and Connor and I walked over to where Antonia sat, sliver-handled cane in hand.

"Good evening, Antonia," Connor said. "We've been admiring the view of your vineyards. They're absolutely superb."

"Thank you. I'm especially pleased with this year's crop. Provided we don't make any mistakes"—her voice faltered a bit—"we should have an outstanding vintage. Tell me, would you like to open a bottle of our 2000 Cabernet? I find it exceptional."

"That sounds perfect. I don't believe I've had the pleasure," Connor said.

Antonia smiled. "It's scarce. We didn't produce a lot, and over the years—Chantal, do you think you should have another?"

Chantal stood at the bar, her back toward her mother. She

didn't turn but raised the vodka bottle off the counter. The sound of ice cubes, slowly and deliberately dropped into a martini shaker, filled the room.

"Yes, Mother, I most definitely think I should."

The splash of alcohol hitting the ice was broken by footsteps in the outer hall. Stephen Martinelli entered, followed by his wife, Veronica. It struck me once again how different he was from his mother. None of the vibrancy was passed along. With watery gray eyes, he even managed to miss the vibrant green eyes that were the Martinelli trademark.

He walked into the room and went directly to the bar, where Chantal added an olive to her drink. Gently, yet with surprising firmness, he removed the drink from her hand, tucked her arm in his and led her to the couch. I was surprised Chantal allowed this. She sank into the corner of the couch, kicked off her shoes and tucked her legs under her.

Veronica remained near the door. She stood in sharp contrast to Chantal, who watched her sister-in-law with a small, amused smile.

"Good evening, Mother." Veronica fingered her pearls. "Can I get you anything?"

"You can have a seat. I'm not an invalid, for heaven's sake."

"Of course not. I just thought . . ." Veronica looked around the room for a place to sit. Chantal saw her eye the sofa. She uncurled her legs and sprawled out, taking over the rest of the couch. Nice.

Veronica moved to a chair near the window. She perched on the edge and smoothed the pleats of her gray skirt.

I stood there, sized up the distance to the bar, and wondered if I could slink over and grab the martini Chantal had left behind. I'd been here fifteen minutes and already the tension in the room had given me a headache.

"I've always wanted to see the famed Martinelli cellar," Connor said to Antonia. "Care to show me?"

Antonia nodded and they walked toward the main hall. When they were near me, she paused. "Perhaps we can talk later? I'm curious if you've given any thought to our conversation yesterday."

"No problem."

Antonia raised her voice. "Veronica, please listen for the bell. I gave the servants the night off."

"Yes, of course, Mother."

Connor and Antonia continued through the main hall toward the wine cellar stairs.

Veronica tilted her head and continued to rattle her pearls. Stephen turned on the couch, eyebrow raised. Chantal even managed to focus on me.

"It's just more festival stuff," I volunteered, to no one in particular.

To my relief the front bell rang, and Veronica shot out of her chair. For a woman in pleats and pearls, she could move. Moments later she led Ross and Thomas, loaded with platters, into the room.

"Hello, everyone," Ross and Thomas chimed in unison. "Pen, would you mind moving that vase over just a bit?"

I helped Ross arrange the trays of food, glad to be busy. Thomas immediately went over and pulled up a chair next to Stephen. Within minutes, they were deep in conversation.

"Look at Thomas. He can get anyone to talk," Ross said.

I cut into the spinach tart. "Stephen doesn't say much, does he?"

"He's never had much to say, and lately he says even less. You'd think with the additional responsibilities around here he'd be more confident, but to me it seems just the opposite."

A loud rap on the glass doors stopped us. Hayley stood outside the door along with Marvin Karp, and neither looked pleased to be there. Hayley had her arms crossed and her cheeks were pink. Marvin was turned away from her and had his hands on his hips.

Antonia kept Marvin because if anyone knew more about wine, I'd yet to meet them. I looked at his sullen face, wondering if he was worth it. I was lucky to have Connor as my manager. Except for their skill, the two men couldn't be more different.

I unlocked the door. Hayley dove through and pulled me over to Ross.

"What a jerk," Hayley whispered. "He told me our Cabernet would make a good cooking wine."

My face grew hot with anger. "He's always got something nasty to say. It's time we had a talk."

Ross handed me a cracker with mushroom paté. "Don't. That's what he wants. Besides, it does make a good cooking wine. I drink it all the time while I'm cooking."

I took a deep breath. Ross was right. Marvin would love to know he'd gotten to me. I ate the cracker while Hayley ran her hands through her hair and smiled at Ross.

Marvin took a seat on the edge of the fireplace hearth and pulled out a newspaper from under his arm. He hadn't acknowledged anyone in the room, and they in turn ignored him. Stephen and Chantal spoke together in soft tones on the couch while Veronica straightened a book on the shelf.

"What's wrong with him anyway?"

"I can't answer in general," Hayley said, "but right now he doesn't want to be here. Said he has better things to do than this. Of course, you'd never know it. If you look closely, that's a horse race schedule he's reading."

Hayley leaned back in her chair and looked out the side window. "There's a car pulling into the drive. Black Aston Martin. Very cool."

Ross nodded. "That would be Francesca and Brice."

"I met Francesca last night." I rolled my eyes. "That was a pleasant experience. What kind of doctor is her husband?"

"A cardiologist. He divides his time between offices in the city and at the hospital here. They come into the restaurant and drive my staff crazy. Impossible to please. Plus she always wants me to comp her bill, just because her mother owns the building. What sense does that make? Of course, I never do. Let her eat somewhere else."

"You know she won't. You have the best restaurant in town."

"Oh, that's right. I do." He grinned. "Anyway, I've heard her talking at dinner. She's always too loud to ignore—"

"Like you try," I said.

"Do you want to hear or not? Anyway, she doesn't get along with Stephen. Apparently she doesn't think Stephen's doing a good job of running the winery. She could do better if given the chance. Of course, she's also angry with Antonia for that."

"That's an understatement. She made it clear to me last night how she feels."

"If you think the stress level in here is high now, just wait until they walk in."

The sound of heels striking the flagstone foyer grew louder. Stephen wiped his forehead and kept his eyes away from the door, while Veronica fiddled with her pearls until they sounded like castanets. Antonia had returned with Connor and as she turned to the door the smile dropped from her face. The only family member who didn't react was Chantal, who looked bored and sullen.

"God, I hate coming here on Fridays. Traffic was terrible."

I caught a glimpse of very expensive but serious shoes as they traveled to the bar, where a Coach attaché and handbag were unceremoniously dumped on the floor. Paperwork fell out of her bag. Francesca snatched it from the ground and slapped it on the bar. She looked up.

"What, a party? And you didn't even invite me?"

Her hair was once again pulled into a tight bun, and she wore the same red lipstick. I was struck by how opposite she was from Chantal, now playing with the fringe on the couch pillow.

Antonia greeted her daughter with a slight nod. It was easy to see she was still upset over last night. She kept a tight grip on her cane, and she wouldn't look at Francesca.

"We're meeting to review festival details, and we haven't started yet. Will you be here the entire weekend?"

"Of course. I'm looking forward to some quality time with the family. Besides, I haven't seen all of the improvements Stephen's made."

The sarcasm was evident in her voice. Francesca enunciated every word, giving it a weight and presence all its own. She must be hell in a courtroom.

Brice stood just inside the door of the library and clutched a cell phone to his ear. He gave a small wave with a manicured hand and turned to continue the conversation.

Francesca poured herself a sherry, perched on one of the bar stools and tapped short scarlet nails against her glass. "I might as well stick around to hear what the plan is."

"We'll wait a few more minutes. The only person who isn't here yet is Todd," Antonia said.

"Why do you need to wait for him?" Francesca asked.

"He's responsible for coordinating shifts in the tasting booths." Stephen had a slight frown.

Connor settled next to me as a brisk knock announced Todd's arrival. He pushed open the glass doors. Once again, he wore jeans and a white fitted shirt. He also had on a Stetson hat that he removed as he walked across the room.

"Hello, everyone."

Antonia motioned to him and gestured toward the chair next to her. He smiled and took a seat, resting his hat on his knee. It was unlike Antonia to be so informal with someone she would consider staff. She must really like Todd, and it was easy to see he was comfortable with her.

Marvin watched them over the top of the racing form. Only his eyes were visible, but his brow was furrowed and his hands clenched the paper.

Now that there were men in the room, Chantal lost the bored look and artfully arranged a pillow into the small of her back. She arched and stretched to the best of her ability. It was quite a performance, and Antonia hadn't missed it.

"How is your fiancée and the plans for the wedding?" Antonia asked Todd, with a side-glance at Chantal.

"Joanne is really good at this stuff. I'm just picking wine

for the reception. We're almost done with everything, now that I've asked Penny to be the photographer and she's said yes." Todd smiled at me.

"That's marvelous," Antonia said. "You don't have any other responsibilities?"

"That's it. Joanne won't let me pick out music or select any decorations. She swears I'm tone-deaf and knows I'm color-blind, so she took charge of everything else."

Chantal uncurled from the couch and stood. "Francesca's right. Let's get started. I don't want to be stuck here all night." She brushed Stephen's hand away and weaved toward the bar.

Francesca looked at her sister. "Why are you even here? You've never taken any interest in the goings-on around here before. As long as your bills are paid, you couldn't care less what happens."

Antonia raised her hand. "That will do. As a family member, I want Chantal to attend portions of the festival." She looked at her youngest. "Besides, maybe Chantal will have something to contribute. Perhaps in marketing?"

Chantal shrugged as she reached for the martini still on the bar. With a toss of her hair she tipped the drink to her lips.

Francesca snorted. "Well, Mother, there's your answer."

A silence descended on the room, broken only by the sound of Brice, still on his phone in the hallway.

"I don't care for cell phones," Antonia gestured toward the sound. "I think they're rude."

"He's a doctor, Mother," Francesca said. "Brice takes his job very seriously."

"Yes, your very important husband, the doctor." Chantal

polished off the martini. "A hundred bucks says it isn't a patient on the other end of that phone."

"Jealous bitch," Francesca said calmly. "Go drink yourself into unconsciousness."

"At least I have an excuse when I'm unconscious. You manage it sober and wide-awake."

"Enough!" Antonia slammed down her cane. "I will not stand for this."

"I agree. This was supposed to be a pleasant family evening," Veronica said.

Francesca laughed. "Get real. How many pleasant evenings have you seen since you married into this family anyway?"

"Please, Francesca." Veronica looked around the room. "We have guests. Antonia, can we go over the agenda for the festival?"

Antonia watched her daughters. "Todd, you start with the overview, and I will step in."

"Sure." Todd's calm demeanor took some of the tension out of the room, and he walked through the following week's activities.

The Autumn Festival was the biggest annual fund-raiser for The Kasey Foundation, the town's foster care center. The participants donated a portion of their profits on wine sales, and visitors paid admission. In addition to the wine booths, the festival had a petting zoo, a farmers' market and gourmet food booths.

The festival theme varied from year to year. This year the theme was medieval, and the booths and participants were expected to be adorned in an appropriate fashion. Throughout the weekend, displays of blacksmithing and soap-making and staged presentations of swordplay would occur in the midway.

Brice came in a few minutes later. He glanced around the room and perched next to his wife on a bar stool. Francesca ignored him, as did Chantal, who'd returned to the couch with her drink.

After Todd covered the basics of the festival and moved on to staging, I wandered over to where Thomas sat.

"Not exactly role models for a perfectly functioning family, are they?" Thomas said under his breath.

"Do they always squabble like this?"

"Are you kidding?" Thomas sipped his sparkling wine. "They're on their best behavior for company."

"The only one who hasn't had anything to say yet is Stephen. Actually that's not true. You got him to talk."

Thomas shrugged. "I asked about Chantal, how she is. She sure doesn't look good today."

We watched as she finished her drink and set her empty glass on the end table.

"He's got to be worried about her drinking."

"That's part of it. The drinking. The inconsistent behavior. There's been talk of prescription drugs. And the men. Always the men. She throws herself at any guy that goes near her. Anyone but me and Ross, that is." Thomas leaned closer. "A while back Stephen thought she was interested in Todd. I mean, beyond flirting. It bothered him. He wanted to fire Todd. Antonia wouldn't hear of it. She said Todd did a great job and increased visits to the winery."

"That sounds like the Antonia I know. The good of the winery before anything else. How did you get all of this out of Stephen?"

"I excel at three things: decorating, dressing and dishing the dirt. I can get anyone to talk."

At half past nine, the rest of the festival details were finalized. Antonia dismissed everyone with a wave of her cane and the family scattered. Todd and Hayley went out the front, Marvin left through the sliding doors and Connor remained with Antonia to discuss a new grafting technique.

"You guys wait here," I said to Ross and Thomas. "I didn't know what prints you needed, so I grabbed a bit of everything. I'll be right back."

I walked down the front steps into the night, where Todd and Hayley stood near Connor's truck.

"I've got postcards for Ross and Thomas. Then I want to bring a stack of prints to the booth."

"I'll take them down for you," Hayley said.

"Did you confirm that Marvin gave us the right booth?"

She nodded. "Finally. At first he tried to tell me the map was preliminary, but it said 'Final Copy' right on the bottom. I told him not to try anything and he dropped it. I'm really not his favorite person."

"I'd be worried if you were."

I handed her a box then reached into the glove box, where I knew Connor kept a flashlight. "Take this. The main lights are up in the festival area, but the path down is dark."

Todd and Hayley started down the path that led to the fermentation building and, farther, down the hill to the festival grounds.

I grabbed the box of postcards and returned to the library. Connor and Antonia had poured out the Cabernet. Ross handed me a glass and I took a sip.

"Antonia, this is superb."

She nodded. "One of our best years." She pointed to the box. "What are those?"

"Postcards and small prints for the gift store. Ross and Thomas sell my work there."

"Let me see."

I spread out the photos by the various seasons and Antonia peered over them. "My winery seems to be one of your favorite subjects."

"It is. It's beautiful." I caught her eye. "I mean it. The only winery I think is prettier is my own."

After I'd given several to Antonia, I boxed up the rest and grabbed Ross by the arm.

"Come on, you two. I'll walk you out."

A short time later I stood in the night air and watched as they drove away.

The evening fog had rolled in, a regular occurrence this close to the water. Below, in the clearing, the light from Hayley's flashlight moved through the mist.

As I walked back up the front steps, someone shouted. It sounded like it came from the fermentation building. I stopped to listen. Nothing. I turned back toward the house but hesitated. If someone was ruining the wines, it would need to be now, when the wine was aging in the barrels, before it was bottled. Also, it would be at this time of day, when it was unlikely that anyone would be about. All in all, this could be a pretty good opportunity for me to find something out.

Oddly enough, the possibility that I might actually surprise someone didn't get my feet moving. I wasn't thrilled with the idea of looking for anyone in the dark.

The thing that got me back down the front steps and moving toward the fermentation building was Connor. He'd said getting involved was a bad idea, and I hated the thought of admitting he was right. A quick look around and I'd be out of there. I didn't have a flashlight and picked my way along the path. The fog now rolled in drifts, moving across the ground around me.

The heavy double doors creaked when I pushed them open. Rows of barrels loomed in the semidarkness ahead. If the goal was to surprise someone, I needed to leave the lights off. I waited for my eyes to adjust and crept to the rear of the building.

The only sounds were my footsteps and the soft hum of the fans. I walked slowly down the center aisle. Nothing seemed out of place. If there had been someone in the building, they were gone now.

I turned around at the large metal tanks and retraced my steps. When I reached the middle of the row, there was a crash from outside to the rear of the building, then the whine of an electric motor. There was a shout and the whirl of machinery beyond the back doors.

I ran back, pushed open the rear exit and stumbled outside. In front of me were the two winery crushers. The crusher to my left was on. The grind of machinery and the whirl of spinning blades filled the night air.

I went to the machine and climbed the four metal steps to where the grapes were dumped into the crusher. The moon broke through the fog and exposed the silver lever. I stepped on something as I reached and turned off the machine. Silenced descended. The moonlight was bright now as I looked down into the crusher.

It took a moment for my brain to catch up and for me to realize the crusher wasn't empty, that it wasn't a simple trick of the light. It took even longer to understand the dark stain that covered the steel beneath me. I looked again and turned away. My eyes landed on what I'd kicked. A Stetson hat.

Seven

I GRABBED the rail, took a deep breath and managed to make it down the stairs before my knees gave out. I collapsed onto the bottom step and stared at the moon until it began to blur. Then I dropped my head between my knees and tried not to pass out.

Crushers were designed to slice through grapes and any remaining stems. There wasn't any need to call for help. The only thing I'd recognized was Todd's hat. My eyes closed against the night, against what I'd just seen. I sat for a few moments, breathing deeply.

When I could, I opened my eyes and waited for my head to clear. The flashlight swung up the front steps as Hayley returned to the house. I started to yell but turned to look down to the clearing, and the sound died on my lips. Hayley stood next to our booth in the festival area stacking boxes.

My eyes shifted back to the house. Whoever held the light

was at the top of the steps. The beam arched across the landscape and the entire yard was illuminated. The light swung my way. Even though it was too far away for me to be seen, instinct took over and I ducked. The light lingered for what seemed an eternity. It finally disappeared, and the front door softly closed.

With both hands on the rail, I pulled myself up. I swayed and stumbled back into the fermentation building. The fire alarm was to the side of the door and I hit the switch. The sound blared through the building and bounced off the steel tanks. I turned on the lights. Whoever had killed Todd hadn't turned any of them on, hadn't touched any of the switches. Not that it would matter. It was someone who'd returned to the main house, someone whose fingerprints belonged there. I walked down the row and reached the front doors just as they opened.

Brice shut his phone as he stepped into the building, with Francesca right behind him. She was pushed out of the way by Stephen. Veronica clung to his arm, and both of them now wore robes.

"I've called the fire station," Stephen shouted.

Connor arrived with Antonia, and he ran to turn off the alarm.

Hayley came through the rear double doors, followed by Marvin.

Chantal was the last to enter the building. She'd changed into red hip-skimming sweats and a midriff top and was out of breath.

"So," Francesca glanced around. "Not that it's any of my concern, but where's the fire?"

"Todd's dead." It came out as a whisper and nobody heard me.

"There isn't any fire." I spoke louder this time. I wiped the dampness from my forehead with the back of my sleeve.

Brice waved his phone in the air. "What kind of game is this? I'm trying to work. I only get coverage in a couple of spots here, and the patient—"

"That's enough," Antonia said. "Penelope must have had a reason for setting off the alarm. Now tell us, Penelope"— her eyes turned toward me—"what it is."

"Brice, call the police. Todd's dead."

Brice opened his phone and moved toward me. "Where is he?"

"He's dead."

"Since when are you a doctor?"

"He's in the crusher. It was turned on."

Everyone in the room knew what a crusher could do. Brice stopped and closed his phone. "I'll go check on him, but I don't need to call. The fire department will bring the police and paramedics." He walked through the rear doors.

Hayley came up to me and pulled me close.

I looked over her shoulder at the faces around me. The shock was evident but seemed to hit Chantal hardest. She moaned, turned pale and grabbed for the door to steady herself.

When Brice came back a few minutes later, he silently shook his head, and Chantal's sobs filled the room.

It felt good to have Hayley's arm around me. I only had a few moments before the police arrived. All I had was the knowledge that one of them had returned to the house. One of them knew something. I took a deep breath and put the image I'd seen from my mind. "Did any of you go outside within the last hour?"

Silence.

"I was in the library," Antonia said. "With Connor. The rest of you answer her immediately."

As the silence resumed, Antonia struck her cane against the cement floor. "Answer her!"

"I was in the breakfast room," Chantal sobbed, tearstains dark on her red shirt.

"Did anyone see you in there?" The breakfast room had glass doors that led onto the patio, just a short walk from the path.

"I saw her." Trust Stephen to be able to account for his sister's whereabouts. "Just as Veronica and I went upstairs. The rest of the time, Veronica and I were both in the west wing."

"I saw Chantal too," Marvin spoke up. "I also saw Veronica in the kitchen." He rubbed his hand across raspy chin whiskers.

Veronica pulled her robe belt tighter. "I came back down to make tea while Stephen was in the shower," she whispered.

"That's true," Marvin said. "She did. I can see most of the main floor from the winery office."

Veronica looked at him quickly, as did several others. It must have been strange for them to realize Marvin was able to observe them at will.

"'Course, if we have to answer, then you do too," Marvin said.

I looked at him. "You know where I was. I'm the one that found him."

"Not you." He pointed to Hayley. "You."

Eight

"I WAS at our booth."

"I saw her down there." I gave Hayley's arm a small squeeze. "She was on the festival grounds when I found the body."

Marvin watched Hayley. "Before that, before you went to the booth, you and Todd were right outside the fermentation building." He nodded his head toward the kitchen. "I was bringing back my dinner tray, and there you were, just the two of you."

"That's where I left him. I walked down the path and he went inside. He said he had something to take care of."

"Sure. I figured that's what you'd say."

"Marvin, I just told you I saw Hayley down the hill, next to our booth."

"Yeah, after Todd was killed."

"How would she get there so fast?"

Antonia stamped her cane once again. "That's enough, Marvin." Antonia gazed around the room. "Francesca, where were you?"

"Thanks for the vote of confidence." Francesca shrugged. "No matter. Brice and I've been working in the study the entire time."

"Not the entire time." Connor looked at Brice. "You walked out the side door at one point. You were out there for at least fifteen minutes."

"Yes, damn it, but I was just on the porch. My phone doesn't get good reception in the house and it was an important call."

That meant Francesca was alone for at least that long as well. Everyone in the house could have slipped away.

Marvin watched Hayley. I tightened my arm around her, but her pale face didn't respond.

CYPRESS Cove doesn't have much of a police force. We don't often need one, and we like it that way. A loud party or a tourist who'd indulged too much was a busy night. The entire force was Chief Lucas and a few deputies. Lucas was young, around thirty, with sandy blond hair and intelligent blue eyes. I liked him.

When he arrived, he had us return to the house while his men taped off the crushers and fermentation building. As he and one of his men questioned us individually in the breakfast room, the rest of us waited with another deputy in the library.

Since I was the one to find the body, he questioned me first, taking notes as I retraced the evening's events. Chief

Lucas listened without comment until I told him I saw some-one enter the house right after I found the body. He put his pen down.

"Do you know if someone in this family had a problem with Todd or might want him dead?"

"No. Chantal's interest was more than platonic and Marvin is jealous of anyone that shows promise, but Todd was only in charge of the tasting room." I thought of his wedding day and the photographs I'd never take. "He was engaged to be married." I thought once again of the sight in the crusher and tried to remember Todd's smile instead.

Lucas nodded. "Go back to Chantal."

"Chantal and Todd seemed to be close at one point and, knowing her, I can only imagine it was romance she wanted, but I don't know the details. Stephen wanted to fire him but Antonia wouldn't let him."

Lucas looked up from his notebook. "Boy, that's an unlikely couple. How'd you hear about it?"

"Thomas told me."

"What would we do without small-town gossip?"

"Okay, there's something else you're going to hear, probably from Marvin. Hayley and Todd were together right outside the fermentation building before she went down the hill. So, they were alone for a few minutes. It doesn't mean anything, but I wanted you to hear it from me."

"We'll ask everyone where they were at the time."

"Huh," I took a deep breath. "I sort of did that already, while we were waiting for you."

Lucas just looked at me.

"It was the flashlight. I'd just seen one of them going back into the house. I didn't want anyone to have time to come up with a plausible story. I thought the less time they had to think, the better."

"Did it work?"

I hesitated. "Not the way I would have liked. From the sound of it, any one of them could have snuck away for long enough to kill Todd and get back." I told Lucas where everyone claimed to be.

He looked up from his notes. "So, let's put the flashlight going back into the house aside. From what you've said, at one point after Ross and Thomas left, it was only you, Hayley and Todd outside."

I kept my eyes on his. "That's because someone is lying. Hayley was in the clearing below right after I saw the flashlight on the front steps. Besides, she doesn't have a motive."

Lucas looked at me. "Thanks, Penny. I'll have to check all the leads, but I don't think you need to worry."

I didn't feel reassured. Lucas didn't have a vested interest in keeping Hayley safe, and I took little comfort in his words.

"Anything else?" I told him about Antonia's suspicions of someone tampering with the wine. Lucas listened but didn't ask anything when I'd finished.

"It seems unlikely to kill somebody for that, but we'll investigate everyone's motives."

Connor was the last to talk with Lucas, and I waited with Hayley in the library. I sat on the couch where Chantal had been earlier in the evening, while Hayley stood by the glass doors and watched the events outside. The coroner had just left with Todd.

I checked my watch. It was one in the morning. All of us

had been in this room at nine thirty. The last time I'd seen Todd alive was outside, at nine forty. I'd given Hayley the prints and the flashlight to take to the booth. Todd and Hayley had walked away together—Todd to the fermentation building and Hayley to the path. I found Todd around ten after ten. Thirty minutes. Time enough to end Todd's life and change the lives of those around him forever.

The outside lights were still on and police tape surrounded the building. I wondered if Todd knew what was about to happen when he was pushed into the crusher. Did he hear it being turned on? He might have still been alive. Still aware.

The room started to spin, and I broke out in a cold sweat.

Hayley was by my side in an instant. "You don't look very good."

It wouldn't help either one of us if I told her my thoughts. "I can't seem to get warm."

I closed my eyes and pictured Todd in this room earlier. I stood and rubbed my arms against the chill.

Hayley had walked back to the window and stared out at the night. "They keep reminding me I was the last person to see him, before it happened."

"Everyone?"

"Mostly Marvin, not that he's said anything more. You can see it in their eyes, though. Now I wish I'd stayed with Todd. I should have followed my instincts."

"Your instincts? You couldn't have known what was going to happen."

"There was something, though. Something about Todd that seemed wrong."

"Like what?"

"He seemed, I don't know, nervous. Excited maybe. He wasn't paying attention, and he stumbled at one point. Just not his normal self. He kept looking at his watch."

"His watch. Why would he care what time it was, unless he needed to be somewhere? Maybe he was supposed to meet someone at the crusher."

Hayley turned to me. "I think you're right. Now that I think about it, he could have been in a hurry to get somewhere. At the time the way he was acting didn't seem very important. Now I wish I'd been paying attention. I feel guilty, even though I didn't have anything to do with his death."

I kicked myself again for the lost opportunity to see who'd returned to the main house.

At the bar, Francesca's handbag still sat on the counter. My eyes fell on the paperwork that had fallen out. Briefs, motions and a bunch of other stuff I didn't understand. There was also a copy of her bio. Under "Education," it said, "Attended Layton Law School, Class of 1998." It didn't say she'd graduated, but it was certainly implied. No mention of any other school. If she'd finished elsewhere, apparently it wasn't as impressive.

Outside, the fog had thickened, and the world was tucked under muted gray. Todd's death would change things. The festival was to start on Saturday, and Antonia had him scheduled for the Martinelli booth. Beyond that, she would need to hire someone for the tasting room.

Lost in these thoughts, I didn't notice when Antonia came to stand beside me.

"Stay for a moment. Please."

"Of course."

Wisps of hair had escaped from the combs at the top of her head and there were circles under her eyes. It was easy to forget Antonia's age, with her perfect posture and tireless energy. Not now, though. Not as she stood and looked out the window at her beloved winery, divided in two by police tape.

When Chief Lucas was through with each of us, he called everyone to the library and addressed the group. "We have what we need for tonight. I may have additional questions for each of you, so please let my deputy know where each of you is going to be for the next seventy-two hours. Also, no one in this room is to leave town."

Marvin mumbled something under his breath.

Chief Lucas held up his hand. "You have anything to add?"

"Just making sure you meant all of us." Marvin turned and looked at Hayley.

Chief Lucas looked over at Hayley as well. "Yes, I meant what I said. Everyone." His eyes lingered on Hayley, but it wasn't a look that held suspicion, and Hayley looked calm as she returned his gaze.

"If there isn't anything else, I'm finished for now."

Marvin moved to the sliding doors to return to his apartment, and the rest of the family moved in separate directions through the house.

I touched Connor's jacket sleeve. "Can you give me a minute with Antonia? She wants to talk."

Connor nodded, and walked with Hayley and Chief Lucas to the front door.

Antonia and I took a seat on the library couch. She clutched the silver handle of her cane with both hands.

Although the skin was translucent and the bluish tint of her veins clearly visible, she grasped the handle with surprising strength.

"What prompted you to go into the fermentation building? Why were you out at the crusher?"

I told her everything. If she had a killer in the house, she needed to know.

"Do you think he was already dead when the crusher was turned on?"

"I hope so. At the very least I hope he was unconscious." A chill once again coursed through me. "What do you think he was doing out there?"

"Todd was a conscientious worker, but I can't imagine any reason for him to be out at the crusher, especially at night. His duties were relegated to the tasting room."

"Hayley said before she left him to go to the festival grounds he was distracted and kept looking at his watch. I think maybe he had a meeting scheduled with someone."

"If he did, I don't know anything about it. It certainly had nothing to do with work."

"Hayley feels like she should have known something was wrong with Todd and she let him down, that somehow she could have made a difference. There's only one way to help her. I want to know who did this. I need to, for Hayley's sake."

"Good. I hoped you'd feel that way. I believe Hayley was the last person to see Todd alive."

I looked hard at Antonia. "Except for his killer, of course."

Antonia waved her hand. "I wasn't listening to Marvin. Of course I don't think Hayley did it. She'd have no reason.

No, Todd's death is somehow connected to this winery. Someone here gained something from it."

"Maybe what they wanted was to damage the winery. The sabotage wasn't enough, so someone resorted to murder."

Antonia pushed herself up on her cane and walked to the fireplace.

"Could someone want to destroy this winery that much, enough to kill?"

Antonia studied her hands, turning the ring on her finger. "I don't know. I don't know what to think at this point. This winery is more than a business. It's my life. You know what I'm talking about."

I nodded. Aunt Monique had felt the same way. I saw it in Connor and Hayley. More than a business. Creating a memorable wine was an art, a passion.

Antonia turned. "Maybe the goal isn't to destroy the winery. Maybe it's to destroy me." There was pain in her eyes. "I admit it. I'm a better vintner than an employer. Certainly better than a mother."

She swept her arms at the glass doors, toward the fields and vineyards beyond. "I realize I'm obsessive about this place. In the early years I had to be. It wasn't easy, you know. Not back when your aunt and I were the only two women owners in California. When my husband died, the kids were even more aware they came second to the success of the winery."

Uncertainty shone in those steely green eyes, a look that didn't suit Antonia.

"Antonia, you might have made some mistakes with your children." I shrugged. "I wasn't there and don't know. Either way, it doesn't matter now. Adults make their own decisions regarding the directions of their lives. Apologize for the person you were then, if you need to, but don't take responsibility for their actions now. They're the only ones who can do that."

She avoided my gaze and nodded. "I thought I was doing what was best for them, ensuring they had everything they could want. I thought a comfortable home, a good education, and a solid place in the community was enough. Now I'm not so sure."

Her cheeks held that same touch of pink I'd seen earlier. Coming to stand in front of me, she rested her hands on the silver head of the cane.

"I've never spoken like that to anyone."

"You need to be careful. There's someone here you can't trust."

Antonia looked at me. When she spoke, there was strength in her voice. "I'm always careful, Penelope. Something here at the winery holds the answer to Todd's death. Maybe it started with the sabotage. Maybe he found out who it was and confronted them. Perhaps he discovered someone out there tonight and they had to kill him."

I'd been thinking along the same lines. "When Todd came to see me about his wedding photos, he was upset about something. He wouldn't talk about it, but there was something on his mind. I just want you to be prepared for whatever we might find."

Antonia's hands trembled slightly, but her voice was steady and her eyes held mine. "You said it yourself. People are responsible for their own actions. My children included."

A few moments later, we joined Connor and Hayley in the hall and Antonia walked us to the door.

The three of us drove home in silence. Hayley turned to

me, her eyes full of fear. I squeezed her hand, but she didn't respond.

I was involved, even if Antonia hadn't asked for my help. There was a cloud of suspicion over Hayley, and I'd do whatever it took to clear her. Beyond that, I'd found Todd and would forever have that image seared into my memory. Finding the person responsible was the only thing that might help.

Nine

I DRIFTED off sometime near dawn. It was a dreamless sleep, which was probably a good thing. When I got up I went to Hayley's room, but she was gone. I made coffee and joined Nanook and Syrah outside in the warm morning sun. Connor joined me a few moments later.

"Have you seen Hayley? She isn't in her room."

"She came into the barrel room early. She seemed okay but said she couldn't sleep. I gave her some work to do. Thought it would help."

"Thanks."

"You okay?"

I shrugged. "I've been better."

"You don't have to talk about it. 'Course, if you want to, I'll listen."

I repeated the conversation with Antonia. Then he sighed.

It was the guy sigh. It's when they want to tell you what to do but know that when they try, it's going to end poorly.

Before he could once again launch into why my involvement was a bad idea, the phone rang.

I hate to answer the phone.

I refuse to answer the phone.

I snatched it up before the end of the first ring.

"Coward," he said.

I shrugged.

"I can't believe Thomas and I missed everything." Ross stopped. "That sounded terrible. I didn't mean to sound callous. Todd was terrific. Are you okay? Todd was hit with a bottle on the back of the head. Then he was pushed into the crusher."

Small-town gossip at work. "One thing at a time. How do you know Todd was hit and then pushed?"

"The chief was in here first thing this morning to talk to Joanne. She works part-time in the gift store."

"I suppose Lucas wanted to ask her about Todd. See if there was anything she could add that could help to explain why this happened."

"I heard most of the conversation. He wanted her to know that at least Todd hadn't suffered."

"I guess that's something to be grateful for. I'm surprised she came into work."

"She isn't working. Said she just wanted to be around people. She doesn't have any family in town."

"When did she start working for Thomas?"

"She goes to school in Monterey. Wants to be a marine biologist, and works there when she's out of school." Ross paused. "Lucas wanted to talk to her, so they decided to meet here. We heard the whole conversation."

No surprise there. "Tell you what. Why don't I come into town for lunch and say hello to Joanne?"

"I think she'll be okay with that, if I tell her you were a witness and want to help Lucas. If you're here soon, you can try my truffle frittata."

"On my way."

By the time I was ready to go, Connor was back in the vineyards. I glanced at him as I drove by. A mistake. I got the look. I waved and became engrossed in adjusting the side mirror.

The morning was bright and brisk as I tooled down the two-lane road connecting Cypress Valley to the coast and the town of Cypress Cove.

Monterey, to the north, would be busy for the weekend as tourists and visitors from the south made their way up Highway 1 from Santa Barbara and Los Angeles. I merged with traffic then took the next right and made a sharp left onto Ocean Boulevard, the main artery of Cypress Cove.

If elves were to design and build a town, it would be this one. Angular and moss covered, with every roof pitched, every doorway arched. A temperate climate allowed for flowers year round, which grew in profusion from every available bit of earth.

I narrowly missed an errant tourist in the middle of the road and pulled into the parking lot. A tree-lined path connected the lot to the front of the building and the lobby. I walked to the main entrance, which was shared by Sterling and Beauty and the Bean, the coffee and gift shop. Flowers flanked the door, large pots of marigolds and chrysanthemums in bright yellow and bronze.

Mouthwatering aromas wafted into the lobby. I opened the front door to the restaurant and entered the main dining area.

I headed to the display of desserts, my favorite food group. Pastries and cakes with mountains of whipped cream were housed in glass cases designed to keep out marauders like me. Autumn blossoms, artfully arranged in hollowed gourds, graced the tops of the cases and tables. The whitewashed stucco walls and rough tile floor made the restaurant cool and inviting, even on the hottest days.

I reached into the glass case for a chocolate-covered strawberry and saw the reflection of a woman on the patio. Her head was slumped forward and she wiped away a tear. Slightly plump, with masses of unruly red hair, she looked like a garden fairy herself. Although the sun was warm, she pulled at the moss green sweater around her shoulders.

I walked over to the double doors and stepped into the morning sun. Joanne didn't look up as I dragged a chair over to her side of the patio table. I hated to interrupt her thoughts, to break the silence, but my desire to learn more about Todd compelled me forward.

She suddenly focused her soft blue eyes on me. "Are you Penny?"

"You must be Joanne."

She held out her hand to shake mine, and there was a slight tremble.

"I feel like I know you. Your photographs are beautiful. I wish . . ." She stopped.

I knew she was thinking of the wedding pictures I'd never take. "I know. Me too."

Joanne took a ragged breath. "Ross said you wanted to talk about Todd." Her eyes held questions.

"Thanks for seeing me. You see, I found him." I hurried on, before she could ask any specifics I couldn't bring myself to answer. "Also, my niece was the last person with Todd before he, I mean, before . . ."

Joanne closed her eyes, but not in time to stop the tears. "Todd was the nicest person I've ever known. I can't imagine anyone doing this to him."

"How long did you date?"

"A little over a year. Todd grew up in Monterey. He was visiting his mother when I met him. He grew up as an only child and was really close to her, especially after his dad died. They came into the Monterey Bay Aquarium, where I was doing research. It took him a while but eventually he asked me out."

"He seemed to like the work he did at Martinelli."

"I guess. Oh, don't get me wrong. He loved his work. Viniculture came naturally to Todd. He was learning as much as he could about the business and about Martinelli Winery. It wasn't easy for him, though. Marvin Karp is the manager over there, and he always acted like Todd was after his job. Todd couldn't go to him for help and Marvin said some things that upset Todd."

"I know Marvin. What kind of things did he say?"

"He pretty much let Todd know there wasn't a future for him at Martinelli. I told Todd not to worry about Marvin, but now I think there was something to Todd's concerns. I wonder, if Todd kept showing promise, if there was a chance Antonia might have offered him Marvin's job."

"Marvin's very good, but if Todd proved better, it's a definite possibility. Antonia's first loyalty has always been what's best for the winery. How did Todd get along with the family?"

Joanne let out a sigh. "Great, at first. Stephen likes whatever his mother likes. And Francesca isn't at the winery very often, so that wasn't the problem."

"But there was a problem," I prompted when the silence lengthened.

Joanne looked out over the patio garden. "Have you ever met a woman who couldn't resist the challenge of a new man?" Joanne didn't wait for an answer. "Chantal is like that. We'd just started dating when Todd went to work for the Martinellis, but Chantal threw herself at him. She just can't help herself. Todd didn't want any part of it. Then Stephen got involved."

"He was angry at Todd?"

Joanne shook her head. "No, funny enough. I mean at first he was. He thought Todd led Chantal on. As if she needed any encouragement. But after Todd told him he wasn't interested in Chantal, Stephen backed off."

"Did Antonia know about Chantal and Todd?"

"I'm sure she did. Antonia doesn't miss much." Joanne turned her face into the morning sun and exhaled deeply. "He was so excited when he got that job. He still enjoyed it, even after the drama with Chantal."

"How did Chantal handle it?"

"Not well. She's used to getting her way." Joanne paused, biting her lip. "She disappeared for a while. That is, she went on a binge. She likes to party and then she likes to go to the 'spa.' At least that's what they call it, but everyone knows the truth. There's a clinic just north of Monterey that the old money in the valley uses."

I knew the clinic. "Did she check herself in?"

Joanne pushed herself away from the table and we both stood. "Antonia insisted. She makes sure Chantal stays hidden when she gets sloppy. It isn't good for the winery if one of the family members has a problem with alcohol. Or pills. Chantal's been on and off of both, for years."

Joanne leaned on the table. "Somewhere around that time, she started seeing someone else, and she and Todd actually managed to become friends. It was almost like she trusted him because he never let her play her games on him."

"Who did she start seeing?"

Joanne shrugged. "Todd didn't know. She wouldn't tell him, but it was clear it wasn't anyone good for Chantal. That was when she got bad—with the drugs and drinking, I mean."

"I wonder if Stephen knows who it was. He seems overly protective, even for a big brother."

Joanne smiled softly. "Oh, you noticed that, did you? Stephen acts like Chantal is made of glass."

"How much time have you spent around them?"

"When I wasn't working I went and kept Todd company, so I saw them when they came into the tasting room."

"Is Stephen always this protective of his sister?"

"Every time I've seen them. It's irritating, but I've never heard Veronica complain about it. She was a nurse in Monterey before marrying Stephen. It seems like she's fit right into that family, but I wonder how it's working. Can you imagine sharing a house with Antonia?"

"Not remotely. How long have they been married?"

"It's been years. Todd heard Antonia tell Veronica to start having children. Antonia wants heirs to continue the family legacy and inherit the winery. Stephen's being groomed to be the lucky recipient."

"I heard about that. Francesca doesn't hide how much she wants the winery."

"Well, you've picked up quickly on all the Martinelli family secrets." Joanne smiled. "It's funny, but Francesca's more like her mother than she'd ever admit. She'd love to get her hands on the winery, but Antonia is determined to leave it to Stephen. I think that's what infuriates Francesca more than anything. Antonia was given an opportunity that she won't give her own daughter."

"I'm not a fan of Francesca's, but I can understand that." Joanne rubbed her temples, her eyes closed.

"Let's go inside." We walked to the patio door. "Just one more question." I thought about Todd, and the wedding photos. "Todd came to my house, to ask me . . ."

"I know, about being our photographer."

I nodded. "He acted like there was something on his mind. Do you know what that might have been?"

"No. To be honest, we've mostly talked about the wedding the last couple of weeks."

"If you think of anything, please call me. It would be something to do with the winery. Something that bothered him. Anything that might explain why he was out at the crusher alone that late at night."

Joanne paled. "Is that where it happened?" She reached out and I grabbed her by the arm. "Lucas said he'd wait to tell me the rest when I was feeling stronger."

Damn. "He was hit over the head. He was unconscious, and felt nothing." I held her eye and willed her to believe me. I needed to believe it myself.

She nodded and steadied herself as I held open the door for her. We chose a window table and Joanne stopped and turned to me.

"I understand it wasn't an accident, but I'd assumed it was

a random murder. A robbery that Todd walked in on, or some terrible chain of events. Why all these questions about the Martinellis?"

"I'm just trying to understand what happened."

Her eyes welled up. She turned to face the window. "I hope you figure it out. I still can't believe he's gone. How could this happen in Cypress Cove? Things like this never happen here."

Outside, a web stretched from the window frame to the potted marigolds. As a trapped honeybee struggled, a spider descended the spindled thread.

Joanne watched for a moment, then shuddered and turned away. "At least, they never have before."

Ten

"To fully appreciate the bouquet, twirl the glass several times. This allows the undertones of fruit, in this case pear, to rise from the glass." Connor held the glass up to the light. "Also, notice the faint amber hue of this wine. This is caused by using more of the Cabernet grapes."

I poured a glass from the bottle in front of me, picking up where Connor had left off. "In this Syrah, on the other hand, you can see the difference in the color, which is a clear, true burgundy."

On the first Tuesday evening of every month, Connor and I teach wine-tasting classes in town at the Cypress Cove Civic Center. The class is just an overview of what many consider an art and a lifelong study, but it helps when trying to distinguish between different labels and vintages. The tourists enjoy it, and it keeps our labels fresh in their minds when they return home and wander down the wine aisles in their local markets. In any event, Connor and I enjoy sharing our knowledge. The evenings can be fun.

When tasting, you're supposed to refrain from drinking the entire taste. You empty the remainder in the vessel provided and move on to the next selection. In classes given on wine appreciation at the college, I've actually seen that happen.

Here, though, you have a roomful of tourists on vacation. They don't grasp we often have six or seven bottles to taste and, by the third or fourth glass, they don't care. Sometimes you get large parties. Those are the most fun. Tonight it was the Ferrari Club, which had driven the coastal route up from Los Angeles. Twice yearly they came and took over the town for a long weekend. You could tell when those weekends occurred just by the number of times you saw the familiar black horse rearing up, the Ferrari logo, emblazoned on every imaginable piece of clothing.

Halfway through the tasting, Stephen Martinelli appeared in the back of the room. The Martinellis frequently gave classes at the civic center as well. Todd had run the classes, and I wondered who would take over. Stephen must have been checking on when they were scheduled next. He looked up and I caught his eye. I waved briefly and got a slight nod in return.

How did Veronica let him walk around dressed like that? This evening's ensemble consisted of a drab green sport coat and weird pink tie combination.

I nodded to Connor to continue, scooted off the platform and weaved through the Ferrari Club members. Stephen saw me as I worked my way toward him, but that didn't stop him from trying to leave. I caught up to him just as he was about to depart through the fire exit. He would rather set off the alarm than talk to me. Great.

"Hi, Stephen. Got a minute?" I wedged in between him and the door.

"Uh, sure." He glanced around the room. His hands were in his pockets, and as he shifted his weight from side to side, I was struck again by how someone as vital as Antonia could have produced someone so, well, bland. Maybe that was why he wore those ghastly color combinations. Otherwise, he would have completely matched the brown wall behind him. Actually the wall had more color. And more personality.

"Good group tonight." That's me. Master conversationalist.

"Uh, yes, it looked like it was." Silence.

Well, that was fun. Let's try that again. "Did Martinelli have a seminar today too?"

"No. We had one scheduled for tomorrow, but the person teaching was supposed to be Todd . . ."

Silence. He wiped his brow and avoided my gaze.

"Stephen, do you mind if we talk about last night?"

"I guess not, but I don't know what there is to say. I thought at this point the police would be looking into that."

"They are, but I have some thoughts on it and I'd really like to get your input." For results, when I can't think of a lie, flattery runs a close second.

"Uh, do you mind if we sit down over there?"

I didn't mind. Stephen had turned milky pale and was sweating. Better to sit down now than scoop him up after he swooned at my feet. We sat on the bench around the fireplace, which was burning low and steady, just enough to take the chill out of the cool night air. Not that Stephen was cold. He immediately removed his jacket and placed it between us on the bench.

"So, Stephen, tell me about Chantal and Todd."

My directness appeared to catch him off guard.

"Hum, I don't think . . . Why do you . . ."

I was out of patience. "Come on. Spit it out."

"Well, I'm not sure what to tell you. Since you've brought it up, I guess you've heard Chantal was interested in Todd." He wiped his forehead.

"Yes, and I also know he rejected her. That must have been quite a shock for someone like Chantal. I'm sure she isn't used to being rejected."

Stephen eyes grew wide. "You can't possibly think Chantal had anything to do with last night. Chantal wouldn't hurt anybody."

"It isn't always easy to know what people will do when they're upset. I heard you weren't very happy either. Didn't like the hired help rejecting your favorite sister, did you?"

"That's crazy." He wiped his brow.

Boy, was he sweating. "Is it? From what I saw last night, Chantal's certainly drinking again. Was she more upset about Todd than you might know? It wouldn't be the first time a broken heart was motive enough to kill."

I didn't like using Chantal's problems as an inducement to get to Stephen. It felt rotten, but I wasn't here to win a popularity contest. I was no expert on looking into murders, but I was a first-class information-getter. You take a deep breath, find the soft spot in people, then press.

Stephen took a ragged breath. "I'm telling you, Chantal wouldn't hurt anyone. Anyone but herself, that is. She didn't have anything to do with last night."

"How can you be so sure? You said you saw Chantal go into the breakfast room and then you and Veronica went upstairs."

"Yes. But while Veronica was taking her bath, I went back down to see how Chantal was."

"How come you didn't say that last night?"

"Veronica thinks I protect Chantal too much."

"Do you?"

Stephen looked away. "Sometimes."

"So, what happened when you came back downstairs?"

"I wanted to stop her from drinking any more than she already had. She was at the table, crying. I helped her up the stairs and into her room. Then I went back to the west wing. Veronica didn't even know I was gone."

"But Marvin said he saw Veronica in the kitchen. She said she made tea."

"She made it before that, while I took my shower."

Inwardly I groaned. Chantal would have had time to go out the door of the breakfast room, meet Todd, kill him and get back before Stephen returned downstairs. Veronica would have had time before she came up, when Stephen was in the shower. Finally, if Veronica's baths were anything like mine, Stephen had easily had as long as he needed to kill Todd and return to help Chantal up the stairs.

Did Todd have a prearranged meeting with someone at the tanks? Why then? Did he hear something, or follow someone? This wasn't getting me anywhere. "While you were downstairs, did anyone else see you?"

"I don't know. I was only concerned with getting Chantal to her room before Antonia saw what a mess she was."

"I take it your mother doesn't like seeing Chantal when she's been drinking."

Stephen gave a mirthless laugh. "She threatened to put

Chantal back into the hospital for another drying-out session if she didn't pull herself together. With the festival this weekend she's keeping an eye on her."

"Sometimes protecting someone isn't the best thing for them," I said in a quiet voice. "Maybe treatment would be good for Chantal in the long run."

Stephen sighed and rubbed his eyes. "Maybe, but she's been in there so many times and it hasn't helped so far. I just want to protect her, and my mother, from more disappointment."

"How many times has Chantal been in?"

"Eight or nine times over the years. Her first was when she was only eighteen. That's when I met Veronica."

"Veronica worked in a treatment center?" I didn't mean to sound shocked, but I'd always found Veronica wound just a little too tight. I couldn't see her as a calming influence on patients being treated for chemical dependency. Stephen's next words validated my skepticism.

"No. Veronica's worked in various departments in the hospital, but never in the drug treatment facility. She was a nurse and now she volunteers, mostly in the office."

Now that Chantal wasn't the topic, he'd relaxed a bit.

"So you met at the hospital. How?"

"I went into the hospital cafeteria for coffee, and we got to talking. One thing led to another. We married soon after."

I waited for details, but that was all he had to offer. He didn't smile at the memory and didn't strike me as a man overly in love with his wife.

"So, that's it, then." Yawn.

It was as if Stephen read my thoughts. "Veronica and I have

a perfectly good marriage. Oh, I know it may seem tedious compared to some, but it suits us."

That, I believed. I couldn't imagine the girls lined up to be married to Stephen, even for the chance to be the next matron of Martinelli Winery, and Stephen had elevated a nervous, high-strung woman to the level of society doyenne. In some circles, this marriage had more going for it than most.

"Back to last night. Did you see anyone else while you were downstairs?"

"No, but I heard Francesca and Brice talking from behind the library door."

"Were they talking to each other, or on their phones?"

I got a small shrug. "I'm afraid I couldn't say. If I had to guess, I'd say they were probably on their phones."

Although I didn't say anything, I knew it was possible they weren't in there at all. People have played taped conversations behind closed doors before. I read Agatha Christie.

"If you're going to suspect anyone in the family, though, I'd think she'd be your first choice." Stephen's voice sounded confident.

"Francesca? Why?"

"Todd's mother owned about a hundred acres of grapes not far from here. She didn't harvest on her own but sold the crop outright to the surrounding wineries."

"Nothing you've said so far makes me think Francesca had a reason to want Todd dead."

"I haven't finished. Three years ago, Francesca went to her with an offer to buy the property. She refused. Somehow Francesca put the squeeze on the surrounding wineries to stop buying her harvest."

"How do you know this?"

"There are rumors. Stories."

"So how would Francesca get the wineries to stop buying the crop?"

"Who knows? Francesca's an attorney. Her specialty is real estate law. You go back in California history far enough and you can find everything here was once owned by someone else. A well-placed threat here or there might have worked wonders. But with Francesca, you never know. She can be vicious and very creative."

"So, what happened next?"

"Like I said, the wineries wouldn't buy the contract for the harvest. It rotted in the fields. Todd's mother didn't have the reserves to suffer that kind of catastrophe. She was forced to sell."

I looked at Stephen closely. He was enjoying this narrative. His shoulders were back and his voice steady. "And . . ."

"Haven't you guessed?" Stephen's smile was grim, not reaching his eyes. "The property was purchased by my lovely sister. Make no mistake, she will have her own winery. Even if she has to steal it."

Eleven

"I HATE to admit it, but Antonia's right. You're too fat and officially on a diet." I struggled to move out from under Syrah. Having been threatened with diets before, she settled into the warm spot and promptly went back to sleep. No crying for breakfast, which meant Hayley had fed her. I walked into the kitchen where Hayley and Connor sat with coffee.

I yawned. "Did you eat?"

Connor nodded. "Leftover key lime pie."

"Oh, goodie. Glad I asked."

Outside the fog was damp and thick. Mornings were like that in Cypress Cove. One day the sky was crystal blue, the next, you could only snuggle under the comforter and wait for a break in the chill morning air.

I walked to the window. "I wonder if this will burn off later."

"Connor started a fire," Hayley said.

"Thanks."

He nodded at me. He never sat still long enough to be cold. Or to gain weight. I, on the other hand, had no problem sitting still for long periods of time, preferably with a good book, which was probably why I couldn't eat key lime pie for breakfast.

Hayley put her coffee down. "Come on, Nanook. Let's go for a walk."

They bounced down the back steps and disappeared into the fog.

"I'm going up to Martinelli this morning," Connor said. "One of their tractors quit and they want to borrow one of ours. Do you want me to bring anything else up to the booth while I'm there?"

I pulled a mug out of the cabinet. "I have some prints of Martinelli Winery that Antonia hasn't seen. The ones I took the other night. Let me get them and some coffee and I'll go with you."

Connor studied me over the rim of his cup. "I saw you grill Stephen last night after the tasting. He sure was trying to get away. If there was a fire, he would have been right in line to be first out the emergency exit."

"Fat chance of a fire with him around. He's such a wet blanket, I'd throw him on the flames. Put it out in no time." I carried my cup over to the window. "And I didn't 'grill' him. I just wanted his take on what happened. According to him, there's no way Chantal had anything to do with Todd's death."

"I can't see her being the one either."

"Imagine my surprise. You wouldn't be defending Chantal out of appreciation for her more obvious charms, now, would you?"

Connor grinned. "She is quite 'charming,' isn't she?"

I rolled my eyes.

"I just can't see her going through everything required to kill him. First of all, she'd been drinking pretty heavily . . ."

"Unless she was pretending. It was a clear liquid. For all we know it was water, not vodka, she was slugging back all night long."

He looked at me. "You just aren't going to give her the benefit of the doubt, are you?"

"I need to balance out your urge to rush to her rescue."

"I'm not rushing . . ." He stopped. "I'm not going to win this one. Let me just say I'm sure she was drinking."

"How?"

"Because she gave me a hug good-bye. I smelled the vodka on her breath."

The pit of my stomach twisted, and I threw my hands in the air. "Fine, whatever. She was drinking. And I couldn't care less who you hug."

Connor watched me. "Well, just so long as you don't care."

I walked to the coffeepot and imagined the kind of hugs Chantal was likely to give. Not a lot of daylight would show between her and anyone she grabbed on to. I poured myself some coffee and when I could continue the conversation, I returned to the table.

"So. It's unlikely she would have been able to carry out any plan to murder Todd, even if she'd wanted to."

Connor nodded. "She'd have to meet him at the crusher up on the platform, then hit him on the head and push him in. And on top of that, to actually turn it on . . ."

An unwelcome memory of that night filled me, and the room started to tilt.

Connor stood to grab my arm. "Sorry. That wasn't what you needed first thing this morning."

"It's still so fresh in my mind. I'm sure it'll get better with time." I tried to believe my own words. "Actually, I know what you're saying about Chantal and, at the moment, I can't see her responsible either. Unrequited love, though, is right up there as a reason why people get killed. She isn't coming off the list yet."

Connor took a sip of coffee. "I'll tell you who should be at the top of your list. Francesca. That woman is chiseled out of solid ice."

I told him about my trip to Layton.

"So she didn't graduate from there. Maybe she went somewhere else. If she doesn't have her degree at all, would she kill Todd if he found out about it?"

"Maybe, and there's more to it." I repeated what I'd heard about Todd's family's vineyard.

"Todd must have held a grudge against Francesca for forcing his mother to sell, especially since he would have been the one to inherit."

"It was clear at the MCWGA he was furious with her, but that doesn't explain why Todd was the one who turned up dead, unless he threatened Francesca somehow, or he found a way to get the land back."

Connor walked to the sink. "Look, you probably don't want to hear this, but I'm going to say it anyway. Someone out there's a murderer, either because they have something to hide, or something to lose. They aren't going to be crazy about you nosing around."

"I'll be careful."

He lifted his brow.

"I mean it. I'll try not to let my nose get me into too much trouble."

He hesitated then nodded. He moved to the fireplace and used the fire poker to push the burning wood to the back.

I felt taken care of. A guardian angel in blue jeans. When I lived in the city, every spare moment was spent at the paper. I think I'd been lonely and hadn't realized it.

It was nice he was here. Someone looking out for me. It'd been a long time.

ALTHOUGH Antonia kept several full-time staff, it was Veronica who answered our knock at the Martinelli home some time later.

"Come in. Come in." Veronica's hand held the door and the other fiddled with the ever-present pearls. She wore a neutral sweater set with a matching wool skirt. Who wore pantyhose and heels just to be around the house? Veronica must be working hard to convince Antonia she was ready to step into those matriarchal shoes. In all fairness, though, it was tougher to run a winery than most people realized. If Veronica was this committed to the winery and the Martinelli family, she deserved some credit.

She was a chatty little thing as she led us into the library.

Antonia sat at the desk, going over papers. "Good morning." Antonia put her pen down. "Would you like some coffee?"

As Veronica turned to get us some, Connor and I declined.

I walked over to the desk. "Here, Antonia." I handed her the photos. "I took these the other day. I think they're probably some of the best photos I've ever taken of your winery."

Antonia peered at the photos. "The shrubs are all overgrown. They're a mess."

"That's part of why I like these pictures so much. It makes the whole place look rooted, older."

Antonia handed the pictures back to me. "The gardeners are here today. You should have waited."

Who's the photographer anyway? "Well, I like them." I took them from her and put them back in my bag.

Connor looked amused. "I have the tractor out on the trailer, if Marvin can help unload it."

"Of course. I'll walk down with you to find him. Veronica, stay and keep Penelope company." She sounded like she was talking to the family pet.

"Certainly, Mother." Veronica nodded as Antonia led Connor through the glass doors and into the morning fog.

Veronica perched on the edge of the couch, ankles crossed, but her foot tapped on the floor and she picked at a button on her sweater. This was not a woman used to relaxing. She was a bundle of nerves.

"I love this room." The walls were covered in peach silk that complemented the cream brocade furnishings. Fresh-cut flowers in Waterford vases rested on gleaming cherrywood side tables. Along the walls, between the sparkling windows, cherrywood bookcases ran floor to ceiling. A ladder on a ceiling track made access to the top shelves convenient. I wondered if anyone had ever taken a flying leap at it to sail around the room. Certainly not the eager-to-please woman sitting across from me.

"It is beautiful, isn't it?" Veronica sprang up. "Would you like to see the family portraits I recently had framed?"

Veronica carried on about old wedding photos and various uncles and aunts. Yawn. I listened to her prattle on about long-dead members of her husband's family and wondered how to bring the conversation around to more recent events.

Veronica solved the problem for me. "The police were here again early this morning, asking the family all sorts of personal questions. I certainly can't believe they actually suspect one of us had anything to do with this nasty business."

"Actually, it seems reasonable for the police to interview the family first. You were all here at the time, and the reality is most homicides are committed by people the victim knew."

Veronica reached for a spent blossom in a vase. "I suppose, but after all this family has done for the community, it seems reasonable to expect some special consideration. And as for the notion someone in this family had something to do with that business"—she gestured toward the back windows—"why, that's just ridiculous! Surely the police must realize it was some-one who wandered onto the property, probably looking for something to steal. If they surprised Todd, he could have fallen into the crusher."

"Perhaps, but would someone who wandered onto the property know how to work the crusher?"

"That machine is easy to turn on. You don't need to be strong. I've seen Antonia work it a hundred times."

Veronica caught my glance and stopped, her hand once again on the pearls. "That sounded terrible. I didn't mean to insinuate Antonia had anything to do with this." She was pale and seemed to shrink beneath her sweater set.

"I know that. In the end, what matters is how everything looks to the police."

"You're right. I'm sure it will all work out, but still, please don't repeat what I said. It sounded terrible."

"Of course Antonia knows how to work the crusher. Everyone who lives on a winery probably knows how to run that machine."

"Yes, yes. Of course you're right. During crush, everyone in the household is pulled in to help."

I wasn't going to point out she'd brought the likely list of suspects right back to where she'd tried so hard to avoid: the immediate family.

I left Veronica a short time later to walk the grounds. Since Antonia had given her implicit instructions to keep me company, she'd been reluctant to let me go, but she'd poured herself a cup of coffee, and I wouldn't be able to take high-strung Veronica in the throes of a caffeine fit.

The police, no doubt, have a system to figure things out when solving a murder. I'm sure they have a formula or a profile they use. Without anything to go on beyond my gut, I was going with my theory that Francesca did it. Nonscientific, but there it was. She was the obvious one to want Todd dead. He might have confronted her about how she ended up with his mother's land, the land that was supposed to be his. Todd was agitated when he came to see me. I wish now I'd pushed him harder to tell me what was wrong. Then, there was that whole thing about her not graduating from Layton. Just one more thing that didn't add up about her.

I made my way through the side yard, toward the back of the property. Gardeners worked in the beds around the house and winery buildings; the bushes and shrubs were all trimmed back, neat and orderly, just as Antonia preferred.

Fog danced around my legs as I walked across the newly mowed lawn, toward the path down to the festival grounds. I passed the storage buildings but stopped at the winery office. Antonia had sent Marvin to help Connor unload the tractor in the front of the house. I nodded at one of the gardeners, who pushed a wheelbarrow of trimmings past me. When he'd turned the corner, I paused at the office window and peered in.

Paperwork and a ceramic coffee cup, white with the words "Viva Las Vegas" in red, sat on the desk. Beyond the office was a doorway that led to a small apartment. There was an unmade bed and I could see a corner of the kitchen, dishes piled in the sink.

I turned my attention back to the desk. Invoices and a letter opener, a couple of receipts and what looked like a racing form.

I really needed to get better at reading upside down.

I swiveled to look back at the house. Sure enough, you could see most of each room from this window. I would have tried the door but Veronica stood at the back windows watching me, so I waved and continued toward the path down the hill. Below me stood the main exhibit tents of soft white muslin, each topped with the flag of the winery sponsoring that tent. The colors looked muted in the misty gray.

To my left was the fermentation building, silent behind the yellow police tape. I was behind the office now, and out of sight of the main house. I stopped. No doubt the police would find anything in there that could help. On the other hand, Lucas hadn't seemed to take the wine tampering very seriously. Hmm, what to do, what to do . . .

The tape left a streak of moisture on my sleeve as I pushed it over my head. I scooted to the entrance, stepped inside, and eased the door closed behind me.

As on the night of Todd's murder, the room was warm and humid. My running shoes were silent on the tile floor and I left the main lights off. No need to advertise that I'd ignored the police tape. Since I wasn't sure where to start, I focused down the center aisle to the double doors that led out the rear of the building. I wasn't in a hurry to open those doors again. The crushers could wait until last.

I let my attention wander to the aisles that ran the length of the building. There were perhaps ten rows on each side of the main walkway, with barrels stacked toward the ceiling. The building was enormous. Four times the size of the fermentation building at our winery.

I made my way to the first row of barrels. It was dark and I walked with care, led by one overhead light. It grew darker the farther I walked into the building. I reached into the pocket of my jacket and grabbed my keys and the small flashlight that dangled from them, an addition after the last time I'd been in this room. I turned it on and swung it side to side. The reflection of the light between the barrels bounced off the floor in the aisles next to me as I moved down the rows. I didn't know what I hoped to find, so I took my time.

Halfway down the second aisle, my brain registered something had changed. It was quiet, with just the hum of the fans in the background. I turned back, retraced my steps and again shined the light between two barrels sitting to my right. No gleam of tile floor. Something blocked the light. Silently I bent down and directed the light between the barrels. Black pants. Black gloves. Someone stood listening in the row next to me.

My heart started knocking around in my chest and there were black spots in front of my eyes.

"Who's there?" I tried to yell, but it came out more like a whimper. The leg moved and glass broke. Steps pounded on the floor as someone ran down the aisle. I started for the main door and stopped; the steps were headed in the opposite direction. With less-than-lightning-fast reflexes, I realized they wouldn't risk being seen in the front of the building and would use the rear exit. As I turned and ran back I could hear the cost of my hesitation: the sound of the rear doors.

Sure enough, the door stood open and I was alone. I avoided looking at the crushers, ducked under the police tape and walked the twenty yards to the edge of the bluff. Nothing. Turning to my right the hillside loomed in front of me, blanketed by trees.

I walked to the edge of the growth and stepped into the brush. It was darker there, the sky canopied by branches. The trees were thick enough to block the house and other buildings from my sight. The crunch of fallen leaves, brittle under my feet, filled the silence, but other than that it was completely still. Either I was alone, or someone waited for me deeper in the shadows. A crow flew overhead and its cry echoed in the stillness. I listened and looked around. Nothing.

I didn't have a plan if I actually found someone. What was I going to do, tackle them in the forest? To be honest, I'm not the bravest person by nature. A chill ran though me. Forget going any farther. I had to fight just to stay in place. I backed out of the woods, returned to the fermenting building, slipped back inside and closed the door. I leaned against the wall and stopped to catch my breath. I really needed to work out more.

Turning on the flashlight, I made my way down the row the intruder had just vacated.

Halfway down the aisle a broken wine bottle was scattered across the floor. I bent over to look. It wasn't just glass. A brownish powder was mixed in and drifted through the air. Someone had dropped a wine bottle full of something that didn't belong in the fermentation building. I felt along the top of the nearest barrel and was rewarded with the feel of the opening where the cork belonged. Antonia was right. Someone was sabotaging Martinelli Winery.

The base of the bottle was still intact and held some of the powder. I used my boot toe to sift through the broken glass. A basic wine bottle without a label. Whoever had done this could walk around the winery at will and not be noticed. The bottle breaking was bad luck for someone. If I'd passed them outside the building holding the same bottle, I wouldn't have thought anything of it.

I used my foot to push the largest pieces of glass under the barrels, where they wouldn't be seen. Without knowing what the powder was, I didn't want to touch it with my bare hands, so I reached into my purse and grabbed the envelope that held Antonia's pictures. Using a photo, I scooped up some of the powder and put it in the envelope. The building remained quiet as I made my way back to the entrance.

With the doors closed behind me, I scooted under the police tape and made my way around the corner of the winery office.

"Looking for something, missy?"

Twelve

M*ISSY?* That used to tick me off, even back when I was one.

I pushed off the wall and towered over Marvin Karp. An easy thing to do since I had five inches on him.

He seemed undaunted. "Yup, there isn't much I miss from that window." He jerked his thumb over his shoulder toward his office.

Okay, great. He'd seen me come out of the fermentation building. Maybe defiance wasn't the best stance, considering he actually had something on me. He couldn't have been in there with me, because he'd been with Connor, and he wouldn't have seen the person run away, since the back door wasn't visible from here. I wouldn't learn anything from him and turned to walk away.

"I just helped your man unload the tractor." He hooked

his thumbs into the loops of his jeans as he rolled back on his heels. "You oughta get going. He's waiting for you."

Damn. Marvin telling me to get going prevented me from leaving just yet. I turned back to him. He scratched at the gray stubble on his chin. Something was different. Today his usual glare had been replaced with something else. Amusement. He was enjoying something. No doubt it was at someone else's expense. Maybe it was that he'd just caught me where I didn't belong, but as I looked at him, I realized it was more than that. He wasn't amused. He was satisfied.

It took a master's touch to turn a bunch of grapes into really good wine. Marvin seemed to have that quality in excess. From what I'd heard, Todd had shown the same promise. With Todd gone, Marvin's position was secure. The timing worked. His office was adjacent to the fermentation building and it would have been easy to entice Todd out on some pretense of winery business.

"So, you said you saw Veronica in the kitchen the night of Todd's death." I nodded toward the winery office. "From that window."

His eyes narrowed. "That's what I said, all right. Chantal too." He jerked his thumb back over his shoulder. "I was right there at that window the whole time, and I'd like to hear some-one say different." His voice rose an octave. "To them, I'm just a hired hand. It would take nothing for them to pin this on me if they could."

"Oh, come on, Marvin. Nobody's trying to pin anything on you."

"You don't know much about this family, do you, missy? If you ain't blood, you ain't. They'd stick me with this, or even you, if it kept their own from going down. I've taken care of that, though." His look of satisfaction returned. "I've taken well good care of that."

"What've you done?"

"All I'm saying is what I already said, little missy. I didn't leave that spot the night Todd died. I saw what I saw, and that's all I'm saying."

With that, he disappeared into the winery office. Marvin was amused by causing discomfort to others. I didn't know what he'd done, but I was sure someone else wouldn't find the situation nearly so funny.

ON our way home, I repeated my conversation with Marvin. I also told Connor about the powder and the unknown person in the fermentation building. I didn't tell him I'd briefly considered looking for the person in the woods. I admitted going under the police tape. That was enough. I didn't feel like facing those piercing blue eyes right then.

When we reached the house we headed down to the offices and the winery lab. Ours was quite small, although some of the labs on larger wineries can be very extensive.

"Let me have the powder."

I pulled the envelope from my bag. "You don't know what it is. Don't touch it with your bare hands."

He held it up to the light. "I've got a pretty good idea."

He poured a bit on a slide and slipped in onto the microscope.

"Yup, it's Brett."

"It's who?"

He stood up and gestured. "Not who. What. Brettanomyces, usually just called 'Brett.' See for yourself."

I peered at the tiny specks. "I think I see something. What is it?"

"It's yeast. In certain wines and in small amounts, it's usually okay. Sometimes it's even a good thing. You said there was a whole bottle of this stuff?"

"Yes, and the cork of the nearest barrel was out."

He raised his brows. "A few tablespoons of this would ruin a barrel in no time. It multiplies in the wine, and the result isn't pleasant."

"What does it do?"

"Makes the wine taste bitter and smell like a wet horse blanket."

Connor carefully folded the envelope and threw it away. Taking the slide, he walked toward the sink. "You need to figure out how to tell Antonia she's got a real problem with someone at her winery. But first, you need to wash your hands."

I walked back to the house, taking a seat at the desk and thinking through the events of that morning. Someone had taken quite a chance, but to carry the yeast in a wine bottle would almost ensure nobody would question the contents, especially if the person belonged at the winery. Some of the surrounding wineries were jealous of Antonia's success, but I couldn't imagine any of them resorting to this. Once again, Francesca and her anger at Antonia's decision to leave the winery to Stephen came to mind. I wondered where she was right now.

Around noon, Hayley came in. Her search through the kitchen cupboards and refrigerator was loud, and I pushed back from the desk.

Wednesdays were reserved for a standing lunch with my

best friend and cousin, Annie Moore, the town veterinarian. Before Annie came to town the closest vet was in Monterey, and I'd convinced Annie to move here not long after she graduated from UC Davis. She fell in love with Cypress Cove the first time she came for a visit, so convincing her to open a practice here wasn't difficult.

We don't look anything alike. Annie is five-foot-two, has auburn hair and weighs around a hundred pounds. I'm eight inches taller, with streaky blond hair, and weigh decidedly more. The giveaway that we're family is the same sense of humor, which typically bursts forth at inappropriate moments, and a tendency to rush into situations without stopping to ask questions. We also have matching hazel eyes we inherited from our grandmother.

The sun had burned off the morning gloom and was high in the cloudless sky, so I lowered the top on my car, waved to Hayley as she ate on the back patio and pulled into the lane. I turned up the local PBS station, and Vivaldi washed over me, smooth as the fresh autumn air.

I was almost at the turn into town when I spotted a car, nose first in the ditch ahead. I slowed and turned down the music. The car was partially hidden beneath an oak tree. I took a good look at the car. Oh, great. A red Porsche. Now, Chantal's car was as easy to spot as she was.

I slowed down to a crawl on the empty road and took another look. Something wasn't right. The car was stopped at an odd angle in the ditch, almost as if it had drifted off the road, and it was pulled too far into the tree. The branches dug into the hood and were going to leave scratches when she tried to back out.

I pulled in beside the car and jumped out, balancing my concern with curiosity. Nobody was inside and the driver's door hung open. The car rested against the trunk of the tree, and the brake hadn't been set.

A sound came from the open field below and I walked toward the embankment. Chantal sat on a rock. She faced down into the valley, toward the creek winding along the bottom. Her normally perfect hair was pulled into a disheveled ponytail, and the loose-fitting jacket and jeans were completely unlike her usual attire.

The car hadn't actually run into the tree, and I could see she wasn't hurt. No longer concerned for her safety, my curiosity took over. While I stood there and wondered how to approach her, she turned. She didn't seem startled. She didn't react in any way. Rather, she released a long-held breath, pushed herself up from the rock and walked toward me. She moved as though the effort was enormous, as if braced against a nonexistent wind.

When she reached me, I was startled at how pale she was. Gone was the red lipstick. Black streaks mapped where tears had fallen. The pain in her eyes was evident and private, and she turned away to face the valley once again.

"I envy you, you know." Chantal spoke without turning back. "You're surrounded by people who love you. You know who you are. You seem fulfilled. You seem happy."

Knock me over. A lonely and vulnerable Chantal hadn't occurred to me. I suppose that could explain why she came on to every man she met. To hear her humble admission made me do a quick mental adjustment of my impression of her life.

"You have friends. People you can rely on. Todd and I had that, at least for a while. I really miss him." She broke

118

off, staring into the valley below. "Just not the way everyone thinks. I never felt romantic about Todd."

"Why do you think everyone assumed you did?"

She turned. "Oh, come on. Look at me." A small smile touched the corners of her mouth. "Not exactly at this moment, but how I normally look." She shrugged. "Everyone always assumes if I'm interested in a man, it's sexual interest."

"No kidding."

"Yes, I admit it. I'm a flirt." Her smile faded. "Never with Todd, though. He was the best friend I've ever had."

She looked back over the valley. "It's just different with everyone else. Like Stephen. Don't get me wrong, he's a great brother, but I feel like he wants what's best for the family before what's best for me. With Todd it really felt like it was about me being happy."

"Did your family know how close you two were?"

She studied me for a moment then shrugged. "I didn't hide it. It must have been pretty obvious I preferred his company to theirs."

"But just as a friend."

"Just as a friend."

"I can't help it. You sound sincere, but it's hard for me to believe you just wanted to be friends with a man—any man, much less one as attractive as Todd." I thought of the boyfriend she'd stolen from me years before. "You forget, I've known you a long time."

Chantal straightened her shoulders and looked me squarely in the eyes. "I understand why you'd have your doubts, but I'm telling you the truth."

I believed her. For the first time in all the years I'd known her, I believed what she was telling me.

"Okay, Chantal, if that's the case, what happened? Everyone knows you and Todd had a falling-out."

"I pushed him away. My best friend. He wasn't happy with what I was doing with my life. He was right, but I pushed him away."

"What were you doing?"

She paused. "I made some really dumb mistakes and one of them, just one of them, was drinking."

"What else?"

She bit her lip and stared down into the valley.

"Chantal, you don't have to tell me, but if we're going to have this conversation, what were you doing that Todd didn't like?"

She didn't answer.

"I can only imagine a man was involved. Am I right?"

Chantal laughed. "Of course. A woman like me can't be alone for long."

"Who was it?"

"You'd think the way Stephen keeps an eye on me he'd have figured it out."

"Who was it?"

She didn't answer, and a hush settled between us.

"Chantal."

She turned to me as color crept up her cheeks. "I guess I feel compelled to stir things up in this family. What better way than to sleep with your sister's husband? It was Brice."

Thirteen

I DIDN'T respond. For once I was speechless. It was bad enough to sleep with your sister's husband, but Brice? Her pale face and eyes that wouldn't meet mine made it clear she regretted her behavior. She'd made a terrible mistake, and because she'd been so open with me, I tried to hide my disgust. It took a lot of effort.

In the end, I didn't say anything, and she didn't elaborate. We stood for a while, looking out over the valley.

Finally, she turned to me. "Look, I really don't want to talk about it anymore. I just want to stay here alone for a while."

My cue to leave. "Yeah. Sure. No problem." I turned toward my car.

"Penny."

I looked back at her, alone with mascara tracking her cheeks, the empty valley behind her.

"Thanks for not saying anything. Thanks for just listening."

I nodded and walked back to my car, glad that for once I'd managed to keep my opinions to myself.

WHEN I arrived at the restaurant twenty minutes late for lunch, Annie was at the bar. Ross was behind the counter, pouring out a Pinot Grigio. They had their heads together, talking in low voices, but they pulled apart when I walked up. I hadn't had a chance yet to talk to Annie about the night of Todd's death, but if Ross knew, Annie knew. Probably the entire county knew.

"Hi there." Annie gave me a quick kiss. She made room for Ross as he came out from behind the counter for a big hug. As I let my friends hold me, I thought once again of Chantal, who had everything in the world but this.

I looked at Ross. "It's slow. Why don't you join us for lunch?"

Ross got someone to cover the bar, and the three of us made our way to a patio table, the same one where I'd met with Joanne the day before. I didn't want to talk about Todd, which Annie understood without a single word being exchanged. It might be soon, it might not be for a very long time, but either way, I knew she'd be there when I needed to talk.

Ross is a different story. He's never met a question he wouldn't ask. No amount of information is too much, and as we made our way to the patio he repeatedly launched into a comment, only to stop. His restraint was admirable.

"So, you were running late?" Annie asked.

"Actually I ran into Chantal."

"What do you mean, you ran into her? In your car?" Ross poured me a glass of wine.

"Just by the side of the road. She was stopped, and so I stopped . . ." I couldn't decide how much to say. I'm no stranger to gossip, but for the first time stirrings of sympathy for Chantal, although faint, held my tongue. "I wanted to ask her about Todd, and we got to talking about some guy she was seeing, and what a really bad idea it turned out to be . . ."

"Oh, you mean Brice," Ross shrugged. "I heard about that months ago. I thought I'd told you."

"No. I think I would have remembered that."

Annie looked at both of us. "Somebody better tell me what I missed."

"You tell us, Penny, since you actually talked to her, and I would just be repeating gossip."

"Big shocker. You repeating gossip."

"You're right. Even I can't believe I just said that."

Since it wasn't going away and Ross knew the story anyway, I gave them a condensed version of my earlier conversation with Chantal.

Annie poured herself some more wine. "I always knew she didn't have her panties on too tight, but Brice? It's creepy, even if he weren't married to her sister."

"I think she's sort of lonely," said Ross.

"Come on," Annie said.

"Well, I do. She doesn't have any purpose in life. In and out of rehab. Nobody takes her seriously. She's kind of tragic."

Annie put her glass down. "HELLO. She's sleeping with her brother-in-law."

"I think you're both right, in a way," I said. "She is tragic, and she was totally out of line. I'll be back. I want some berries."

Ross sets out fresh fruit for customers to nibble on while they wait for their lunch. Today it was blackberries, just picked that morning. The last of the season.

The mound on my plate was conspicuously large when I picked up a clipped, short voice rising above the rest. I knew that voice. I popped a berry into my mouth and peered around the plaster column separating me from the table. Well, well. Francesca and Brice. Francesca sat with her back to me, her shoulders held rigid and stiff. Brice shook his head, and his hands waved about as he stressed some point that, unfortunately, I couldn't hear. He finished talking, stopped shaking his head, and waited for an answer. In one of those still moments that happen occasionally in crowded situations, there was a complete lull in the chatter, and Francesca's answer carried across the restaurant.

"I just realized something. Not only are you a cheating bastard, you're stupid too."

Brice's face visibly paled and he looked like he was carved out of stone.

Francesca threw her napkin on her untouched plate. The scrape of the chair as she rose to leave filled the ensuing silence.

She stomped toward the front door. Every diner watched her go, her snappy little Ferragamos carrying her as fast as they could. I popped berries into my mouth and made my way back to Annie and Ross, where Chantal was still the topic of conversation.

"She makes it hard to like her. Her biggest problem is herself," Annie said.

"I'm absolutely starving," I said. "I'm eating."

"Isn't that the truth." Ross took a berry from my plate.

"It absolutely is the truth. What's up with Brice? I see him alone all the time. I don't think he and Francesca spend much time together. I'll have the lemon sole. It's delicious," Annie said to the waiter, who had just arrived.

"Ha, you're right about that."

"You're both right. The sole *is* delicious," Ross said.

"No, she isn't right about that." I waved off the injured look on Ross's handsome face.

"What's wrong with my sole?" Ross asked.

"I thought you liked sole," Annie said.

"The Chicken Buena Vista is delicious," the waiter suggested helpfully.

I snapped the menu shut. "I'll have the sole. I was talking about Francesca and Brice. He spends a lot of time alone. As a matter of fact, he's alone right now." I repeated what I'd heard.

"Ouch," Annie said. "How embarrassing, but certainly no more than he deserves."

Ross stood. "I can't believe I missed it and it happened in my own restaurant. I'm going over to see if he's still there."

I looked at him. "At least be discreet."

Ross sniffed. "I'm six-foot-three, I weigh two hundred thirty pounds, and although I humbly submit it's almost all muscle, I must say I do walk with a bit of a sway. Exactly how discreet do you expect me to be?"

I rolled my eyes. "Already you're making a scene. Just go."

He returned a few moments later. "Nope. What rotten luck."

WHEN lunch arrived, I assured Ross the sole was perfection. We spent the rest of the meal discussing the fight between Francesca and Brice, and whether it was about Chantal or possibly some other indiscretion.

By the time coffee arrived, we'd exhausted the Brice topic and Annie entertained us with stories of several of her patients, including a twenty-eight-pound cat with a thyroid problem. I figured Syrah, at eighteen pounds, wasn't that fat after all. Of course, I didn't say this to Annie, who I'm sure would be inclined to disagree.

After we finished, we wandered through the gift shop, said hello to Thomas and made sure they had my posters and postcards well stocked. I picked up a shot of Martinelli Winery, taken in the early spring, when the vines were just getting their leaves. I still preferred the one I'd taken earlier in the week, with the plants and shrubs large and full.

Annie and I left, turned right on Ocean Boulevard and walked along enjoying the last of the day's warmth. Tourists filled the street, cameras at the ready, their bags filled with souvenirs and local wine, some of it hopefully from Joyeux Winery.

We turned the corner and spotted Chief Lucas and Hayley a short distance ahead. Their heads were bent close and they held hands.

Annie nudged me. "Why didn't you tell me they were seeing each other?"

"I didn't know. She said she was seeing someone but didn't want to talk about it. Didn't want to jinx it. She said it was a new thing."

"Well, they look pretty cozy. Maybe you'll have a police chief in the family."

"That explains it."

"Explains what?"

"Hayley was the last one to see Todd before he went into the fermenting building, and Marvin tried to make it look like she was the most obvious suspect. Lucas told me he didn't think I needed to worry. He was trying to reassure me."

They made their way toward us. "I don't want to put Hayley on the spot. She said she'd tell me when she was ready."

"So let's avoid them. Move it."

We each made a sharp turn, right into each other. Annie, being so much shorter, took the brunt of the impact. She flailed into a group of sightseers and landed on the sidewalk, along with cameras, bags and a couple of tourists. Stealth mode. Catlike. Yup, that's us.

As I apologized to tourists and helped Annie up, Lucas and Hayley stopped in front of us.

"Hi, you two." Hayley blushed. "Connor insisted I get off the vineyard for a while. He said working ten days in a row, even during crush, was too much."

I nodded. "I quite agree."

"We thought we'd grab a bite, just a quick sandwich, and then I need to get back to work." Lucas took Hayley's arm.

Hayley blushed a pretty pink and smiled. I don't think I'd ever seen her look quite so happy. "Great idea. Enjoy."

"Actually, Penny, this saves me a call. Can you stop by the station? There's something I'd like to ask you about."

"Sure. When do you want me there?"

We agreed to meet in an hour. Annie and I watched as they walked away, Lucas's hand resting in the small of Hayley's back.

"They look so cute," Annie said. "So, you've got an hour. Come on. I'll keep you company."

We made our way into Neiman's while Annie speculated

on what Lucas wanted. "You must tell me absolutely everything."

"I'm glad he wants to see me. I was going to call him anyway. Lucas doesn't know about Francesca getting Marilyn's land."

"Are you going to tell him about Brice and Chantal?"

"I don't know yet. Chantal made a mistake, but it was stupidity more than anything. I'd like to leave her out of it, but it could be important. If Todd confronted Brice or if Brice felt Todd was interfering in his relationship with Chantal, who knows what might have happened."

"I'd love to know what Francesca and Brice argued about at lunch," Annie said. "It might have been about Chantal, but, in reality, Chantal probably wasn't the first one, or even the only one, that Brice was 'playing doctor' with."

I rolled my eyes. "You have such a way with words."

"I bet 'Hide the Thermometer' is one of his favorite games."

"Stop." I pushed her toward the elevator. With unspoken agreement, we made our way to the second-floor shoe department. No surprise there. I wanted to try the new style, which, of course, had changed in the last week. I wasn't sure about it. They were back to stiletto heels, only this time the toes were extra pointed. I held up a cobalt-blue pair. The reed-thin, all-dressed-in-black waif of a salesgirl slinked over.

"I'd like to try these on."

She eyed my feet and all but snickered. "I don't know if we stock them that large. What size do you wear?"

"Nine, which isn't large for my height, by the way."

"You go up two sizes in these because of the narrow toe. I'll bring a size eleven."

Already I wasn't sure. Nothing took the shine off a new pair of shoes faster than watching your foot grow two sizes.

We found chairs and waited. When the waif returned with the shoes, I opened the box and held one up.

Annie stared at the shoe.

"What?"

She rolled her hand side to side. "I'm not sure about the color. They sort of remind me of this special I saw on water-fowl. This one duck had blue feet. A 'blue-footed booby.'"

"Right. Size eleven? More like a big-footed booby."

I tugged the shoe on. It felt like I had my foot crammed into a pencil sharpener.

Finally, I got the second shoe on. I looked at Annie. "Well?"

"Stand up so I can see."

I braced myself on the arms of the chair, rose and plunged headlong into a rack of marked-down platforms. By keeping my thighs firmly clamped together and swinging my feet out to the sides like boat rudders, I managed to walk down the aisle, leaving a wake of mismatched shoes.

I paused in front of the mirror and looked back at Annie. "Do you think these are sexy?"

"Not the way you're walking."

Afraid to do any more damage, I managed to peel them off where I stood, handed them to the waif and apologized for the mess. Having once again donned my sensible flats, we made our way out of the store and into the afternoon sunshine. When we were out on the street, Annie resumed the conversation of Brice and Francesca.

"The reality is that his marriage to Francesca has opened a

lot of doors he might have otherwise found closed, hotshot doctor from the city or not. You know as well as I do few things impress people in this town like a local family connection. What I'd like to know is whether or not Francesca knew all the time what he was up to?"

"That's a good question." I stopped at the police station. "She isn't a pushover, not by a long shot, but sometimes people put up with amazing things in the name of love. If she doesn't know about Chantal yet, I don't want to be the one responsible for her finding out. Nobody, not even Francesca, deserves to have their husband fool around, especially with a younger sister."

Fourteen

At the door of the police station, Annie extracted from me a promise to tell her everything and walked off. The bounce in her step and diminutive stature would have suggested someone twenty years of age instead of the thirty-eight I knew her to be.

I entered the station and recognized the clerk behind the counter. He waved me in and signaled to Lucas that I was there. Lucas came out of his office, swung open the waist-high counter gate and asked me if I wanted some coffee. When I declined, he poured himself a cup and led me into his office, closing the door.

I caught a glimpse of a file on the desk with Todd Ryan's name on it. Lucas followed my glance and casually scooped it up. He tilted his cup toward the chair in front of the desk. "Have a seat."

If I wanted Lucas to share with me, I didn't want the desk

between us. Instead of the chair I chose the couch under the window, open to the afternoon breeze. He seemed to understand what I was up to, but he smiled, turned the chair he'd indicated toward me, and sat.

"Have you remembered anything else about that night you want to share?"

"Nothing I didn't tell you. Why?"

"I'm inclined to believe you were right about that light disappearing into the house. There weren't any footprints at the fermenting building or around the crushers that didn't belong to family members. No fingerprints unaccounted for, no unusual car tracks, no reports of vagrants or people that aren't from here, and believe me, in a town like Cypress Cove, we hear about all of them." He looked at me. "That means right before and after the murder, you were alone with Todd and his killer."

I nodded. "Trust me, that's crossed my mind more than a few times."

"I was just hoping something else might have occurred to you. Let's work it backward. If it was a family member, then it was someone with all of you earlier that evening in the library. What if something was said, something the killer wanted kept hidden?"

"I see what you're saying. I was thinking the killer already knew they were going to try to kill Todd later that night, but what if something was said or done in the library that forced the killer to act?"

I got up, paced around the room, and replayed the evening in my head. Finally I shrugged. "I don't know. I can't think of anything. Everyone seemed to behave normally." I counted off the names on my fingers: "Marvin, obnoxious as usual. Stephen tried to keep Chantal away from the bar. Chantal, of course, flirted and drank. Veronica didn't say much. Just sat there and rattled those damn pearls. Francesca was her usual condescending self, along with Brice, who had his cell phone glued to his ear, and, of course, Antonia, who seemed fine. Todd came in late, after everyone else."

"Why?"

"Why what?"

"Why was he late?"

Good question. "I don't know. Stephen said Todd was responsible for coordinating the shifts in the tasting booths. The wineries take turns. Otherwise it's too crowded. Maybe he was late because he was finishing up the schedule."

Lucas looked over his notes. "Do you think his death had anything to do with the festival?"

"Doubtful. The festival happens every year, but this is the first one since Todd's been with Martinelli Winery. If I had to guess, I still think it's something to do with the winery. I told you the night Todd died that Antonia thought someone was up to something, and since then I've confirmed it." I told Lucas about the person in the fermenting building. When I mentioned going under the police tape, he raised his brows but didn't say anything. "Todd could have found out who was sabotaging the winery."

"Okay. Any other reason why you think someone would want Todd dead?"

"Well, Francesca owns some land outside of Monterey. She got it from Todd's mother, and it doesn't sound like Todd was very happy with the way she acquired it."

"You know you should have led with all of this at the beginning of the conversation. Anything else you care to tell me?" He gave me a stern look and waited.

In the end, I told him about my roadside chat with Chantal, along with finding out Francesca didn't graduate from Layton, as well as her fight with Brice at the restaurant. I didn't know what would help him, so I gave him everything I knew. Besides, I didn't like the look I was getting. He wasn't happy, and I couldn't help it—I cracked like a walnut.

Lucas crossed his arms. "Sounds like I need to have a talk with Brice and Francesca, as well as Chantal. You've been busy."

"Hey, most of this just dropped into my lap. Except for going to Francesca's law school. And the fermenting building visit. Sorry about that sneaking-under-the-police-tape thing."

He just watched me.

I stared back. "What?"

"I'm trying to decide if I should tell you what we know or lock you up for unauthorized entry of a crime scene."

"If those are my only two choices, I'll take the first one."

Lucas walked over to the open window and watched the street as he spoke. "We didn't find much, but there was one thing of interest. In the crusher next to Todd was a torn corner of a document."

"A document? What do you mean? Something official? Like a deed or something?"

"Yes. It's still up at the lab, but the preliminary reports show it's older and there's a mark, part of an embossed shape, like an emblem." He turned to me. "You were a reporter?"

I nodded, confused at the turn in the conversation. "Of sorts. Photojournalist."

"What are you working on now?" He watched me.

"Nothing. I had a disagreement with my editor at the paper. Since then I've been focused on my own photography. Landscapes mostly. Why?"

Lucas turned back toward the window. He didn't respond. He just sipped his coffee as I started to squirm. "If you see or hear anything, I want to be the first to know."

"Sure."

He turned and walked to the door of his office. As he opened the door, he caught my eye. "I'm serious about this. And don't enter any more of my crime scenes."

"I promise." Yikes.

I walked back to the car and thought about what Lucas had said. An emblem. Something embossed. Like a diploma. Or maybe the deed to property. Or maybe just about anything else.

What I needed was to put the problem away for a while. I pointed the car toward Pacific Coast Highway. The late-afternoon sun was low over the ocean as I pulled the car out of town and made a right on Highway 1. Here, the sea breeze met redwood forests and the air was cool even on the hottest days.

I drove south until I hit Big Sur, where I finally turned around and headed back. I arrived home just as Hayley placed vegetable and shrimp kabobs on the outside grill.

I went inside to make rice, one of the few things I reliably cook. Hayley came in behind me and I spoke without turning. "So you and Lucas looked pretty cozy." I turned, expecting to see the happy smile I'd seen earlier, but the eyes that met mine were strained and red as though she'd been crying. I put my arm around her. "What's happened?"

"I just keep thinking about that night and if there's anything I should have done that I missed. Lucas is great and I think he might be the one, but Todd's death and my being there has strained our relationship. He doesn't want to talk about it and I understand he can't, but when he said for you to meet him at the police station it scared me. I tried to ask him about it but he got all official with me. I'm just worried." Hayley looked toward the back door. "Connor's coming up in a few minutes." She took a seat at the counter. "Can I ask you a question?"

I looked at her. She dug her teeth into her lip and there was a line of tension between her brows.

"Sure. Go ahead."

"It must have been pretty bad when you found him. I guess I just want to know what to do to make it okay. How do you put it behind you?" She gave me a soft smile touched with sadness. Todd had been around Hayley's age. People with that much ahead of them weren't supposed to have their time cut so short.

"Here's the thing. Sometimes things happen in life you can't control." I brushed back her hair. "There were times at the paper when I hid behind the camera because I didn't want anyone to see my tears. You think you're making a difference when you cover a story and you bring it into the spotlight, but the sad reality is that sometimes things still don't change. It can make you feel helpless. Make you want to hide."

"So there's no way to make it any better?"

"Sometimes you can't prevent things from happening, and once they're done, you can't change the past. There is a way to deal with the pain, though, because you always control your response. You cry, if you need to. You hurt for a while. But then you look for a way to make a difference." I held her by the shoulders. "Todd's dead and we can't change that, but if the person that did this to Todd scares me and keeps me from living my life or from finding the truth, then I'm a victim too. I'm not about to let that happen. Sometimes, you fight back."

Hayley nodded. "I understand."

"Of course you do. You're my niece."

AT dinner we discussed the harvest. Connor started with the white grapes first, determined by the varietal and location on the property. Those areas with the most sun ripened earlier. The reds needed more time on the vine and came in at the end.

We didn't talk about the murder, on his part probably because he hoped I'd forget about it and let Lucas solve it, and on my part because I knew he hoped I was going to forget about it and let Lucas solve it.

Let sleeping dogs lie, let men in denial, deny. Connor's sidelong glances throughout the evening told me he wasn't as deep in denial as I would have liked.

I woke up to a rare morning without a hint of fog. I rolled Syrah off, let Nanook out the back door and threw on my Michelin Man sweatsuit.

After I turned on the coffeemaker, I went out to the garden to see what was ready to pick. I pulled one weed, then another. An hour went by.

When I returned to the kitchen, Connor was finishing a wholesome breakfast of strawberry shortcake. I rolled my eyes.

"Hey, it's fruit and dairy."

The phone rang. I let the machine answer, only to hear Ross on the line. "I know you're there, Pen. Pick up."

I grabbed it. "Hi."

"Hi, yourself. I saw Annie at the gas station. She said Lucas asked you to go to the police station yesterday after lunch."

"He just wanted to know if I remembered anything else."

"Oh, come on. Surely you've found out something."

"Um," I mumbled, noncommittal. "How is Joanne?"

"As you'd expect. She went from wedding plans to funeral arrangements for her fiancé. She wants to work, but she doesn't eat and spends a lot of time crying. I don't think she's sleeping either. I'm cooking her favorites to try and restore her appetite, at least."

"She's in good hands with you and Thomas." I stood up to stretch. "I might stop by the restaurant later. I'm going over to the festival grounds this morning to finish decorating and leave some more postcards at the booth."

"While you're there, stop by our booth and we can talk. I have to finish our decorating as well. See you in a bit."

IT was sunny but cold when I arrived at the festival grounds an hour later, a day of crisp sunshine but not much warmth behind it.

At one point the festival grounds had been owned by Martinelli Winery, but years ago the land had been donated by Antonia's family to the town for public events. To get to the parking lot, you had to circle around the winery on a back road, which then led into a parking lot for the last fifty yards.

There were only a handful of cars, and I recognized the

catering van used by Sterling. Ross had it parked right up front. I pulled in next to him and grabbed the box of photographs.

The festival was spread out in a grid of five rows, with ten booths each. The ones in the center were reserved for local wineries by invitation only. Only a few of them held any activity.

I cut over to the food section to find the Sterling booth. Two rows over, Ross was hanging a banner over the front counter. He had a good spot in the row of specialty and gourmet food, between the organic turkey sausages and Swedish pancakes. I looked at Ross balanced on a ladder. He nodded at me as he hammered a tack through the banner and into the wooden frame of the booth. I did a double take at his outfit: a purple robe with a faux-fur collar and a large gold crown.

Thomas came out of the booth and waved me over. "Come check out our menu. In honor of the medieval theme Ross is doing leg of mutton. It makes one feel so 'King Arthur.' Speaking of which, I designed our outfits." He turned to model a full knight's outfit. He wore leggings and sleeves of mesh silver chain, and his chest was covered in a silver-plated sheet. A helmet topped with a purple feather plume sat on his head.

"Why are you wearing them now?"

"We wanted to see if we could cook and move around in them." He tapped on his chest. "It's a little hard to walk in. I cut the pieces from the solid aluminum strips they use to make cookie sheets." He pointed at his head, and the purple plume flopped in the breeze. "This was my silver bike helmet."

"You look terrific." I nodded my head toward the box I held. "Let me put this in my booth. I'll be back in a few minutes."

Joyeux Winery was midrow on the first aisle. The winery

flag, a golden fleur-de-lis on a background of royal blue and burgundy, fluttered on the roof. The booths were covered with temporary weatherproof curtains to protect the contents between now and the festival. I pushed the corner open with my shoulder and turned to enter the tent, box first. The curtain closed behind me, leaving me in the dark. With my hands full, I couldn't grab the flashlight on my keys and I crept to the tables just ahead of me. As I felt the edge of the table with my thigh, something exploded against the back of my head. The pain was blinding, and I could hear glass breaking as the world tipped away from under my feet. I dropped the box, grabbed the edge of the table and landed on my knees. Through the roar in my ears, I heard a soft laugh. I tried to concentrate, but my eyes closed. A shove into my shoulder ripped the table from my grip and I fell to the ground.

Just before the world went black I heard a soft whisper. "Just like a bad penny, always turning up in the wrong place. Bad, bad Penny."

Fifteen

"I'LL get some ice. Don't move her."

"Of course I won't move her. I'm not the village idiot."

"Penny, if you can hear me, try not to move." It was Ross. "We couldn't find you, but your car was still here, so I called the police. Lucas should be here any minute. I would have made it to you sooner, but these tents all look the same with the curtains down. I only found you because I recognized your flag."

A few moments later the front curtain was rolled up and the light hit the backs of my eyelids.

I blinked and saw Ross's worried face staring at me. Then the world swayed once more, sweat beaded my forehead and I shut my eyes against the wave of nausea that rolled through me.

"What happened? Your hair's wet. Is that wine?"

"Somebody hit me."

His hand felt the back of my head. "They sure did. That's quite a lump you've got."

"Lucas will want to see this. You were hit with a wine bottle."

Thomas returned. "Here's the ice."

Ross pressed the ice against my scalp.

I waited, reopened my eyes, and this time everything stayed in place.

"Should we call an ambulance too?" Thomas leaned on his sword to get a closer look.

"I don't need one. It hurts like hell, but I know who both of you are and who I am. No concussion. No ambulance."

There were footsteps outside the booth. Lucas stepped into view and surveyed the scene before him: Ross dressed as King Arthur, Thomas kneeling before me in his knight's attire and me flat on my back.

"I see you found her."

I hated to look foolish in front of Lucas, so I struggled to sit up. Lucas waved me back down. I wasn't feeling so great and was happy to fall back into the folds of Ross's robe.

"Are you okay?"

I nodded. Pain shot through my head and settled behind my eyes. The earth tilted.

"At the risk of sounding unprofessional, you don't look so hot. What happened?"

I told him what little I could while Ross and Thomas listened with rapt attention. When I finished, Ross joined in.

"She said she'd be back, but when half an hour had passed, I decided to look for her. There were only so many places she could have gone and I just knew something was wrong, so I phoned you."

Lucas looked up from his notes. "Did you recognize the voice?"

"No. They spoke after they hit me, so I was hardly conscious. I only remember what was said because it kind of freaked me out, if you want to know the truth."

Lucas boxed the bottle, soggy bits of our blue-and-burgundy wrapping paper still clinging to the broken glass. Hayley had prepackaged some of our bestsellers in case we got busy during the festival.

"You're lucky this bottle was gift-wrapped. Otherwise, you'd be on your way to the emergency room right now, having glass removed from your scalp."

"If you say so, but lucky isn't exactly what I'm feeling right now, to be honest."

"I do want you to go to the hospital." He raised his hand at my protestations. "If you don't agree to go there immediately, I'll drive you myself after I get done here. Although I doubt I can get any prints off of this."

Thomas, who still knelt at my side, looked around. "I don't understand how anyone could have known you were here. Were they just waiting in the dark?"

"My car is easy to recognize. Someone could have seen it coming down the back road."

Lucas and I looked at each other. Anyone from the Martinelli house might have seen me. They could have walked down the path with plenty of time to get into the tent before me.

"We'll be talking to everyone here, but did either of you see anything that seemed unusual?" Lucas asked Ross and Thomas.

Thomas spoke first. "Well, I don't know about unusual,

but I haven't seen anyone that doesn't belong here, if that's what you mean."

Ross nodded. "I was on the ladder hanging the banner and facing our tent. I didn't see a thing."

I felt the back of my head. It hurt, but the skin hadn't been broken and there wasn't any glass. Lucas was right; I was lucky. I looked around the booth. Whoever had hit me hadn't been intentionally kind. The wrapped bottles were lined up on the counter and the easiest to grab. If someone was trying to warn me, they could consider the message received.

I signed the police report Lucas had filled out and handed it back to him.

"Go to the hospital."

"I will."

He just stood there.

"I can't believe you don't trust me."

Lucas looked over at Ross and Thomas. "Follow her."

In truth, my head was pounding, and I felt no compulsion to do anything else.

KASEY Hospital is set into the hillside north of downtown. The land for the entire facility was donated years ago by a silent screen actress, and the facility has been operating for the last seventy years. Surrounded by redwoods and pines, the main building was brick and faced west, with large windows out toward the sea. To the right and behind a high chain fence was the Kasey Children's Home. To the left and behind an even higher fence was the Kasey Recovery Clinic. The hospital sat in between.

I swung into the parking lot, near the swings and slides for the Children's Home. The Sterling van pulled in next to me, and I rolled down the window.

"See, I made it. Thanks for the escort."

Thomas leaned out, the silver-plated chest piece bright in the sunlight. "You were just lucky it was all side streets, otherwise we wouldn't have let you drive yourself. Do you want us to come in with you?"

He was getting stares from the kids on the monkey bars. "You're dressed like Lancelot."

"Right. Call us later." They pulled back onto the main road, my own private band of merry men.

I walked to the hospital entrance, watching the children on the playground. The little ones, jumping rope or on the swings, were bundled up in bright knitted caps and scarves, while the teens, ultracool in their low-waisted jeans, played basketball. All of the play sets appeared to be new, the rubber matting beneath the swings decorated with a jungle theme. Large murals of orange and yellow dinosaurs covered the outside walls of the cafeteria and dormitories.

The Children's Home worked with kids of all ages, some given up at birth, some removed from dangerous home environments. They lived here year-round and even attended school right at the facility. The home was a model example of how this type of establishment should work.

On the other side of the hospital, away from the children, were the bungalows used for drug and alcohol recovery. This facility was voluntary, and was one of several in the state preferred by celebrities from Hollywood. The doctor who ran the facility was the author of *And Now You Don't*, a self-help book that had spent ten weeks on the bestseller list. The bungalows looked like little bed-and-breakfast cottages, and the specialty treatment received there didn't come cheap. I thought of Chantal and the times she'd been here. Antonia had paid dearly to help her youngest daughter.

The double glass doors swung open with a blast of that same antiseptic smell of hospitals everywhere, and I walked to the admittance counter. A pretty receptionist reading a schedule looked up and smiled.

"Can I help you?"

On impulse I asked, "Is Doctor Brice Shapiro in today?"

She flipped through her paperwork. "He isn't scheduled until this afternoon at two."

"Where's his office?"

"Room two fifteen. Did you have an appointment?"

"No. I took a fall and wanted this bump on my head looked at."

"Oh, then you don't want Doctor Shapiro. He's a cardiologist."

"Oh, that's right. He and my regular doctor have such similar names."

Before she could ask who my regular doctor was, her phone rang. I slipped around the far side of the counter and down the hall.

I turned left, into the corridor that led to the nursery. Not having kids, these places made me jumpy. I hadn't heard any clocks, whistles or any other signs I'd ever need to be here myself. I got to be an aunt. It was like skipping to the good part.

This place looked nothing like the old maternity wards. According to the sign on the wall, this area was now referred to as the "Birthing Center." Apparently, the latest trend was that fathers were not only encouraged, but expected, to be active participants. The rooms along the hallway confirmed this. When doors opened, there were fathers and other family members, some with video cameras. Just a little too much information for me. Here I was averting my eyes while some-one's uncle Clyde captured the whole thing on film. The viewing womb. I needed to get out of here.

The chemical dependency and birthing facilities had separate admittance counters but shared a common reception area. The commonality seemed to be stressed-out patients and the nurses who could handle them.

Although it was quiet in the rest of the hospital, it was hopping here. Voices were louder. Patience was shorter. Stephen had told me Veronica had never worked in this area. Good thing. I could picture it now: her foot tapping, the jangle of pearls.

To the left of the counter a nurse stood and flipped through a chart. She was in her late fifties and her name tag declared she was "Greta, Head Nurse." I glanced at the birthing room to my right, peeked at the name on the door, scooted around the crowd at the counter, and went up to her.

"Excuse me, can you tell me where the Harrison room is? The delivery date is today and I know they're here, but I forgot the room number."

"Suite one oh one, right behind you." She pointed over my shoulder with her pen as she continued reading.

"Thanks. Oh, quick question. A friend used to work here, but I'm not sure if she still does. It was ages ago. Her name is Veronica. I think her married name is Martinelli."

With a sigh, she lowered the chart to her side. "You mean Veronica Strand."

"Yes, that's it. She wasn't married back then."

She looked at me. "I guess you really don't keep in touch. She hasn't worked since she got married."

"That's too bad. I'd really like to see her."

Greta folded her arms. "Oh, she's still around, just as a volunteer. Behind the scenes. She doesn't spend time in the trenches anymore."

"Right, she was a nurse, wasn't she?"

"I remember when she started working as a candy striper. She put herself through school and became a nurse."

"You've got a terrific memory, Greta."

"I've been around a long time."

"I'd really like to see her again. How often does she come in?"

Greta shifted. "All volunteers work one day a week." She raised the paperwork between us. Apparently the conversation was over.

"Okay. Great. Thanks for your help," I said to the back of the chart.

Instead of backtracking, I walked around the other side of the counter and worked my way down the corridor. Because the hospital was a large rectangle, eventually I'd come back to the main entrance. I rubbed the back of my head. It still hurt, but at least I wasn't feeling any worse.

As I walked, I mulled over Nurse Greta's information. Veronica still came to the hospital. Brice was here on a regular basis. Chantal was too, although unfortunately for treatment. Did it mean anything?

I reached my doctor's office, Dr. Armstrong, which, of course, sounds exactly like Dr. Shapiro. Judy, the nurse practitioner, managed to squeeze me in and checked my pupils, pulse and blood pressure and announced I might have a minor concussion and needed to go home and rest. Feeling like I'd fulfilled my promise to Lucas, I thanked Judy for her prediction I'd live and continued down the hall.

I stopped at the cardiology wing. I'd just go for a walk and see how things turned out. I rounded the corner. The offices were even numbers on the left, odd on the right. Eight offices down on the right, and I was outside number 215, Brice's office. There now. If I wasn't meant to find it, it wouldn't have been so damn easy. The door was open and the office empty. I looked up and down the corridor, but there wasn't anyone around. If I continued to stand in the hallway I was sure to be questioned. Hmm, what to do. What to do . . .

I scurried in and shut the door. That wouldn't work. If they found me in Brice's office with the door closed, the police would be getting a call. I didn't want to have that conversation with Lucas.

It worked better with the door partially closed. Just the desk and bookcase behind it were hidden from the corridor. If anyone asked, I could always say I was leaving Brice a note. I walked behind the desk and paused. His cologne was so strong, I could have found this office blindfolded.

I pushed the oversized leather chair back against the bookcase and scanned the desk. No pictures, mementos or personal touches of any kind. Just a keyboard and flat-screen computer monitor, turned off. There was also a white bust of Hippocrates, probably marble, on the corner. The words "First, Do No Harm" were engraved at the base. I bet Chantal could answer how much harm Brice was capable of.

If the desk was sparse, the wall across from me made up for it. In one corner there was a white examination coat, which hung from a suit hanger on a coatrack. Next to it, shelves rose to the ceiling above two leather chairs. Brice fancied himself quite the athlete. Mementos and trophies made up the majority of items, and the awards were mostly from tennis, lacrosse and polo.

Personal pictures filled the rest of the shelves. Brice smiled out of photos of him with the governor, and there were several of him and the last three mayors of San Francisco. None of them looked particularly happy, and my opinion of politicians rose slightly. There was also one of Brice and Francesca. She looked even less happy than the politicians.

Well, if I was leaving a note, I should have a pen and paper. Good thing there wasn't anything on the desk to use. The top drawer slid open with ease. Several Montblanc pens and a leather address book. I breezed through the names. I recognized several, and there were more I didn't. No big surprise female names outweighed males four to one.

I closed the drawer and opened the right side. Tickets to *La Bohème*, a prescription pad and a well-thumbed copy of *Playboy*. Brice's idea of a medical journal. I poked around. The prescription pad separated in my hand into two pieces. I looked at the binding. It was coming apart in several spots. My thumb lifted the sheets, letting them fall as I scrolled through the pad. Wait a minute. Something was wrong. I flipped through a third time, just to make sure. The printed count was definitely off. Prescriptions were missing.

I froze at the sound of the door being pushed open. Brice walked into the room. His back was to me as he pulled off his blazer. The fully opened door kept me cornered behind the desk and prevented me from leaving the office. I couldn't do anything but quietly close the drawer and wait for him to turn around. He pulled on the white exam coat and hung the blazer in its place. I reviewed my options. Nothing brilliant came to mind. I considered diving under the desk, but I was too tall.

Brice buttoned up the coat and turned. "What do you think you're doing?"

"Oh, good." Yeah, this was great. Just terrific. "I was hoping I'd catch you . . . See, my doctor isn't in, and I had a nasty spill this morning. I thought maybe you could take a look at this bump on my head. Make sure it isn't anything serious."

Brice didn't answer, his face utterly still. Finally, he straightened the collar of his coat. "I'm a cardiologist."

Duh. I knew this. Everyone in town knew this. "Oh, right. I totally forgot. Could be the hit to the head."

He didn't answer.

"Okay. Not a problem. Thanks anyway. See you." Penny Lively, master of the exit strategy.

Brice stepped forward and blocked my way. He rested one hand on the bust of Hippocrates and smoothed his perfect salt-and-pepper hair with the other. Confidence glittered in his eyes. "You know, if I had reason to suspect you were going through my desk, I'd have a responsibility to report you to the authorities. I'm sure you understand my position."

He expected his remarks to unnerve me and, for the life of me, I don't know why they didn't.

I thought of the prescription pad and took a gamble. "You know, if I had any reason to suspect you were using your position as a doctor for illegal and illicit purposes, I'd have a responsibility to report *you* to the authorities. I'm sure you understand my position."

His face turned crimson, and I thought I was about to see a cardiologist have a heart attack. He tightened his grip on the head of Hippocrates and squeezed until the blood drained from his hand. His fingertips were as white as the marble. With visible effort he let go, backed up, and pointed to the hall. "Get the hell out of my office."

I pushed past him and made my way down the corridor. His door didn't close and there weren't footsteps, so I knew he stood watching me. From his reaction, I'd hit a nerve. Maybe it was just because I was in his office. Maybe his reaction had nothing to do with my comment. Maybe Brice had just lost the missing prescriptions. Maybe someone from over in rehab had taken the same walk I'd just finished and stolen them. Maybe.

Sixteen

W HEN I arrived home, Annie was leaving a message.
Nanook recognized her voice and howled at the
machine.

I grabbed up the phone and shouted over the noise, "Nanook
says hello."

"Let me say hi to him."

I put the phone down and went to get him a biscuit, tossed
it across the room, wiped off the phone and settled back into
the couch.

"You know that little Maltese I've been treating for stomach
problems? The one that could use a few more walks and a few
less chicken livers? She was in today."

"How's her mom?"

"Ivy's fine. She just started in on husband number four.
A film producer."

"Does she still own that winery up the river?"

"She sure does. A parting gift from husband number three. She told me something I knew you'd find interesting."

"Give." I kicked off my shoes, let Syrah curl into the corner of my arm and buried my feet in the warmth of Nanook's back.

"Peterson's Jewelry offered to let people drop off donations for the festival. If you're donating jewelry for the silent auction, you can leave it and Peterson's will clean it and get it ready. Anyway, Ivy was dropping off a bunch of stuff this afternoon, including those pearl studs I've always liked. I want to make a bid on those. I wonder if I have a chance. There will be hundreds—"

"What about Ivy?" I shifted Syrah to the other arm, grabbed a notepad and pen from the end table and wrote *low-fat cat food*.

"Oh. Well, you know Peterson's also buys old jewelry, estate stuff and all that. While she was in there, guess who came in to try and sell a necklace? Marvin Karp. She recognized him because Ivy's third husband had offered him a job as winery manger. Ivy said the piece he was trying to sell was really old, an antique, but when he saw her looking at it he shoved it into his pocket and left right away. He didn't even wait for Peterson to tell him what he thought it was worth."

"Where would Marvin get something like that? He doesn't have any relatives I know of. He certainly doesn't have friends he could've been selling it for. Was she sure the piece was an antique?"

"Believe me," Annie said, "if Ivy said it was an antique, it was. The one thing she knows is jewelry."

A throbbing began behind my temples and I rubbed the back of my head. "Different subject. Let me tell you about my morning."

Annie listened without interruption. "I can't believe someone hit you and I really can't believe Brice caught you in his office. Usually things like this happen to you when I'm there."

"Be glad you weren't. What painkiller can I take with a head injury?"

"You realize you're asking your veterinarian for medical advice?"

"Come on, Annie. Don't answer like a doctor. Just give me your personal opinion."

"Acetaminophen, ice pack and a nap with Nanook and Syrah."

I followed her advice.

I woke to the sound of Connor stacking wood in the fireplace. The long-handled lighter clicked in the semidarkness and outlined Connor's profile. He must have just come up from his quarters, because his hair was damp.

Pushing back the sleeves of his soft green flannel shirt, he added fire-starters made from wax-dipped pinecones. In the flickering light he looked tired. On a winery this was the busiest week of the year. If the weather held, this was also the most satisfying time to be a vintner. An entire year of work came down to a few crucial days of labor, harvest and love.

I sat up on the couch. My left arm was completely numb. "Ouch." I pushed at Syrah and rubbed my shoulder.

Connor looked up. "You doing okay over there?"

"Just getting circulation back."

The room filled with a rosy glow and the chill dispersed.

"Yum. Nice fire."

"Hayley went out to dinner. I told her if she didn't take the night off, she was fired."

"Good." I moved Syrah off the quilt and shifted closer to the now-glowing warmth.

"I was going to make pasta and thought you might want some company."

"The company sounds good but I'm not very hungry tonight."

He pushed away from the fire and sat with his back against the couch, keeping his eyes on the flames.

My knee barely touched his shoulder.

"I can understand why you wouldn't necessarily have much of an appetite. You going to tell me what happened this morning?"

I didn't move. "How did you hear about this morning?"

"Lucas. Who do you think took Hayley to dinner? Asked me if you went to the hospital. I'm not sure why Hayley and I are finding out from the police you were ordered to go to the hospital. I had to promise Hayley I'd come back here to check on you. She wouldn't have gone out if I hadn't." He glanced at me. "Not that checking on you wasn't something I would have done anyway."

My cheeks warmed.

"You were asleep, so I decided to let you rest for a while. Why didn't you at least call?"

"You know we get lousy cell reception in the valley, and by the time I went to the hospital I knew I was okay. Besides, even if I'd tried from a landline, you were out in the vineyards." It was weak even to my ears, but it was the best I could do. The reality was I'd been independent for so long it hadn't really occurred to me he'd be concerned. Even with Hayley, having family around to worry about me was something new.

He pushed off the floor to sit on the couch and raised a hand to the back of my head, to the still-tender bump. My skin tingled, and not just on the back of my head.

"They got you pretty good." He turned once again to the fire.

I had to strain to hear him.

"You think you can take care of yourself. Sometimes you can't. Sometimes the bad guy has the advantage. That's just the way it is. I'm sorry Todd's dead, but we need you here. Hayley needs you. This winery needs you." He turned to look at me. "I need you. I don't know how we'd make it without you. Don't make us try."

"I keep thinking if I'd been just a little sooner, I'd have been able to make a difference. Todd might still be here. I feel like I missed a chance that night. I don't want to miss my chance now."

Connor nodded. "I figured as much. Even if you tried, you wouldn't stop thinking about it. You couldn't. So, the only suggestion I can give is to take care, Penny. Just take care."

"I promise to be more careful. Thanks, Connor."

He nodded then turned to hide a yawn.

"You must be exhausted. Do you have time for a full night's sleep?"

"This feels pretty good right here."

He put a pillow behind his head and leaned back against the couch. He was asleep in five minutes. I covered him with the quilt and watched him sleep.

He was right. I couldn't just turn off the need to know what happened that night, even if I wanted to. Insatiable curiosity. It was why I'd become a photojournalist. It was probably what was going to get me in trouble someday.

Because of my late nap I was wide-awake. I changed into my sweats and made some hot chocolate. I needed to get everything I'd learned about the Martinelli family down on paper. The motive for murder was at that winery, but I couldn't see all the connections. I turned over the shopping list headed by *low-fat cat food* and started writing.

Todd: 28. Victim. Ran tasting room at Martinelli Winery. Degree from San Luis Obispo in viniculture. Wanted to one day run a winery. Talented. Engaged to be married to Joanne.

It was hard to imagine anyone wanting him dead. Everyone liked Todd. No. I sat tapping the pencil. Not everyone. Was he pushing for Marvin's job? Did he fight Francesca for his mother's land? That light I'd seen return into the Martinelli house was pointing the way to someone who hadn't liked Todd very much at all.

Marvin Karp: 50ish. Manager of the Martinelli Winery. Good at his job but not well liked. Understands wine better than he understands people. Lives alone at the winery. Appears to know more than he is letting on. Spotted selling jewelry that would be unlikely for Marvin to own. Likes to gamble. Connection?

Todd was very good at his job and well liked. In addition, he had a degree and appeared to have settled into Martinelli

Winery for a long stay. Could Marvin have been threatened enough to kill Todd? There was a racing form and a Las Vegas mug on Marvin's desk. Did he need money? Where did the jewelry come from?

Chantal: 32. Long history of problems—alcohol, drugs. In rehab on numerous occasions at Kasey Recovery Clinic. Uses her extraordinary looks to attract men, even her brother-in-law. Per conversation, feels lonely, isolated from family. Angry. Appears to have been attracted to Todd but it turned into a close friendship.

I knew from Joanne that Chantal and Todd were only friends. Chantal told me the same. Did Todd find out it was Brice that Chantal was mixed up with? Could Chantal have been acting under the oaks that day and be protecting Brice? Even though she denied it, could Chantal have wanted more from Todd than to be friends? "Hell hath no fury . . ."

Francesca: 35. Chantal's older sister. Attorney. Lives in San Francisco. Acquired acreage from Todd's mother through dubious means. Smart, shrewd and tough if you get in her way. Went to Layton Law School but apparently failed to graduate, at least from there. Angry at Antonia for letting it be known Stephen would inherit winery. Concerned about two things: reputation and land ownership. Married to Brice.

Was Francesca angry enough at her mother to sabotage the winery? Did Todd catch her at it? Where was she yesterday morning? Did Todd know how Francesca got his mother's land? Did he have proof? Would he have used it? Did he threaten to?

Stephen: 38. Brother to Francesca and Chantal. Martinelli heir. Protective of his family, especially his youngest sister, Chantal. Naturally uptight demeanor. Appears to feel the weight of responsibility for the winery heavily on his shoulders. Married to Veronica.

With his lack of personality and presence, what would Stephen do if he weren't running the family business? Todd was an asset to the winery. I couldn't see how Stephen benefited from Todd's death, and yet when I spoke with Stephen, he was clearly uncomfortable talking about the winery or about Todd.

Veronica: 35. Married to Stephen. Nervous and high-strung, a perfect partner for Stephen. Former nurse, now a winery matron. Protective of her husband's family. Involved in numerous clubs and organizations.

I thought about Veronica, in her pleated skirts and pearls. Veronica cared about what her husband cared about—namely, the winery and the Martinelli family. Once again, I couldn't see how Veronica could benefit from Todd's death.

Brice: 40. Married to Francesca. Cardiologist. Practices at both Kasey and in San Francisco. Perfect Armani suits. Perfect bedside manner. Admitted to by Chantal and confirmed by Francesca in her restaurant outburst, has been perfecting that bedside manner in far too many beds.

I didn't like him, but I couldn't think of any reason for him to kill Todd, unless there was some connection to Chantal. If Todd was Chantal's confidant, did she tell him about her affair with Brice? If he'd known, Todd might have confronted him.

The firelight was dying. I hadn't narrowed the list of suspects and didn't know more than when I'd begun. I closed my eyes. One thing I was sure of, the one thing that brought me back to the list of names before me . . . that flashlight as it disappeared into the Martinelli home.

Seventeen

A T some point in the night I must have dragged myself to bed, because that's where I woke up the next morning. When I opened my eyes Nanook stood beside the nightstand and had his head next to mine on the pillow. He prodded me with his nose and I slowly sat up, expecting a painful headache at the very least. It was a surprise to find my head no longer throbbed. I ran my fingers through my hair, gliding them across where I'd been hit. It was tender but not nearly as bad as it might have been.

I let Nanook out the bedroom sliding door and reached for a fleece sweatshirt and pants. The sky was a mass of dark clouds carried in on a cold ocean breeze. We needed the rain to hold off for a few more days, to give Connor and the rest of the wineries time to pull in the harvest.

The bed was still occupied by Syrah, who eyed my

movements and waited for the promise of breakfast. When I found my walking shoes under the bed, she stretched, leaped to the ground and led me from the room.

I fed Syrah and grabbed a banana smeared with peanut butter for myself. As I ate, I dropped to the living room floor for a good stretch. Nanook saw what I was up to and howled at me through the glass door. He knew my stretching meant walk time.

I finished stretching, clipped his leash around my waist and slipped on my walking shoes.

It would have been easy to stay inside, where it was warm and cozy, but my pants were tighter than usual and I needed the exercise. Nanook was perfect company for these adventures. He was happy to let me set the pace and was always ready to turn around at the same point I was. Moreover, although he was a baby, he was big and scary-looking, which was just fine with me.

I thought about Hayley and her efforts to put Todd's death behind her. I'd told her we can always control our response to what we see and experience. I believed that, for the most part. Then I thought about Todd and what someone had done and realized even in this idyllic spot I wouldn't feel completely safe ever again.

About thirty minutes into our walk, I thought Nanook was reacting to my dark mood when he tensed beside me. As we came to the corner of our property, he gave a soft growl.

"What's up, boy?"

Nanook's fur stood on end. His body was stiff.

We were on a bluff that overlooked the rest of the valley. The breeze stirred the grasses on the slope below, silent except the occasional blue jay. Another growl. I barely recognized Nanook. His teeth were bared, something I'd never seen, and he stared down the hillside. I grabbed his collar and clipped him onto his leash.

I still couldn't see anyone.

A voice came from the scrub brush below me. "You control that dog, missy."

My own hackles rose. "You're trespassing and not in a position to give orders, Marvin. Come out of there." No answer. I let the leash slide in my fingers, and Nanook pulled against my grip. "I mean it. I can't keep this hold on him much longer."

I held my ground as Marvin made his way up the side of the hill and back onto the path. Binoculars swung from around his neck.

Marvin changed tactics when he saw Nanook's teeth up close. "Keep a tight hand on the leash of that animal. I wasn't doing nothin' wrong. Just looking at birds. I didn't even know this was your property."

"How could you walk onto my property without knowing it? You had to go through the gate below. You couldn't have missed it. I can see it from here."

"The gate was open when I came by. I forgot this section was part of your land."

He turned to go down the path toward the gate, looking back at us over his shoulder. "I'll be sure to close it when I go out. Wouldn't want anything to happen to that animal of yours."

Marvin made his way down the slope. He knew this was my land. He made his living knowing what stretch of grapes belonged to who. He didn't turn back as he walked the dirt trail to the property boundary, a small cloud of dust behind him. Just before he darted through the gate, he looked over his shoulder. His arrogance had returned. He made a slow, sweeping bow to me as he swaggered through the gate, failing to shut it behind him.

Next to me, Nanook whined and strained against the leash. I started down the path after Marvin to close the gate. "I promise you, sweetheart, if we find him up here again, you get to eat him."

After I had securely fastened the gate, I let Nanook off the leash and walked back up the slope. Marvin out bird-watching? Right.

As I reached the crest, I walked off the path where Marvin had been moments before. The hill dropped off sharply to the north, the mountain range in the distance. I walked to the edge of the bluff. Well, would you look at that. Below me, in a glorious checkerboard of grape varieties, was the rear of Martinelli Winery. The house, fermentation building and other structures, although somewhat distant, were in plain sight. I couldn't make out faces, but workers in the fields and people around the house were visible.

With a good pair of binoculars there wasn't much you'd miss. What had Marvin watched from here? Was it something to do with the sabotage? With Todd? The answer was hidden in plain view before me. I was sure of it. Concealed in the idyllic setting stretched out like a travel brochure. I knew it, and so did someone else.

I thought again of Marvin. Maybe he wasn't looking for someone. Maybe he was looking for something. Was he up here to ensure something he did remained hidden or because he wanted to find something that someone else was trying to hide?

Todd's death had given Marvin job security. Just how much was that worth?

We were both out of breath when we returned, Nanook from running in circles and me because I didn't get out there often enough. We made it to the winery office, where Connor sat at the desk with Hayley. The time schedules for the remainder of the harvest were in front of them. Nanook threw himself down on the cold cement floor, but I couldn't relax.

"Marvin was on the property. Down at the south gate."

"What was he doing?"

"He said he was bird-watching, but when I took a look myself you can see Martinelli perfectly from there. He also said he forgot the section he's on is part of our winery."

"I'm going to be talking to Marvin." Connor slammed the ledger shut.

I looked at him. "You remind me of Nanook. All that's missing is the bared teeth."

"Did he try anything?"

"Like what? He comes up to my shoulders. Besides, he's afraid of Nanook. I just want to know what he was watching."

"Or *who* he was watching," Hayley said.

I nodded. "I wish I'd been able to see faces, but I needed Marvin's binoculars."

"Here," Connor said as I turned to leave. "These orders came in a little while ago. They might keep you out of trouble, at least for the rest of the morning."

I smiled and took the orders. "Don't count on it."

Connor looked over at Hayley. "She has such a *sweet* smile, too."

BACK at the house I put the orders on the patio table and turned on the hose to fill a small kiddy pool, which doubled as Nanook's water dish.

The banana and peanut butter seemed like ages ago, so I heated some tomato soup, my favorite. While I read over the orders, one for twenty cases, the phone rang. I was tempted to ignore it but thought Annie might call to check on me.

"Hello," I mumbled between bites.

"Penelope Lively, are you eating and talking on the phone?"

"No." I swallowed and vowed never to answer the phone again. "Hi, Antonia. How are you?"

"Well, frankly, I'm a bit disappointed." Antonia sniffed. "From the looks of it you haven't made any progress on the sabotage, and now with Todd's murder it's even more crucial this is all cleared up quickly. Don't you understand how vital this is to my winery, to all the wineries, including yours? Tourism in the area is down, you know."

Talk about single-minded. It wasn't a surprise her winery was the most successful in the valley, nor was it any surprise her family was a complete mess.

"Antonia, I'm trying to find out what I can, but you know the police "

"The police have their own agenda, and it certainly isn't what's best for this winery." There was a pause. "I liked Todd. He was a nice person and a good employee, so I have several reasons for wanting to get both the sabotage and murder cleared up. I'm sure the police are doing everything they can, but I'd have thought that you, being the person who found Todd, as well as a fellow winery owner, would want it resolved as much as I do."

This woman had shared a lot of history with my aunt, and I worked to keep my voice calm. "It'd be better if we talked in person. Why don't I come by tonight and tell you everything I've come up with so far. Not all of it is flattering, especially about Chantal and Francesca. I'll tell you everything I know, but I just wanted to give you some warning."

There was a pause. "Yes. Well. I appreciate that. Now, what are your plans for this afternoon?"

"This afternoon?"

"Yes, this afternoon. Surely your hearing isn't going along with your phone manners."

I fought off the impulse to slam the phone down. "Actually, I was planning on heading up to Monterey to talk with Todd's mother."

There was a sharp intake of breath. "Ah, there, you see? A fine idea. Well, good luck in your search, and I'll expect a full report at seven this evening. Sharp."

The line went dead. So much for phone manners. I took a quick shower, threw on a knit sweater and jeans and piled my unruly hair on top of my head. When I was finished, I called the restaurant and got Ross on the phone. "It's me. Got a minute?"

"I've got more than that. Get over here. I have a new creation for dessert and I want your opinion. The pastry is lighter than air."

"Maybe, but I won't get any lighter if I take you up on every dessert. Is Joanne working in the gift shop today?"

Ross dropped his voice a notch. "Why, has something happened? If I tell you whether or not she's here, will you tell me what you want with her?"

"That's easy. I just wanted to know if Todd's mother still lives in Monterey."

"Oh. Nothing exciting. Well, anyway, this is your lucky day."

"So, can I talk to her?"

"No, she isn't here."

"If she isn't there, why is this my lucky day?"

"Because not only do I know for a fact that his mother still lives in the area, I have her address."

"I hate to ask why."

"It's a perfectly legitimate reason." Ross sniffed. "When Todd and Joanne were engaged, Marilyn called to see if I'd cater the wedding. Her contact information is all I really know about her, other than the fact she has exquisite taste in caterers. Hold on and I'll get you the address."

Eighteen

I FINISHED the sales orders, printed directions to Marilyn's house and walked back down to the winery office. "Nice couple of sales. It's been a good month."

Hayley looked up. "In more ways than one. I'm checking the sugar level in a bit." She held up a refractometer. "It's going to be a long day."

Hayley would squeeze the juice of a grape sample into the refractometer to measure the sugar in the grapes, the best way besides actually tasting the grapes to determine when to pick.

"Before I go, do you want me to make you something to keep on the stove?"

Connor and Hayley looked at each other.

"What? I can manage something."

"We'll just grab a pizza later."

"So pizza sounds better than something I'd make. Home-made."

Connor smiled. "Yup. Pretty much."

Hayley nodded in agreement.

"Fine. I know when I've been insulted. Heathens. I'm heading to see Todd's mother. Be back in a while."

I started the car, pushed up my sweater sleeves in the warm autumn sun and tied a scarf around my head, à la Grace Kelly. Very dramatic.

I pulled out of the drive and scanned the horizon. The clouds were gone and the sky was clear. One more day for the grapes to ripen. Basically we were farmers. We lived at the whim of the weather. A thunderstorm right now would be devastating. I knew from Connor the grapes needed to be picked soon because the sugar was almost perfect, but if the rain came first the fruit would be waterlogged, and the entire vintage would taste diluted.

I drove north to Monterey, past the famed seventeen-mile drive of Pebble Beach. The Monterey Peninsula's famous landscape swept before me, an oasis of coastal bluffs, sandy beaches and a forest of pine and cypress trees.

A short time later I took the central off-ramp into downtown, pulled to the side of the road and checked my directions. Marilyn lived on a street in an older but well-maintained section of town. I drove along the tree-lined residential streets and considered my options. Here was a woman who'd just lost her son while employed by the same family responsible for the loss of her land. Granted, Antonia had nothing to do with Francesca's behavior, but no doubt Marilyn had made the connection. I'm sure she wished neither one of them had ever met any of the Martinellis.

I parked across the street from the house, a little brick-and-ivy-covered Tudor. Moss grew in between the stones of the flagstone walk, and lush flower beds in russets and yellows framed the front of the house. The effect was warm and inviting. As I sat and contemplated my next move, an English Springer Spaniel raced around the corner of the house, ears flying. I didn't want it to run into traffic, so I opened the door, ran across the street and knelt down. The dog cleared the ground and sailed into my arms, tail wagging furiously. I heard the voice before I saw anyone. "Dollie, please come here. I just can't do this today."

A woman came around the corner of the house, a towel in her hands. I judged her to be about fifty, with sandy brown hair cut short and puffy around her face. She was a tiny thing. Even with high-heeled sandals made from that jute material, she couldn't have been more than five-foot-two.

Still on my knees, I continued to hold Dollie.

"Thanks so much. She loves her bath and usually we play catch for a few minutes beforehand. I just want to skip that part today."

"You must be Marilyn."

Marilyn walked over and took Dollie's collar, the question in her eyes.

"My name is Penny Lively. I was a friend of Todd's and I wonder if I could have a few moments of your time." I stood.

Marilyn looked blankly at me. "You were a friend of Todd's? I'm sorry, but I don't ever remember him mentioning you."

"I knew him through his work at the winery. I own a winery nearby. Also"—I searched for connections—"I'm good friends with Ross and Thomas. They own the restaurant and gift shop where Joanne works."

"Oh." She was clearly undecided.

"We can talk and give Dollie a bath at the same time if you like."

At her name, Dollie spun her head toward me, straining to come say hello. I reached for the little dog, who pulled away from Marilyn and began running in circles around me.

In spite of her reservations, Marilyn began to smile. "I'm a great believer in the intuition of animals. Recommendations don't get much better than seeing that Dollie approves. Come on around back. If you don't mind watching her, I'll get us some iced tea and an extra towel. I hope you don't mind getting wet."

I smiled. "I have a dog that hates bath time. He makes sure I get every bit as wet as he does."

Marilyn led the way to the rear of the house. It was a big yard, neatly kept, with a side garden and play area. While she went across the patio with its potted geraniums and daisies and through the rear door of the house, I played fetch with Dollie.

Marilyn came back out, placed the iced tea and towels on the picnic table and walked to the yellow plastic basin at the side of the house.

"Normally at this time of year I heat water and give her a bath on the sunporch. In the nice weather, though, I like to give her baths outside. It's easier for me, and then she gets to air-dry in the sun."

I looked over at the garden. Autumn crops of squash, pumpkins, cucumbers and late tomatoes were ripe and ready to pick.

Marilyn saw my interest. "Usually in October I spend two or three hours a day out there and in the kitchen pickling and canning. I decided this morning I'm not up to it this year. I'm taking it all to the food bank."

I scanned the back play yard, complete with swings and a slide. "Do you have other children?" I turned on the hose.

Marilyn squirted eucalyptus-scented doggie soap into the streaming water.

She smiled. "At my age? Heavens no. Oh, I know the trend now is for women in their forties to have children, but even if I could, to still have children playing on swings at fifty? I don't have the energy. No, I kept the swings because the neighborhood children like coming over, and then after Joanne and Todd married . . ."

Her voice broke off and she turned to wipe her eyes on her sleeves.

I gave her a minute while I turned off the water and set Dollie into the soapy tub.

"It's funny," she reached into the water. "I keep thinking I've cried all I can, that at some point I'm going to be empty. I am empty, completely, yet the tears keep coming."

She sat back on her heels and looked out at the garden. "Gardening gives you such an awareness of the seasons. You plant, you watch it grow and you reap the rewards of your hard work and loving care. There's a rhythm, an order to things." She turned to look at me. "I'm burying my son on Saturday, and my world will never be the same."

I massaged Dollie behind the ears. "I'm truly sorry for your loss. Todd was a good man. I'm sure he was a wonderful son."

"Thank you." Marilyn wiped her eyes once more and turned toward the squirming dog. "And now, Miss Dollie, kindly hold still while we rinse off this soap."

Dollie was soon towel-dried and chasing the ball I threw from the deck.

"Have a seat." Marilyn handed me a glass of the tea.

"I understand you used to be a vineyard owner as well." I took a drink of the tea. "Wow, this is delicious."

"Thanks. I make it with lavender and lemongrass from the garden. Now"—Marilyn took a deep breath—"vineyard owner. Yes, my husband and I owned nearly one hundred acres of grapes at one point. Pretty land. Out on Colony Lane. Of course, we never ran our own labels, but we took a certain amount of pride in our harvests. We made a good income from them too." Marilyn paused. "If you know I no longer have the vineyard, then perhaps you also know Francesca Martinelli is now the owner."

"I was told she wanted to purchase the property and that you refused at first."

"Yes, I did refuse. She offered an extremely low price. Not that I had any intention of selling. As you know, people don't sell land here. It runs in families. That land was Todd's. I would have refused at any price."

Marilyn poured herself more tea. "But my refusal to sell wasn't enough to make Francesca go away. Not nearly. After about a year of her calling, insisting and finally threatening, I found out just how much Francesca wanted my vineyards when all of the regular wineries I'd been selling to for years wouldn't touch my crop. Not at any price.

"None of them actually said that she was the reason, of course. Some of them loaned or even offered me money outright to help out, but several of them made strong hints I should consider Francesca's offer. They made it clear they wouldn't be buying my crop. Not that year or any other."

"I know how important the Martinelli family is around here, but why would they refuse to buy your crop just because Francesca asked them to?"

"She didn't use her family connections, although I'm sure it didn't hurt. For one thing, as often as I've heard Antonia is tough, I've also heard she's fair. I can only imagine she wouldn't want her daughter using the Martinelli name in a way that would hurt the family image."

"You know Antonia better than you think. If she found out Francesca used her family connection to strong-arm other wineries into refusal of your crop, especially for Francesca's own gain, she'd be livid."

"That's what I've always thought. I suppose I could've gone to her at the time, but frankly, I didn't think of it. I would never have guessed Francesca would sink to the depths she did to get the land from me, and by the time I understood what she was capable of, the damage was done."

"What did she do?" I waited. That is, I waited as long as I could. About five seconds.

"Marilyn?"

"Let me think how to say this." She paused. "One of the wineries—I made a promise to keep their name out of this— told me Francesca was telling all of the wineries if they bought my crop, she'd get a court order saying my grapes had been contaminated with DDT. Once the grapes are mixed, it's impossible to separate contaminated from noncontaminated, and they'd lose their entire year. For a functioning winery, the loss would be insurmountable."

"That's crazy. If one or some of the wineries decided to buy from you, Francesca wouldn't know who it was and couldn't touch them."

"That's what I thought, and I was ready to fight, at the urging of some of the winery owners. Most of them are good people who were put in bad position." Marilyn looked out over the garden.

"I would have kept fighting, but then one day I got an

anonymous letter telling me to have my crop analyzed. Sure enough, they *were* sprayed with a fertilizer contaminated with DDT. Not a lot, but enough to make my entire crop unusable. It's easy enough to find a crop duster to spray. It's possible to find one willing to spray for money under the table. Or, even more likely, the duster didn't question the job or the authority of the person asking. Why would anyone fertilize a crop that didn't belong to them?"

"Where did the DDT come from? I thought it was illegal."

"It isn't hard to find. It's still around in small amounts, even though it was banned years ago. At that point, I didn't have a crop to sell, or any proof of who was responsible."

Marilyn took a drink. "She's an attorney. Something she often reminded me of. Even if I had some way of proving it, fighting Francesca would have taken everything, more than I had. Todd would have helped as much as he could, but when he heard I was going to have to use my house as collateral to raise money to pursue a lawsuit, Todd told me to let it go."

Marilyn pressed her hands to her face. I had to lean in to hear her words.

"Even though that land was really being held for him, he told me to let it go."

Nineteen

THE story I'd heard was that most of the land in Monterey
was once owned by a man named David Jacks, a Scottish
immigrant who arrived in Monterey in 1850. He obtained
work as the county treasurer. Once he got to know the citizens
on the delinquent tax rolls, he began to lend them money to
pay their taxes, using the land as collateral. When tax pay-
ments were missed, he foreclosed. By this and other legal
chicanery, he acquired more than thirty thousand acres
by 1859.

I drove through Monterey thinking of the colorful ways
people had acquired the land of others throughout the region.
I had to admit, in an area known for clever land swindles,
Francesca's, as nasty and rotten as it was, was every bit as
clever.

I headed south and was on the edge of town when I spotted
Colony Lane. Marilyn had said her land was out there. I

wouldn't know it when I came to it, but on an impulse, I made a sharp right onto the narrow road.

The afternoon showed the vineyards at their best; a mixture of purple and russet hues, the rows of fruit ribboned across the rolling hills. Such a contrast to how these same fields would look in a few short months, when the vines were pruned, the plants readied for their winter rest.

Winding roads like this are where my car is at its best: smooth, tight in the turns and fun to drive. However, it was without a doubt the worst thing to drive when you wanted to go unnoticed. When I passed Francesca at a front gate, padlock in hand, I knew where the land was. Of course, Francesca recognized the car and also knew where I was. I could tell by the way she stopped and stared. The fury that tightened her face wasn't a bad clue either.

Since she'd spotted me, snooping was out of the question. I slowed and pulled to the side of the road, next to where she stood. The gravel crunched beneath my tires and sent a soft cloud of dust into the still air.

"I suppose you were just driving by. First, you happen to find Todd, and now here you are. My, my, aren't you just the one for showing up at inopportune moments."

"I was in Monterey for something else." I cut the engine and opened the car door. "I do know that Marilyn used to own this land and now you do, so I decided to drive by and take a look."

I leaned against the side of the car. "Actually, I'm glad you're here. I have some questions for you." It was time for some answers from Francesca, and I had a chip to play.

Francesca raised her brow. "Now, don't get me wrong. I like your style, I really do. But, honestly, why would I tell you anything?"

"Because"—I took a step forward—"if you don't, I'll tell Antonia how you got this piece of land."

No reaction. She was good, I'd give her that. I could see her as smooth in a courtroom as she was with me.

"I know the whole story. Marilyn was quite forthcoming. Really nasty, Francesca, even for you."

Francesca remained still but her shoulders stiffened. "If there was anything to that old rumor, Mother would have heard about it by now."

"From who? The other wineries? Come on. Do you think they'd tell her that her daughter is a thief and a cheat? Antonia, the largest winery owner on the central coast? And at that point, to what end? You already had the land."

A small, nervous tic started above her right eye.

"You're still part of the Martinelli family. You don't get the winery but you're still an heir. You still have access to the family name, to Antonia's public support. How long would that last if she knew the whole story?"

I looked over her shoulder. "It's too late to help Marilyn now. The land is yours, and there isn't anything to be done about that. Otherwise I wouldn't be making you this generous offer. If I keep silent, though, I want some answers." I didn't like it, but I didn't have to.

She studied me. "I'll give you five minutes."

"Fine."

"What do you want to start with, this land? Well, here it is." She swept her arm behind her. "It's as pretty as my mother's. Prettier and more productive. At least it will be when I get done. In terms of size, it's small, but I was never interested in producing a lot of wine. Just the best. Antonia has never given me credit, but I have more natural ability than she does. In a few years, we'll have vintages to rival anything she and my insipid brother can turn out."

I turned at the venom in her voice.

Francesca smiled. "Oh, come now. I'm sure you know there isn't any love lost between us."

"Sure I know. It'd be hard to miss. I'm just surprised you feel that strongly about your brother. Your mother made her decision. Stephen didn't ask to inherit the winery."

"No, but he sure didn't protest either. I was born knowing more about wines than he'll grasp in a lifetime working those hills. But, thanks to my mother, he'll get a lifetime to find that out."

"So now you've got your vineyard, but you still need a winery." I looked beyond the fence. "Marilyn sold her grapes outright. I don't know how you expect to produce your own label from here."

"My, my, Penny Lively doesn't know something. Amazing." She shrugged. "I've been busy. The buildings are finished, and I'm hoping next year's harvest will be bottled under my own name."

"What name is that?"

"F.M. Vineyards."

"Francesca Martinelli Vineyards. Original. For all your anger at your mother, you still managed to pull in the family name, didn't you?"

"I'm not relying on the Martinelli name."

"Right," I said. "I'm sure nobody will figure out what the *M* stands for. Also, it's just you. Can I assume Brice isn't involved in the winery?"

Francesca's eyes narrowed. "This is my vineyard. Brice doesn't know anything about wine. Anyway, it takes money, a lot of money." She stopped and turned to padlock the gate.

"Brice must make good money as a cardiologist."

"Decent." Francesca rattled the locked chain. "He also has expensive habits. Very expensive habits." She looked at her watch. "You have three minutes."

She seemed pretty calm about it, and I decided to press. "Well, he certainly has expensive habits when it comes to ordering wine. That was a nice bottle you two shared at Sterling yesterday. Of course, he had to finish the bottle himself after you stormed out of there. I'm sure the wine was much smoother than the conversation."

She threw her head back and laughed. "You missed your calling, Penny. Putting the defense attorney on the defensive, are you? You'd have made a decent lawyer."

"Now you're just fighting dirty."

Her smile faded, and the red lipstick emphasized the hard lines around her mouth. "Brice and I were arguing about what everyone in this fishbowl town already knows: namely, that my husband can't keep his pants on and his hands off." She gave the padlock one final tug and turned to me. "Now that I think about it, we weren't actually arguing. What's there to argue about? I'm just sick of hearing it discussed behind my back. At a volume intentionally loud enough for me to hear every word."

I wondered if Francesca knew about Brice and her sister. "Hearing the news from others must be very painful for you."

"Heard it from others? Is that how you think I learned about his wandering? Oh, no. That implies he took pains to keep it from me. Brice has been coming home with the proverbial lipstick on his collar almost from the day we were married. And, to be perfectly honest, I couldn't care less about his wandering if only he was capable of being the one thing he isn't: discreet."

Francesca's voice rose. "We live in San Francisco, damn it! You'd think he'd have enough trophies there, even for a man who likes collecting them as much as Brice does. But no, he has to bring it to Cypress Cove, my town, where I know everybody and everyone knows me and where nobody can keep their damn mouth shut."

She continued to talk as she walked toward a silver Lexus parked under an oak nearby.

I moved with her.

"The one thing I have in this town is respect, and that's tough to keep if every available female who lives here has slept with your husband. That's also where his money goes. Hideaways with views of the Golden Gate Bridge for numerous special friends pretty much keeps Brice low on funds."

Not to mention exhausted. "So why not leave him?"

"Because I like being married," she snapped. "I like having a ready escort, the well-respected doctor to dress up in a tux and cart around to openings and premiers. And forget him ever leaving me. He wouldn't be able to afford so much as a postcard of the bridge when I got through with him."

On second thought, better she stayed with him. They deserved each other.

"Besides, he likes being part of the most successful wine family in the valley. He'd never want to leave that behind. It amazes me how much power the Martinelli name still carries here." Francesca paused. "Even with the problems the winery's been having the last couple of years. Shockingly inconsistent. And with all those improvements Stephen is undertaking. I can't imagine what could possibly be going on."

The sarcasm was thick in her voice. Either she was responsible for the sabotage, or she just enjoyed the situation.

"No ideas at all?"

She brushed aside the question with a wave of her hand. "Either Marvin's losing his touch and doesn't know how to manage a vintage anymore, or my mother and brother are making mistakes. It's as simple as that."

I looked at her. She really seemed to think it was just someone at Martinelli making mistakes. If she was the one I surprised by the barrels that day, she wasn't showing it.

"Where were you two days ago?"

"I was in the city in the morning then drove down here. Why? What does that have to do with anything?"

I ignored her questions and considered the timing. She could have driven down early and been in the barrel room with me. "I wouldn't worry about Martinelli Winery, Francesca."

"Believe me, I'm not. The Martinelli name still pulls as much weight as it ever did." Her laughter was shrill. "For example, don't think for a moment the bit of success you're enjoying with your little winery would've come without the blessing of my family."

I turned in front of her and brought her to a stop.

Her smile widened. She savored getting to me.

My heart raced, but I plastered a smile on my face and forced myself to relax. "If you come after me, Francesca, or my winery, all bets are off."

Never losing eye contact, Francesca stepped around me.

"I'm not concerned with your modest efforts, Penny, and there are two points you fail to see. One, my mother will do anything to avoid scandal. She will outwardly support me as a show of family solidarity and will stand against me only if there is any proof of the way I acquired this land. Which brings me to point two. Proof, dear Penny. There isn't any."

Twenty

WITHOUT a second glance Francesca got in her car and drove away. She was right. It did all come back to proof. She seemed damned sure there wasn't any. When the sound of her car faded and I felt sure she was gone, I walked back to the padlock and gave it a tug. Locked up tight. I eyed the fence. It was a little over my height, with simple slats. Easy to scale.

When I landed on the other side I made my way down the dirt road. It curved and ended at a trio of buildings, all new and painted a moss green. The winery logo was mounted over the door of the largest building. It was a capital F in the same moss green seated over a capital M in gold patina, and was surprisingly attractive. Damn it. Francesca Martinelli Vineyards. I wondered if Antonia knew how far Francesca had taken this.

The buildings were all locked and I couldn't get a peek

through any of the shuttered windows. I hopped the fence and returned to my car.

Had Todd been looking for evidence? If he'd been able to prove Francesca had cheated Marilyn out of her land, would he have gone to Antonia? Had he taken the job at Martinelli Winery with that in mind?

Between lack of food and adrenaline from my little field trip and conversation with Francesca, I was light-headed. Low blood sugar.

I drove through town, spotted my favorite burger place, pulled into the drive-thru and ordered a well-done burger with extra pickles and grilled onions. I managed to keep the bag closed until I reached the bluff over the Pacific, near the famed cypress tree the town was named after. I settled in to watch the beach while I ate.

The car top was still down and the last of the sun, like liquid warmth, fell over my face. Down on the beach a few people enjoyed the sunset with me. A man and his Labrador ran along the shore, the dog more in the water than out. An elderly couple sat bundled against the breeze, which was chilly if you weren't moving about. Three kids braved the waves, while their dad watched from shore.

I swam in those same waves when I was their age, but now it was too cold for me. California had sandy beaches, gorgeous weather, palm trees down south and redwoods right up to the shores in the north. But warm water? Forget it.

It was a little before six and the sun had slipped over the horizon. I finished my burger and made my way back down the coast into Cypress Cove, where I turned in to Beauty and the Bean for coffee.

The fragrance of roasting beans, rich and amazingly complex, welcomed me before I'd reached the front door. Barrels of cooling coffee, with exotic names like Coatepec and Ankola, beckoned to me, but I resisted the urge to run my fingers through the glistening beans.

All of the coffees Thomas sold in the gift shop and coffee bar were shade-grown organic. They used the same coffee next door in the restaurant. Rain forests weren't cut down. Songbird habitats were saved. Virtue and vitality in a recycled paper cup.

The restaurant was accessible from the coffee bar through an arched open area. Diners were enjoying their meals. Thomas waved as he went by with a tray and from somewhere in the restaurant I heard Ross laugh.

While the restaurant was open and spacious, the gift shop and coffee bar was cute and cluttered, a place sprites would feel at home. Everything looked fragile, delicate and surreal. Connor breaks out in a sweat any time he comes into the gift shop. He says he feels claustrophobic, but I think it's the hugs Ross and Thomas insist on giving him.

To my right was a grouping of my latest prints. Some were inserted into frames. Nearby a bowl carried the same prints, but reprinted as postcards. I absently picked up the top postcard. I remembered taking the picture last autumn. It was a shot of my vineyard, although, at the time, it had still belonged to Aunt Monique. What a turn my life had taken in one short year.

I returned the postcard and walked to the coffee bar counter to study the daily coffee list, with just a quick peek at the dessert display.

Behind the case the top of Joanne's head appeared. She spotted me through the glass and waved over the fruit tarts she was arranging in the case. She stood and smiled, but she looked pale. She wore an emerald green dress, and with her masses of red hair and ethereal beauty, she could have been a sprite herself.

"Hi, Penny. I heard you went to see Marilyn today. She said she enjoyed the visit. Of course, anyone who likes Dollie is okay in her book."

"I liked both of them too. Can we sit for a minute?"

"Sure. Coffee?"

"I'd love one. You too. My treat."

I sat at one of the tables and Joanne joined me, two steaming cups in hand.

"Did Marilyn tell you anything helpful?" Joanne asked. "You know, about Todd."

"She told me the entire story about how she lost her land to Francesca."

Joanne nodded. "Todd wanted to let it go, more than Marilyn. He hated what it was doing to his mom and wouldn't let her risk her home to fight Francesca in court."

"They seemed really close."

"Oh, they were. Todd and Marilyn spent a lot of years alone."

"What happened to his dad?"

"Car accident. Years ago. Todd always talked about how great his childhood was before that. His dad was adopted, and Todd said family was really important to him." Joanne slapped her forehead. "Oh! I'm sorry. Ross and Thomas told me about the attack. How you are feeling?"

I rubbed the back of my head. "Lucky, I guess. Just a quick trip to the hospital. If the bottle hadn't been wrapped, it could have been worse."

The hospital reminded me of Brice. "I know Chantal and

Todd talked. Do you know if she ever mentioned her relationship with Brice?"

Joanne's eyes grew wide. "Chantal and Brice? I've never heard anything, and if Todd knew I think he would have said something." She paused. "He did know she was seeing someone who was putting her in a tailspin, though, so it sort of makes sense if you think about it. Guys like Brice dream of girls like that. He'd be especially bad for Chantal, you know, because of her problems."

"Her drug problems?"

Joanne nodded.

I thought of the missing prescriptions in the pad in Brice's desk. "Did you think he could ever have given her anything?"

Joanne looked away and took a deep breath. "I'm not sure about this . . ."

"Joanne, someone was determined to keep Todd quiet. If Todd knew something, don't you think you ought to tell me what it was?"

She pulled her gaze back to me. "I just don't see how it will help, and I don't want to hurt innocent people."

"You need to tell me what you know. Someone out there isn't that concerned about people getting hurt."

"Including you. Getting hurt, I mean. That could be why you were attacked. Someone sees you as a threat too."

"Believe me, I've thought of that. What happened with Chantal?"

"A few weeks ago she was out of control one afternoon in the tasting room. Singing, twirling around on the bar stools, that kind of thing."

"Was she drunk?"

Joanne shrugged. "If she was, she came in that way. Todd

never gave her anything to drink. I was there, waiting for Todd to get off work. Stephen was there too, and he didn't want anyone else from the family to see her that way."

" 'Anyone' meaning Antonia."

Joanne nodded. "Everyone knew if Chantal fell off the wagon again, it was back to the clinic for her. She hates it there and her brother knows it. He grabbed her around the waist and sort of half carried, half dragged her around to the back, where he had his car. I remember she dropped her bag when Stephen picked her up. Stephen had his back to us, but Todd and I picked everything up. There must have been ten prescription bottles that fell out."

A couple came into the shop. Joanne stood to return to the counter. "When I asked Todd later what all of the prescriptions were for, he said they looked like sedatives. He didn't elaborate. I didn't mention it again and sort of forgot about it, but when I thought of his reaction later, about the way he answered, I think it really bothered him. He didn't say anything else, but I remember him being distracted for the rest of the day."

Joanne glanced at the couple standing at the counter, ready to order.

"One more quick question?"

She gave me a small smile. "I know what you're going to ask. I didn't read the labels, but I bet Todd did. Did Chantal get those pills from Brice?"

Twenty-one

I LEFT Joanne and drove to Martinelli Winery. Chantal could have taken prescriptions out of Brice's pad and forged his signature. She'd have access if they were spending that much time together. Or Brice could have written them for her and, as a precaution, removed the prescriptions in random order. Then if it was ever discovered, he could always claim Chantal had taken them.

If he'd given her the prescriptions, it was possible she wasn't the only one. Brice might have supplied all his girlfriends with pharmaceutical party favors. Francesca said Brice had expensive hobbies. Was dabbling in drugs one of them? Or he could have been selling them to help finance his other hobbies. Did Todd ask him straight out about Chantal? I was full up on questions. Now I needed a few answers.

The fog had begun to creep in from the coast. It swirled around my car and I turned on my lights, though it was still early. I was glad to see it, as it would keep the heat from the earlier sun close to the ground. This time of year the clear, cloudless nights were the ones to worry about. They could bring an early frost and ruin an entire harvest.

I parked out in front and took a few minutes to snap the car roof in place. The evening was quiet around me as I walked to the front doors, with only the crunch of gravel under my feet and the whirl of the fans from the fermentation building in the background.

The police tape was gone and there was a light in the winery office. I didn't see Marvin at the desk, and wondered again how much he'd seen from that window.

In less than a day the festival would begin. I couldn't see through the fog to the festival grounds, but there was a halo from lights in the clearing and voices echoed as I made my way up the steps. I'd just begun to knock when Stephen opened the door.

"Oh, hello. Mother said you were stopping by. She's in the library. Go on in."

As I stepped into the hall, Stephen went out into the night and closed the door behind him.

I walked through the doors to my left, once again in that beautiful room with the peach walls that now glowed by firelight. The scent of freshly cut roses hung in the air.

Antonia sat next to the fireplace. One hand rested on the reading glasses I hadn't known she needed. She glanced up, pulled the glasses off and tucked them into her sleeve.

"Don't hover over there. Close the door. I don't want us overheard or disturbed." She waved me over with the newspaper she'd been reading.

"Hello, Antonia. How are you?" I didn't really expect a

greeting in return. Good thing because she plunged right in, shaking the papers in her hand.

"Do you know what this is?"

I glanced at it. A copy of the industry newsletter, the *Winery Review.*

Her hands shook as she crumpled the pages. "It's tripe, that's what it is. The reviews of our last vintage."

She threw the paper into the fire and quoted from memory, " 'The acid is too high, the finish much too short, and the oak overpowering.' I can't understand it."

After a long pause, she turned to me. "If I were to be honest, the worst part is they're right. I wanted to turn the winery over to Stephen officially this Saturday at the festival—he's worked hard to prove himself—but with reviews like this, I don't know if I can."

"Things happen—"

"What things happen? Specifics, Penelope."

"The problem isn't Stephen—"

"The only thing I've changed is giving Stephen more responsibility. If this isn't sabotage, then he clearly isn't ready for the job."

"Someone has been—"

Antonia shook her head. "Who?"

"Antonia, stop! I'm trying to tell you something and you just won't listen. You have the reputation of being impossible, and I've got to tell you, it's well deserved."

To my surprise, Antonia didn't respond. She sat there and watched the paper burn in the fire, her only movement the palm of her hand as it cradled the silver handle of her cane.

Finally, she turned to me. "Well? I'm listening, and I don't hear a whole lot."

Right. I ticked through what I'd found: the person in the fermenting building with the yeast, the jewelry Marvin tried to sell, the missing prescriptions in Brice's office and Francesca's anger at Stephen's inheritance. I told Antonia everything except how Francesca had forced Marilyn to sell her the land. I didn't know how I would solve that one, but for now I'd keep the deal with Francesca.

The only difficult part was telling her about Chantal and Brice. It wasn't easy to watch her face register that her younger daughter was sleeping with her older daughter's husband. The pain she felt over Chantal was evident in the glisten in her eyes. It was possible Todd had discovered this and confronted Brice, but either way, Antonia needed to know the source of so many of Chantal's problems.

I spoke at length, the chiming of the grandfather clock letting us know when it reached eight. The sound echoed through the room. It was only when it stopped that a soft knock was heard at the door. When Veronica stuck her head in, apologetically asking if we wanted tea, Antonia waved her away with a flick of her hand.

Veronica disappeared.

"So basically you're telling me my son is incompetent, my older daughter petty and vicious and my son-in-law has been cheating on his wife with my other daughter, not to mention possibly giving her drugs." She gave me a small smile. "What? Nothing to add about my daughter-in-law? No, I don't suppose you need to. I know she's a ninny."

Antonia paused. "I'm a realist. I know my children. I love

them, but I know who they are. They're impossible, all of them. I didn't spend the time with them I should have. I realize that now." Antonia twisted her cane. "There's something else. I don't know if you remember my husband, Fiorentino."

I shook my head. "I was too young."

"He died shortly after Chantal was born."

"He was still young," I said. "What did he die from?"

"Heart attack." She paused. "Not much older than you when it happened."

"I'm sorry." It felt unnatural to offer condolences for someone lost so long ago, and Antonia dismissed my condolences with a quick wave of her hand.

"We were wholly unsuited for each other. He wasn't a particularly nice man. Unreliable as a husband. A lot like Brice, now that I think about it. However, my father liked him, which was important. I needed help with the winery, and my father didn't have anyone else to leave it to, which was a problem. He didn't want to leave it to me to begin with, truth be told. My being a girl, his only child, was something he could never forgive." She shrugged. "It was a different world back then. My father made me promise to leave it to one child. The battles he had with his brother over it tore the family apart."

"Did you keep your maiden name?" I asked.

"No. That just wasn't done back then, but shortly after he passed I changed it back to Martinelli. The children were so young I changed their names as well."

Antonia stamped her cane. "I did what I needed to do. That's what women did back then. If it had been up to me, I wouldn't have married at all." She paused. "There was someone. I was in love with someone I couldn't have. As time went on, my father threatened to sell the winery if I didn't have a husband. I wasn't letting that happen. So, I got married. Married and had children. My father was happy and, because I had the land, I was content."

She was content because she had the winery, not because of her three children. She seemed to realize the inequity and lifted her palms. "I was single-minded and I realize that now. It wasn't far to them."

Antonia turned toward the fire. "And now here we are, discussing the possibility one of my children is trying to destroy what I've built. Ironic, isn't it?"

My voice was soft. "I know it hurts, but I'm not wrong about what I saw in the fermentation building. I can show you the broken bottle. I left it where I found it. Someone is clearly trying to hurt Martinelli Winery."

She spoke, facing the fire. "I don't suppose you have any good news out of all this?"

"Well, no, not actually."

"The obvious person is Francesca, but to take such a risk to see her brother fail? She doesn't get the winery, but she still shares in the profits, even if Stephen's in charge."

"Some people aren't motivated by money."

"Is there any way to prove who was out there with you in the fermentation building?"

"No. I don't have any way to know for certain."

"Fingerprints on the broken bottle?"

"The person wore gloves. They were careful not to leave evidence."

"Yes, I'm sure they would be. Well, I think we better work on finding some, don't you?"

Here I'd been feeling sorry for her. "Gee, Antonia, that's a great idea. I've just been a little busy, getting over a concussion from being attacked and all."

Antonia tapped her reading glasses against her palm. "Yes, I know. I heard about that. Do you think it had anything to do with Todd?"

"I'm fine, thanks, and yes, it probably has something to do with it. I can't think of any other reason why someone would take a bottle of Chardonnay to the side of my head."

To my surprise, she chuckled. "Good. Good, you're angry. A bit of anger goes a long way to motivate. I always use it to my advantage."

She rose and stood with her back to the fire. "Marvin having jewelry to sell. Now, that is quite a puzzle. He likes to gamble. Bets on anything. I pay him good wages, the best, but I've seen him clutching racing forms and watching football games with sweat dotting his forehead often enough to know where most of those wages go. If the apartment behind his office didn't come free with the job, I think he'd be in real trouble."

I sat up. "So Marvin's here all the time, basically."

"Usually, yes."

"All night too. Antonia, do you lock the doors?"

"Never. I don't believe anyone else thinks of it either. We've never had to. If you're asking whether Marvin has access, the answer is yes. If you're thinking he was selling jewelry he stole from here, that's quite impossible. I would have noticed some of my jewelry missing."

"What about Chantal?"

"She doesn't have much. Unfortunately, I had to stop giving her expensive things some time ago. All Veronica wears are those pearls."

"What about Francesca?"

"Unlikely. She isn't here all the time, and besides, she doesn't waste money on anything as frivolous as jewelry. She has very few pieces, all of them ugly, in my opinion. Quite stark. Modern."

I'd been staring into the fire when something clicked into place. "What did you just say?"

"Francesca likes stark, new jewelry. She has simply wretched taste. Really, Penelope, if you aren't going to listen . . ."

"I'm sorry, Antonia, but the jewelry Marvin was trying to sell was old, like maybe family pieces. Antique. Like things stored in an attic."

"The noises I've been hearing at night."

"I think so. Maybe."

Antonia was halfway across the room, any hint of frailty now gone. "Are you going to sit there and make me wait for you, for heaven's sake?"

"Right behind you." I made it to the door just ahead of her and opened it.

With an unspoken agreement, we looked about before we moved across the hall to the flight of stairs. We didn't see anyone between the library and our arrival at the attic, three stories up. Antonia managed the climb almost as well as I did.

"I call it the attic, but originally it was the children's nursery." She turned the knob. The light from the hallway filtered in around us as we looked through the doorway.

Into chaos.

Twenty-two

A NTONIA switched on the overhead light. The curved walls were high, perhaps eleven or twelve feet, and painted a soft yellow. The roof ended in a peak. We were in one of the cupolas visible from the front of the home. The ceiling was red and gold, trimmed with tassels of woven brocade. It was designed to look like the underside of a merry-go-round. At floor level, the walls were decorated with horses, tigers and hippos, caught midprance in a never-ending parade.

This whimsical backdrop made the destruction in the room more violent. Neatly labeled boxes were torn and discarded, their contents scattered around the room. Shredded children's artwork covered the floor. Several cedar trunks were open or turned over. Beaded dresses and several boas had been ripped to pieces. A mahogany vanity sat empty, its drawers flung across the room, the mirror shattered.

A rolltop desk stood to one side. The drawers were out,

the contents dumped. I walked closer and tried to avoid the papers that cluttered the floor. There were old diplomas, certificates and land deeds among the strewn papers. Antonia came up behind me.

"Last week when you were up here, after you heard the noises, was it like this?"

Antonia surveyed the damage. "Of course not. I never would have left it like this. Things had been moved, but this . . ."

I picked up the papers at my feet. "There are certificates and land deeds in here. Look, it's your high school diploma."

Antonia took the yellowed paper. "A long time ago." She pointed to the floor. "What are those?"

I knelt and studied the yellowed forms. "Birth certificates."

Antonia took the papers. "The three of them."

"Right. One for each child."

"Don't be sarcastic." She looked around the room. "These are duplicates. All the originals are at the bank, in the safe deposit."

I placed the papers on the desk. "Why the anger, the destruction? If this was Marvin, why would he be filled with such hate?"

"I don't have any idea. There isn't anything here anyone would want. Not anyone outside the family. Just things of sentimental value. Except the jewelry, of course."

She stopped and moved toward the vanity.

"Antonia, what is it?"

"There's a gun—was a gun—in the bottom drawer here." She reached in. "It's gone."

"We need to call Lucas. This is more than anger. It's desperation." I looked around the room. "Where did you keep the jewelry?"

Antonia pointed to one of the drawers on the floor. It was empty. "Here, in an old pink cigar box announcing the birth of Chantal. Men used to pass around cigars, you know, when their children were born. Their big accomplishment. I wonder if they still do that."

I searched and found the box lying on its side. It had a baby picture on a pink background and announced, "It's a girl!" on its cover. Picking it up, I showed it to Antonia. "Nothing here."

Antonia set the diploma and certificates on the top of the desk and made her way to the door. "It's time to have a talk with Marvin."

We made our way down the stairs, where Antonia grabbed a heavy black shawl. The fog was thicker than when I'd arrived, and it danced around us as we walked from the back of the house to Marvin's office. We didn't speak. The night air swallowed any noise our steps might have made.

When we reached the office, the sounds of a televised boxing match drifted through the window. We made our way around to the front door of the apartment. The lights were off but through the curtains the television glowed, and the announcer declared the winner of the match.

Knocking, we waited. And waited. Antonia tapped her foot. She was clearly losing patience.

"Try the knob."

"I'm really not sure that's a good idea."

She moved forward. "I'll do it."

"What if he's asleep or we surprise him in his underwear?"

Antonia looked at me then started to reach for the door handle.

I *really* didn't want to catch Marvin in his underwear. I grabbed her cane and, using the silver handle, started pounding on the door.

Antonia reached for my arm. "Stop that racket! You're giving me a headache. I don't think he's here."

"Where else would he be?"

"Maybe he went into town." She walked down the front steps and peered through the fog. "No, his truck's still here."

"Let's check the office."

We turned and made our way to the other side of the building. The office light was on and there wasn't any movement.

Antonia came up beside me. "I'm never here this time of night. Usually when I need him it's during the day and I just walk in."

The image of Marvin, clad in nothing but his underwear and a scowl, was still with me.

"Just do me a favor and knock first."

I stepped over the flower border and looked in through the window. Nothing seemed out of place. Bookcases ran along one wall, with a small seating area to one side.

Antonia used the head of her cane to rap on the door.

"It's open." She pushed it with her cane.

My eyes settled on the desk just below the window. The papers and racing forms were still there, shoved to one side. So were the "Viva Las Vegas" coffee mug and the letter opener. Actually, just the handle of the letter opener. I couldn't see the rest because it was buried in Marvin's back.

I wanted to run, but my legs wouldn't move. His face was about six inches from mine and his eyes were shut. Without the letter opener and the big red spot that had now reached his collar, he could have been asleep.

Dots appeared before my eyes and I choked down air in short, quick breaths.

At some point Antonia came up to stand beside me. "Right in the back."

I looked at her. She craned her neck to get a better look and was taking it pretty well. Better than I was, I had to admit. I wasn't so good with bodies. Or blood. I kept trying to breathe.

"I want to go in and look around."

"You're kidding, right?" I nodded toward Marvin. "Do you see him?"

"Of course I do. I don't think we both have to go in."

"I can't let you go alone." What was I saying? "I mean, we don't need to go in at all. What we need to do is call the police."

"I'm the most familiar with this room and Marvin. I might see things the police won't. It simply makes sense."

"I think the police might have a different opinion if we asked them."

"Five minutes isn't going to make a difference." Antonia nodded toward Marvin. "Not to him, anyway."

"Antonia!"

"Well, look at him. He won't mind. One quick peek and we call Lucas."

I peered through the darkness to the main house. We'd left the lights on in the library. The peach walls glowed. The smell of wood smoke from the fireplace reached me. The night was quiet, without the sounds of sirens announcing that, against my better judgment, I was about to enter the scene of a murder. Again.

Antonia moved to the door. "Look. We won't even have to touch the doorknob."

I took a deep breath. "Well, then, no problem. Stroll right in."

The sarcasm was wasted, and Antonia entered the office.

"I agree with your assessment the police won't grasp the necessity of our entering the premises. We'll keep this to ourselves."

Right. Good idea.

Antonia crossed the room and walked up behind the skewered Marvin.

My options were to follow her or remain in the doorway. I followed.

We stood there for a few moments behind the body. He sat in the desk chair. His head rested on the winery ledger, opened as though at some point in the evening he'd been working. The "Viva Las Vegas" mug was half-full. I stuck one finger into the liquid.

"It's still warm."

My eyes drifted across the room to the bookcase next to the front door. Something under the bottom shelf caught the light from the desk lamp.

I walked over and with the edge of my shoe I nudged the shiny item out a few inches.

Antonia followed. "My mother's brooch. I last saw it in the cigar box upstairs."

I moved it back into place. "We need to leave everything as it is."

Antonia returned to the center of the room, directly behind Marvin. "It looks as though someone came up on him while he was sitting here and stabbed him."

Marvin's chair was rolled squarely up to the desk. "Wait a minute. This isn't right."

"What isn't right? He was sitting at his desk."

"Yes."

"Possibly working."

"Okay, yes." I nodded.

"Somebody crept in and stabbed him in the back."

"No."

"What do you mean no? Clearly he was stabbed in the back."

"Yes."

Antonia thumped her cane. "Explain."

I pointed at the letter opener. "Do you recognize it?"

"Of course I recognize it. It's my letter opener. Marvin kept it on the desk."

"He was stabbed in the back with the letter opener. *In the back*. The letter opener was kept on the desk." I moved behind Marvin. "There's no way someone could have reached the letter opener without Marvin knowing the person was there."

I turned toward the door of the office. "The murderer didn't sneak in here planning to kill Marvin while he was sitting at his desk. Anyone coming here to stab him would have had a knife on them. This was spontaneous. Marvin knew the person was here. Marvin knew them. He invited them in. What about the brooch? How did it get on the floor and what does it have to do with anything?"

Antonia crossed back to the bookcase. "Maybe the murderer was stealing it and that infernal racket you made with my cane on the door startled them. They dropped it and couldn't take the time to look for it. That's why the door was ajar. Or maybe the killer was someone Marvin owed money to. Marvin liked to gamble. We know this."

I held up my hand. "It doesn't fit. Unless you think someone came in here earlier and took the letter opener to use as a murder weapon later, Marvin turned his back on whoever was here, to sit at the desk. While the person was still here. Why would he do that?"

Antonia nodded. "To look at something."

"Yes."

"The brooch."

"Yes."

Antonia appeared to be working through it. "But that means he hadn't seen it before."

"I don't think so, no."

"But then, that means Marvin wasn't the one who stole it from the attic. Someone else was up there."

I rubbed my eyes. "I told you how I found Marvin watching the winery from the top of my hill. What if he was watching someone?"

"That was after Todd's death. What would he be watching?"

I shrugged my shoulders. "Beats me. I'm working through it as I go along. Let's say he saw something or someone the night of the murder. If it was someone here, he's had time to tell them, maybe threaten or blackmail them. Maybe he was just keeping an eye on the person. Maybe he had them do something."

Antonia held up her hand. "Maybe your imagination is getting the best of you. You said it's possible someone came in here earlier and got the letter opener to use at a later time."

"Why?"

Antonia waved her hand. "Maybe the killer wanted to cast suspicion on someone here, so they made a point to use the letter opener. We know Marvin liked to gamble. Maybe he owed someone money, someone outside the family. Possibly there was a confrontation."

"Antonia, he was stabbed in the back. No confrontation.

And Marvin turned his back on the person, so it must have been someone he knew, someone he wasn't especially worried about. Besides, people who are owed money, especially money from gambling, aren't very likely to kill the gambling goose, so to speak. It just doesn't make much sense to kill them. If Marvin owed money, how likely is it he's going to get around to paying it back now?"

Antonia walked toward the door without responding. I knew what she was doing.

"Antonia, I know it was easier for you to ask for my help when there was a chance someone outside your family might possibly be the culprit. I'm sure you were still hoping I was wrong about that night. A flash of car lights against the window, anything other than someone you know returning into your home after doing something unspeakable."

Antonia turned at the door. "I won't deny what you're saying. I was hoping your approaching it from a different perspective would lead to a different solution, possibly a solution that doesn't have someone close to me capable of doing something like this."

"Antonia, if you want me to stop right now, I will. The police will figure it out. Chief Lucas is a bright guy. But I have to tell you, it's someone you know, probably someone you care about. You know it too. It isn't going away."

I walked up to her and edged the door open with my shoulder.

Antonia pushed past me. "I'm hardly one to hide behind denial. You can't stop. Whoever did this can't either. Let's go call the police."

Twenty-three

WE were in the library having a much-needed brandy when Lucas walked in. The look I got was a bit unnerving. Apparently one body per week was my limit with him. We waited while he inspected the winery office, posted two officers, and called the coroner.

The rest of the family had pooled together at the sound of sirens and now hovered out in the hallway. Lucas asked them not to go anywhere and shut the library door. He sat in the chair farthest from the fire and took statements from the both of us. Palms together, fingers laced, he read over his notes.

"Why were you two looking for Marvin at this time of night?"

I glanced at Antonia. "We thought he might have had something to do with a theft. Some jewelry is missing from storage in the upstairs playroom. There's a gun that's gone too."

Lucas rubbed his eyes. "And you saw Marvin dead through

the window of the winery office. Why didn't you go to the front door of the apartment? He wouldn't normally be working this time of night, would he?"

"No. We knocked on the apartment door first. We heard the television, but there wasn't any answer."

Antonia chimed in. "So we went around to the office. That's when we saw him. Through the window."

I shot her a look.

Lucas shifted his gaze between us. "You said you think he might have something to do with a theft, which"—he cast a quick glance at me—"I haven't heard anything about. Care to fill me in?"

We told him about the theft and destruction upstairs. Lucas left a deputy with us while he spent a few moments in the playroom. He returned and instructed the deputy to look for prints.

"So you think Marvin's responsible for that?"

"We thought it was possible because he was seen trying to sell some antique jewelry at Peterson's. We suspected it might be Antonia's so we went to talk to him. That's when we found him, well, stuck to his desk."

Lucas didn't respond.

I took a deep breath. "I have a theory."

Lucas raised his brow.

I stuck my chin out. "Well, I do. Whoever killed Marvin tonight didn't come here planning to kill him, or they would have been armed. They decided to kill him after they were alone with him in the office. That's why they used the letter opener from the desk."

Lucas just sat there and watched me over steepled fingers.

"Think about it. Marvin invited them in. He knew they

were there. He turned his back to them, so he didn't think he was in danger."

"We think Marvin was blackmailing someone and they went there to pay him off. My mother's brooch must have been part of it," Antonia said.

Lucas listened, his clear blue eyes steady. "I assume that when you found him, the very next thing you did was phone me. You did call me right away, didn't you? Because"—he leaned toward us—"earlier you said you thought jewelry was missing. Now you specifically mention a brooch. Why?"

No answer for that one.

"See, it's odd. There is a brooch. It's near the front door on the floor. The funny thing is, it can't be seen from outside through the window. It's partially hidden by a bookcase. You would have had to be in the room to see it."

Great. I turned to look at Antonia. "Tell Lucas how we know there was a brooch on the floor where you can't see it from the window."

"We meant we saw him *first* from the window. Then, of course, we went in, to check his pulse. You'd have wanted us to try and help him, had he still been alive, wouldn't you, Lucas?"

Oh, please. She had to be kidding. You couldn't get any deader than Marvin was when we found him and we all knew it.

Lucas held up his hand. We waited. The room was unbearably warm. It took all my focus to not say something, anything, to fill the silence. I looked over at Antonia, unperturbed and as cool as could be. The sweat began trickling down between my shoulder blades.

Lucas rested his chin on his fingertips. He was great at

this. The clock chimed eleven and still he sat and watched us. Finally he tapped his fingertips together and nodded.

"Okay. Let me go down and take another look. I know it's getting late, but I need you to wait, Penny. I want to meet with the family, and I might need to talk to you again afterward."

I started breathing again. "Okey-dokey." Okey-dokey? "I'm just going to call Hayley and Connor and tell them what's going on."

Lucas allowed himself a brief smile. "Sure. Go ahead and tell them you found another body. That's a call I'd like to hear."

I phoned, prepared to leave a message. Connor answered. Lucky me.

"So, why are you still there?"

I gave him the short version. Connor was even better than Lucas at the art of silence. I got to the end and waited.

"I'm coming over."

"No. I'm fine, really. I'm with the police. Lucas just wants to talk to me after he's done with everyone else."

"I think he should follow you home. If he can't, I'm coming to get you."

I have to admit it was nice to have someone concerned about me like that. "Okay. That's a good idea. Don't tell Hayley anything. I want to tell her myself. See you in a bit."

I hung up the phone. Lucas commandeered the library to talk to the family members, so I went to the kitchen. A small light glowed from across the room as I sat in the semidarkness. There was something I'd missed, something I'd either seen or heard, or both, that fit together, but I couldn't make the connection.

My stomach growled. It had been hours since my burger

by the sea. The kitchen was huge, miles of granite with four separate sinks. Who needed four sinks? I found what I was looking for just as the main light came on.

"Caught with your hand in the cookie jar, Penny?" Francesca moved toward the refrigerator. "I thought you had better manners than that."

I grabbed a couple of the oatmeal cookies. I will not react. Count to ten. One . . . two . . . ten.

"I'm here because Antonia invited me. What I'm wondering is why you keep showing up."

She pulled out a bottle of water and closed the door. "Strange, isn't it? I feel compelled to stop in every few days, just to remind everyone I'm still around. Of course, now that I've gotten sucked into this mess with Marvin, I'll be stuck here all night. It's funny, now that you bring it up. Much as I hate Stephen inheriting this place, you'd think I'd want to stay away, but the opposite is true. I want to see what he's done. I want to watch him fail. And he will. He just doesn't have the touch."

"Antonia's let him make some changes . . ."

"Oh, give me a break. Stephen couldn't change a tire. Most of the improvements were Todd's, and he was only a beginner."

"Stephen wouldn't tell you that and Todd wouldn't even speak to you, so how do you know who's been doing what?"

"Marvin told me when I asked him to come work for me."

"When was that?"

"Months ago."

"I take it he turned you down."

"Then. I've asked him a couple of times since, and today when I asked again he said he'd get back to me."

"You asked him today? What time?"

She smirked. "It was in the morning. I spoke with him before lunch, Ms. Sherlock."

"Did you see him again?"

Francesca took her time. "No, I didn't. Why would I tell you even if I had or, for that matter, why would you believe me? Anyway, back to the topic. Months ago Marvin confirmed Stephen wasn't cutting it . . ."

"That's a lie!" Veronica stood in the kitchen doorway. She trembled and her hands were clenched into fists at her sides. "I can't believe you'd say such a thing. Stephen's done a remarkable job. Don't you ever say he hasn't. Ever."

Veronica's face was a splotchy red. Very attractive.

Francesca looked amused and took a sip of the water. "Don't get so upset. At least he was smart enough to make the changes, no matter who thought of them."

Veronica glared at her. "Stephen thought of them. Of course he's capable of running this winery. You can take your spite and jealousy and leave. Nobody wants you here."

"Veronica, this is my family home. I've got as much right to be here as you. More. Now leave me alone."

With that, Francesca strolled from the room.

Veronica stared after her. Her chest heaved with the effort it took to inhale and relax her shoulders. After a moment, she turned to me. "I won't listen to her talk about Stephen that way. She's so hateful." She paced the kitchen and took deep breaths.

"You take the good with the bad when you marry someone. Try to relax a little. Francesca can't do anything to you or Stephen. Antonia has made her wishes clearly known."

"Yes, that's true, isn't it? I just can't wait until Antonia makes Stephen's running the winery official. Then he'll get the recognition he deserves."

I debated telling her Antonia might make the announcement this weekend but changed my mind. For once I was going to keep my mouth shut. I yawned.

"You must be exhausted, as well as shaken up. I'd forgotten you and Antonia found Marvin. That must have been terrible. I don't know what else to do, but I can make you coffee, or tea perhaps?"

"I can't drink coffee this late, but I'd love some tea."

While we waited for the water to heat, Lucas came in. He looked at the two of us and asked Veronica to give us a few minutes. She set out the tea and watched us as she left the room. "Make yourselves at home."

Lucas took a seat beside me and rubbed his eyes.

I waited. Again. The teapot finally whistled, and I gratefully made myself busy. "Want some?"

"Not tea, but I could use some coffee."

I set my tea down and walked over to where the coffee and coffeemaker sat on the counter.

At home I had something you put grounds in, added water, pushed a button and coffee came out. This was a beautiful piece of equipment, something called a Fiorenzato Bricoletta. Made from stainless steel and copper, it boasted impressive features. I looked at the programmable touch pad options, which included something called "espresso extraction," and gave up.

"I can't make coffee with this. I can't even pronounce the name."

Lucas walked over. "Let me see if I can work it." While he turned the knobs and switches, I looked over the yard from the window. I could see right into Marvin's office, where several people moved around the room. Outside, an officer roped off the area with the familiar yellow tape.

"You need to figure that thing out. It's going to be a long night for a lot of people."

"Got it." Lucas joined me at the window. "Curious to know what's going on down there?"

"Lucas, I found Marvin. I found Todd in the crusher, and don't forget I was attacked with a wine bottle. I guess you could say I want to know what's led to this."

Lucas nodded. "I'll tell you what will be in the public records. Killed shortly before you found him, nothing else appears to be touched. Nothing is missing that we can tell. Fingerprints everywhere, both Marvin's and Todd's. Other fingerprints we'll compare to the Martinellis. We found some receipts of wagers, some online gambling and racetrack tickets. Looks like he owed a few thousand. There was something else."

"What?"

"We think Marvin was stealing from the winery."

Twenty-four

"MARVIN couldn't have been stealing from the winery.
Managers don't have access to the actual profits. Just
the wine."

"That's what he was taking."

"What?"

"Wine."

"How would he manage that? Antonia keeps an eye on
everything."

"We don't think he recorded everything going through the
barrel room. We think he took it out later and then sold it on
the side."

"Wait a minute. That makes sense. It must have been
Marvin who stole the account ledger."

"What are you talking about?"

"Antonia said the ledger was taken a while back. It must

have been Marvin trying to hide his theft. If the account book was missing, how did you find out?"

"We found a production report taped to the bottom of the desk and it doesn't match the tax reports. They should match, right?"

"Always. Barrel rooms are bonded wine cellars. This winery, just like mine, wouldn't remove wine from the cellar until they planned to sell it because they have to pay the sales tax right away."

"How do you keep track of it?"

"Mandatory monthly reports are filed with the Alcohol and Tobacco Tax and Trade Bureau to make sure everything is compliant."

I looked at him. "So Martinelli was producing more than was accounted for, and Marvin was able to take it out and sell it without the winery ever knowing because it wasn't recorded in the first place. He could keep all the profits."

"We think it's possible. Production varies from year to year, as you know, so he would have gotten away with it for at least a couple of years. We don't think he's been at it for long. Antonia would have caught on," Lucas said.

"It also explains something I heard earlier from Francesca. She'd offered Marvin a position with her new winery and he'd turned her down. Today he said he'd let her know. Maybe he was afraid it was catching up to him. Of course, instead of Antonia catching on, what if it was Todd who figured it out? That's a real motive for murder."

"A great motive. Of course, then the question is who killed Marvin?"

"Someone who cared for Todd. People act in unpredictable ways. Or what about this: if Marvin had gambling debts, maybe someone he owed money to convinced him to skim winery profits. What if it turned into something the partner wanted to continue? Todd finds out, and either Marvin or the partner kills him, but then the partner gets nervous and kills Marvin too."

"There's a lot going on in that theory. I'll run some scenarios. There's also the sabotage in the fermentation building. Someone could have been paying Marvin to do a little extracurricular work."

"I thought maybe Marvin was responsible, but when I surprised that person in the fermentation building he was with Connor unloading a tractor. Francesca is angry enough to do something like that. Either Todd or Marvin could have discovered what she was up to. Threatened to expose her. If that happened, who knows what she'd do. She has a nasty streak."

IT was the middle of the night when I arrived home. Hayley was still up, but Connor wasn't there.

"So I guess Connor decided I would be all right after all. I did tell him not to worry and that I'd have the police follow me home."

Hayley must have heard the sound of disappointment in my voice. I could hear it myself. "Didn't you see the car lights in your rearview mirror?"

"Yea, Lucas was right behind me."

Hayley smiled. "I mean the lights right behind those. He left right after you called. Said he might as well, he wasn't getting any sleep until you were back here either way. Neither of us were. Want an omelet?"

Warmth flooded me and I nodded.

"So if you're ready, tell me what happened tonight." She listened in silence as I told her about finding Marvin.

"So, are the murders connected?"

"They must be. I thought Francesca was the obvious suspect. Still do, but if Marvin was stealing . . ."

"What do you mean Marvin was stealing?"

She added cheese to the pan and I told her about Marvin skimming profits.

"Todd would have gone to Antonia right away if he had proof. Maybe that's why he was out at the crusher the night he was killed. To get proof. Then, after Todd's killed, Marvin started acting funny. Maybe he thought Todd was onto him and thinks his troubles were solved after Todd was dead."

Hayley slid the omelet on a plate and handed me a fork. She reached for the list of suspects, still on the side table. "I see what the motives are for Todd's death, but who benefits from killing Marvin?"

"Nobody that I can see." I took a bite of the omelet. "This is delicious."

Hayley stretched and fatigue pulled at the corners of her eyes.

"You can't stay up until I calm down. Morning is coming at the same time as usual and there's so much going on here now. You have a long day tomorrow."

"This was supposed to be a fun time for us," Hayley said. "Our first year as participants in the festival. The weather's been perfect, the grapes got that last bit of ripening, the harvest is right on schedule and here you are running around finding bodies." Hayley smiled at me. "Sorry. That didn't come out right. I'm just worried about you. So is Connor. He wanted to be here now, but for once I had my way. I told him he needed to sleep."

I yawned and threw myself on the couch. "Good. I appreciate you being here for me, I really do. We don't have long before this is over. Whatever's going to happen will happen soon. Two murders. It's clear Marvin's wasn't planned. It was out of desperation. Desperate people make mistakes."

Hayley stood. "People who don't sleep make mistakes."

"Forget it. I'm too wound up to even think about going to sleep."

Hayley grabbed the quilt, folded it around me on the couch and tucked Syrah behind my bent knees. "Just try. Humor me."

She threw more wood into the fireplace. Anything else she may have said was completely lost. I was asleep before she closed the fire screen.

I woke with a start, hot and damp. The last of my dreams swirled around my head in the darkness. I lay back against the pillows, lifted the damp hair off my neck and kicked the quilt off. Nanook's steady breathing next to the couch calmed me, and I tried to remember. I'd touched on something in my unconsciousness. I could recall the significance, but not the details. It moved just ahead of me, pulling away from my mental probing, like a sensitive nerve.

I struggled to remember until the last of the night air chilled me. The fire had died to embers. I rose, stepped over Nanook and reached for another log. If I relaxed, it would come in its own time.

That, of course, was the problem. I had the feeling I was

low on time and that someone even now was awake elsewhere, equally determined to keep the secrets safe in the dark. How would they feel right now? It was difficult enough to find the body. To kill someone and try to move on as before was beyond my comprehension. I closed the fireplace screen and made my way into the kitchen.

The predawn was spectacular, vivid pink folded into azure blue. Puffy white clouds spun in from the sea as though pushed along by an invisible hand. I fed Syrah, made a pot of tea, then grabbed the quilt from the couch and padded out onto the deck with Nanook.

The hillsides looked purple in the early light, and I breathed in the soft morning air. Sweet and earthy, the smell of a vine-yard when the grapes were ready for harvest was unlike any other. Mix it with equal parts clean ocean breeze and deep rich soil, and you have the best fragrance on earth.

I curled up on the deck chair and started picking again at the unconscious thread that drove me out there. Watching the pink of the early morning fade away, I knew it was close. I could almost see it in the colors of the sky. The colors. The colors . . .

"Couldn't sleep?" Connor asked from behind me.

I looked up. "Not my best night. Thanks for offering to come get me, and also for the escort home."

"You okay?"

"Not really, to be honest. It's going to take a while."

Connor sat next to me. "What do you do now?"

"Now"—I took a deep breath—"I spend the day as the owner of Joyeux Winery and a participant in the Autumn Festival."

"That's what I wanted to hear. I hope you're able to enjoy

this. We're in good shape, all set up at the booth, but I still want to be there early. I'm not sure what to expect from the crowds and I don't want Hayley there alone. She's already on her way. Want to ride with me?"

"I'll take my car. I want to walk Nanook first." I finished off my tea and stood, resolutely pushing from my mind the unanswered questions in my head.

Still, as I turned to the kitchen, I shot one last look above me and could almost see the answer written in the vivid hues of the morning sky.

Twenty-five

"MAYBE I'll wrap some more Zinfandel." Hayley turned around so I could tie her apron, patterned with grapes and emblazoned with the winery logo. Under it she wore a purple maiden dress that laced in the front and complemented her lithe figure. My attire consisted of one of our winery sweatshirts and clean jeans. All things considered, I thought I looked pretty good.

I counted the brightly wrapped bottles on the front counter. "It looks like there are plenty. Maybe we can do a few more Cabernet, though."

Hayley scooped up the wrapping paper, walked to the back table and moved the postcards and posters I'd brought. She picked up a postcard, once again featuring Martinelli Winery. I'd shot it at a different angle exactly one year ago during last year's festival. It showed the house, winery office and fermentation building with the festival and valley in the foreground.

"This is my favorite." Hayley walked to the front of the booth with the photo and looked up at Martinelli Winery. "The house has a medieval look to it, with the circular towers in front. When you add the festival tents, it looks right out of the middle ages."

I took the postcard from her. I couldn't see Marvin, but I could imagine him sitting at the window that day, in the same spot where I'd found him. The place where he never missed anything, and where someone else hadn't missed the chance to kill him.

I shivered in the early morning air, feeling like the one who'd missed something. I stared harder at the picture and again the answers danced just beyond my grasp. There was something there and I knew with absolute certainty I was looking at it.

My view of the postcard was blocked by a steel mesh glove holding a foaming cup.

"A tall latte for the fair festival maiden."

Ross was decked out as King Arthur. His steel mesh glove rattled as he handed me the cup.

"How are you going to cook in that outfit? You'll suffocate."

Ross gave a shake of his head, the jewels of his crown bright in the morning sun

"The food is prepared for the morning stretch and my staff can manage the counter for now. Later I'll take this off for the afternoon rush and let Thomas work the crowd. He's around here somewhere. Look for the fool."

Hayley looked up from the bottles she was wrapping. "That's a bit harsh. You two having a tiff?"

"No, I mean really look for the fool. He has two outfits. One is the knight you saw the other day and this one is a fool, as in the town jester. It's his morning outfit. Although, I must say, perfect casting."

"If you hadn't brought me this latte, I might have been tempted to tell him you said that."

"Tell who what?" The fool in question came up beside Ross, looking foolish indeed in a yellow and red tunic, tights and a multipointed hat tipped with bells.

"Nice tights." Only gay men were manly enough to brave tights in public. Go figure.

"Actually, I'm partial to the shoes." He tapped his heels together. Curving up to his shins, the bell-tipped toes gave off a delightful sound.

The jingle of bells was joined by the blast of trumpets as the main gates opened. The early arrivals moved as a group to the coffee and food booths. In minutes the crowd around the Sterling booth was three people thick. I stood with Ross and Thomas as their competent staff handled the caffeine-deprived crowd, and soon everyone had that first cup. As we watched they began to head in different directions, some to the arts and crafts booths, while others grabbed seats for the scheduled entertainment of the morning, a joust at ten.

I threw my cup in the recycle bin as Stephen walked down the path from the winery and paused at the bottom. He shifted the case of wine he carried and took in the festivities. A moment later he strolled to the Martinelli booth and set the case on the counter. The wineries tried to have at least two people in the booths at all times. Most of the wineries were represented by the winery managers, like Connor in our booth. It helped to have someone that worked well with the public. I didn't remember Marvin ever attending the festival. Todd would have been the obvious choice, given how well liked he was. There was an assistant in the booth now. He spoke briefly with Stephen, ducked under the front counter and strolled into the crowed. Veronica walked up the aisle and nodded at the assistant as she passed him.

Apparently the request to dress for the occasion didn't apply to Veronica, who wore a dark gray Saint John knit suit and pearls. She must have driven, because she hadn't walked down the footpath in that outfit. She smiled at several people in the crowd and skirted into the Martinelli booth.

Stephen, attired in a beige suit, looked warm in the morning sun. His cheeks were already shiny and pink. He patiently stood while Veronica straightened his tie and smoothed his hair. He reached to kiss her cheek and she smiled at him. They must have seen something in each other the rest of us didn't. It was sweet. Weird but kind of sweet. Maybe Stephen was right. Maybe their marriage did work for them.

FOR the wineries, the important part of the festival weekend was the tasting competition. It wasn't a formal affair, where judges sat and tasted all of the competitors at once. Rather, the tasting went on throughout the weekend. Identifiable by the yellow sashes they wore, the judges staggered their tastings throughout the day, at different temperatures and with different foods. This better mimicked the tasting and drinking patterns of the general public who would later rely on the awards when buying wine. As the judges walked down the aisles they were also able to converse with the crowd and get their input as well. The judges were the experts, yes, but their being invited back was dependent on their making crowd-pleasing decisions.

The morning vanished as I helped Connor and Hayley with tastings and sales in our booth. After several hours, the collective growl of our stomachs sent me out to find lunch. The early afternoon breeze off the ocean swirled the aromas of various foods around me. Everything looked good, from the gourmet pizza to the chocolate-dipped strawberries, but the weekend would be filled with temptation. I settled on a salad of mixed greens, pine nuts, sun-dried tomatoes and goat cheese. I dropped off the requested sausage sandwiches at the booth and went to find a seat in the eating area.

From my vantage point I was able to watch most of the ongoing entertainment, which at the moment highlighted a band of medieval jugglers. They grabbed people from the crowd and Thomas in his fool outfit was a visible target. Not the shy type, he jumped in to give it a try.

As I finished my salad, Thomas threw a ring into the crowd and Chantal caught it. She tossed her hair, waved the ring above her head and made her way toward Thomas.

She looked fetching in a red lady-in-waiting costume. It fit every curve and exposed as much of her ample bosom as possible. Damn, she really got under my skin. Now, though, I could also see her as I found her on the hillside, with her car wedged under the oak and her tearstained cheeks, and I also felt a faint stirring of sympathy. Very faint, but it was there.

She handed Thomas the ring and awarded him a kiss. She carried bottled water, and I hoped she stayed away from the winery booths. To be part of the most prominent wine family in the valley and be unable to enjoy it seemed unjust in the extreme.

"Chantal and Thomas. Now, that's funny."

Brice stood so close to the picnic table I couldn't get up. "Where's Francesca?"

"She's around." He took a sip of Chardonnay, still staring at Chantal and Thomas. "Look at him. Like he knows what she wants. I could show him what to do with a woman."

My stomach turned and I swung my legs away from Brice. As I pushed myself up, Chantal glanced our way. Her smile faded, and she moved deeper into the crowd. She had to live with the memory of sleeping with Brice, and the look on her face showed her regret.

Seeing how she felt helped my feelings toward her go a long way in a short time. I wouldn't ever completely let my guard down around her but she was doing the best she could, just like the rest of us. Actually not all of us. I studied the man beside me.

"Brice, what if these women are addicts? Are you giving them what they want then?"

Icy blue eyes met mine over the rim of a glass. "If I did, you'll never prove it. What, do you think I'd write a prescription for her? Make it easy for you?"

I thought of the missing prescriptions and took a chance. "You were writing them for someone."

Brice turned to face me, his hands on his hips. "If you have any accusations to make along those lines, you can share them with my attorney first."

"I can do that. And furthermore, I'd enjoy having that conversation with your attorney. Would that happen to be your wife, Chantal's sister? Or doesn't she want to handle the cases that involve your girlfriends?"

Brice turned to me, his mouth open.

"Surprised? It's gotten out that you're keeping it all in the family, just not necessarily in the same bed."

Brice tightened his grip on the wineglass. The color faded from his face. "Go to hell, you little bitch."

I took in the slicked-back hair, the perfectly fitted clothes, the manicured hands and manufactured tan. I thought of all the women who relied on their doctors in their times of need and vulnerability.

"Go to hell, Doctor? You first."

Twenty-six

I TURNED on my heel and walked away. Brice's stare bored through me and I turned into the nearest aisle. The two worst traits to find in people are arrogance and stupidity, and Brice had plenty of both. I closed my eyes, forced myself to breathe and took a look around.

I was in the arts and crafts section. Some people dismissed this part of the festival as too quaint, but usually it was one of my favorites. I swiveled my neck to let go of the tension and wandered through the homespun yarn booth, with its lamb's wool in a rainbow of colors. From there I chatted with the honey guy. He specialized in honey-based creams and body lotions, the honey gathered from his own hives. There was everything from jewelry and garden gnomes to pet clothes and bath soaps, but I didn't buy anything until I came to the Christmas booth. There was a tree covered in glass ornaments shaped like dogs and cats. Annie decorated for the holidays at the vet clinic every year, and I bought two of the ornaments: a tabby and a pug.

When I returned to our booth I stashed the ornaments under the counter. The look on Connor's face made it clear he'd witnessed the exchange with Brice. Having Connor put Brice into the hospital as a patient wasn't in the plan, so I forced a smile.

He put down the case of wine he carried and moved closer. "Did he threaten you or try to scare you?"

"No. Nothing like that. I all but accused him of giving drugs to Chantal. He didn't like that much."

"I bet."

The tension left my shoulders. It was a new experience, somebody watching out for me. I liked it. A lot.

A crowd surrounded our booth. "I want to see what they have to say." Connor nodded, and I slipped back around the counter to listen to the comments. The praise was strong and far outweighed the few unenthusiastic responses. All we needed was the majority to appreciate our efforts. Joyeux Winery was receiving its share of accolades. We were going to be fine. I smiled at Connor and Hayley and received a small wave in return.

Near the Martinelli booth, Antonia held court with a group of local politicians. It was easy to tell they were politicians because none of them looked directly at her and all of them squirmed. Never shy about what she thought of local policy, it was a reminder once again of the sway she held in this community. Antonia spotted me and stopped midsentence. She sliced between them with her cane like Moses parting the Red Sea and walked over to me.

"Brice looked upset after your chat with him this morning." She pounded her cane. "Good."

232

Did everyone see us?

A wicked grin papered her fine skin with gentle lines.

"You like my getting to Brice, don't you?"

"Of course. Pompous ass. I knew what he was capable of before you confirmed it. He's just never realized I've been on to him from the start. Another mistake, thinking he was getting one over on me. He's the worst kind of man. I try to let my children make their own decisions, their own mistakes, but he's the worst mistake my daughter ever made." She paused. "The worst mistake *both* of my daughters ever made."

Antonia was silent for a moment then stamped her cane and pushed back her shoulders. Her gaze took in the grounds and rested on the Martinelli tent. "Look at that. I understand sometimes crowds ebb and flow, but there isn't anyone at my booth. That's never happened in the past, not even momentarily." She shook her head. "However, at the moment it works to our advantage. Stephen and Veronica are alone. Go talk to them."

"You know something? So far my offer to help you has turned into a lot more than I bargained for. I'm not getting ordered around on top of it."

Her eyes softened and she rested her hand lightly on my arm. "Please, Penny. I need your help."

I sighed. "Okay, I'll go see what I can find out."

She smiled, and I saw a glimmer of the woman my aunt had called a friend for so many years.

The festival was packed with people, and by the time I reached the Martinelli tent, both Stephen and Veronica were busy once again pouring tastes. The judges had just been served, and I held out a glass for a sample of what they now held up to the sunlight, checking for a deep burgundy color.

"Hold on, Penny," Stephen said. "Time to open up another bottle."

Veronica waved from her side of the booth. While I waited for my taste I listened to her inform her audience on the history of Martinelli Winery. Intent on her narrative, she seemed at ease and happier than I'd ever seen her.

I handed Stephen my glass and watched as he poured. "This is our special reserve Merlot." He filled several glasses at once. When the crowd had moved on, I stayed put and tasted the wine. The flavor of a wine depended on the variety of the grapes used. In Merlot, the fruit in the wine, reminiscent of black cherries and plums, came through first.

"Stephen, this is wonderful. You've got a winner with this one."

He looked up as though surprised to still see me there, and gave a short nod of his head. Mr. Talkative.

I tilted my head toward his wife and tried again. "Veronica's in her element. She really knows about the history of the winery."

Stephen looked over at Veronica, his face showing the faintest of smiles. "She knows the history of my family better than I do. At this point, she even knows more about wine."

As he left me to open more bottles, I joined the crowd around Veronica. A short time later the crowd wandered off and we were alone. Without her audience, Veronica's nervousness returned. She raised one hand to twirl her pearls and poured from another bottle into my now-empty glass.

"Here, Penny, try this Zinfandel. It's Stephen's favorite, and he's convinced Antonia to plant another ten acres of it. It's another example of the good ideas he's implementing. You know, I really can't get over last night, can't get over the nerve of Francesca saying Stephen wasn't right for this job. Every time I think of it I get angry all over again." Her hand trembled on the neck of the bottle.

"It's obvious how much help you are to Stephen." I twirled the glass and studied her face. "You didn't know much about wine before you married, did you? You were a nurse up at the hospital, right?"

Veronica looked confused then nodded. "I didn't know a thing about wine back then, but after Stephen and I married I made a point to learn as much as possible. Before that, yes, I was a nurse for a good many years. I started as a candy striper."

A taster joined us and Veronica poured Zinfandel into his glass. When he'd walked away, she once again turned to me. "Don't you think nursing is such a noble profession?"

"Actually I do." I took a sip of the wine. "Do you ever miss it?"

Veronica smoothed the front of her skirt. "I still find time to volunteer at the hospital, you know. Plus I'm involved with a number of other charity organizations the family supports. It all keeps me very busy."

I wasn't going to learn anything this way. I tried a different tactic. "Everything worked out so well for you."

Veronica eyed me. "What do you mean?"

"Well, I'm sure as a Martinelli you're quite active in charity and social events." I leaned in over the counter and offered what I hoped was an innocent smile. "But let's be honest: this is a whole lot better than dealing with bedpans, isn't it?"

Twenty-seven

W HATEVER response Veronica made was lost behind
Stephen's arm as he reached for the bottle in front
of her.

"Now, Veronica, we can't hoard all of Penny's time. Surely
she wants to go try what some of the other wineries are
offering."

Stephen led Veronica to the other side of the booth, where
a number of tasters had gathered. I walked away feeling unset-
tled. Stephen's arrival hadn't been a coincidence. He didn't
want her talking to me.

Distracted, I turned and walked smack into the group of
judges still tasting the wine from Martinelli. I bumped the glass
of the judge closest to me. Wine landed on his lapel and yellow
judge's ribbon.

"Oops, sorry." I backed away.

One of the other judges leaned over. "Careful. That just might eat through your sash."

Through quiet laughter, I heard the response: "That's okay. I don't want to be a judge if I have to drink any more of this."

It's hard to become invisible when you're five-foot-ten and just managed to run into the group you wanted to avoid. Nonetheless, I did a full turn and popped into the nearest booth, Jammin'. I picked up a jar of pomegranate jam to examine. Yup. That's me. Very slick.

The judge that I'd splashed continued. "A shame, really. Can't understand what the trouble is."

Another judge spoke up. "You know, I've stopped drinking Martinelli wines altogether. This is the first taste I've had in ages."

"Your first and my last, if I can help it."

The clerk came up to me. "Would you like to buy that?"

"Sure." I handed her the jam. By the time we were finished, the judges had moved on. I returned to our booth and put the jam next to my Christmas ornaments.

Connor came up behind me. "Shopping and snooping at the same time?"

"It's a perfect cover." I told him the short version of the judges' conversation.

"I don't get it. You tasted the wine. What did you think?"

"It was terrific, but it was from a different bottle. The judges finished one and Stephen opened a new bottle. That's the one I tasted."

"They need to find out what's going on before the damage to their reputation is permanent."

"The big question is whether or not Todd had figured it

out and if that had something to do with his death. Or Marvin's."

Connor rubbed his eyes. "I need a break. Meet me under that oak."

I walked back to where I'd seen Brice earlier and took a seat in the shade.

A few minutes later Connor swung his leg over the picnic bench next to me. "So what happens now?"

"Let's go over the motives."

Before he could say anything, Annie came up. "I can't believe you and Antonia found Marvin dead last night."

Connor looked at Annie. "I'm surprised you weren't there." He claims Annie and I get into more trouble when we're together than when we're apart. He's usually right.

"I know. Me too." Annie didn't always catch Connor's sarcasm. Then again, neither did I.

"Did I hear you say you were going over motives? Maybe I can help." Annie took a seat beside Connor, who started to rub his temples.

"Isn't the clinic open? Aren't there any dogs and cats that need emergency attention?" Connor asked.

"Nope. I hired a part-time doctor. I get weekends off now." Annie took a pencil and writing pad from her bag. "Okay, we can do this. Look, I'll be the note-taker. You just let me know what you want me to write."

Connor was about to say more.

"Motives," I said. "Let's just go over the people who benefit from what happened."

"Okay, good," Annie said. "Who do you want to start with?"

I looked around the festival. Most of the people who had any interest in Martinelli Winery were right there.

"Let's start with Francesca."

"That's an easy one." Annie tapped on her chin with the pencil then started writing. "The land from Todd's mother. After he thought about it, Todd might have decided to fight for it. Now who?"

"Well," Connor said, resigned. "There's Brice."

"Two motives," I said. "One, the land deal. He isn't running it, but it's his wife's. She might have convinced him to help. Or threatened him with a nasty divorce. Then there's Chantal. Brice denies it, but what if Todd knew Brice was giving Chantal prescription drugs. Nice thing to do to a recovering alcoholic. Not to mention what the medical board would say."

Annie was writing away. "Okay, okay. Good." She stopped and looked around the festival. "Who's next?"

"Well, we have to put Chantal on the list." I shrugged my shoulders. "I don't see it, but there's a motive. Everyone thinks she and Todd were just friends, but that comes from her, and if she was interested and he wasn't . . ."

"Uh-huh. That's good. I like that one. The woman scorned." Annie watched Chantal, still with Thomas in the center area of the grounds. "Look at the cleavage. She got a license to carry those things? They're concealed weapons."

"Barely concealed."

Connor's head pivoted toward the dancing.

I punched him in the arm. "Pay attention. What else on Chantal?"

"What about this?" Annie waved her arm in the air. "What if Chantal lied to you about how involved she and Brice were? What if it's all an act and they're still together? When Todd found out about the drugs Brice was giving her, maybe she killed him to protect Brice."

Annie bounced on the bench and waved both arms in the air. "Or, what about this! Maybe Brice got scared because Todd found out, and Brice threatened to cut Chantal off. If she really needed the fix, maybe it became more important to protect her drug source." Annie waved the pad in the air. "Just look at this list. We're good. We are so good. Too bad Marvin's dead, 'cause he was our best suspect. Who's next?"

"First," I said, "I have some questions."

"Go," Annie said.

I counted the items off. "One, who made the improvements to the winery, Stephen or Todd? Two, who stood to gain if the improvements worked? Three, who wants Martinelli Winery to fail? Four, was that why Todd was killed, or was the motive something we don't even know about? Five, Marvin was stealing. Did someone else know?"

"Six," Connor said.

I stopped to look at him.

"You need to be careful, Penny. If you come up with the right answer to the right question, somebody's going to want you to keep it to yourself."

Twenty-eight

THE sun dropped below the horizon. The restaurant booths were still busy with the last of the dinner crowd, but the winery booths were finished for the day. Hayley yawned and Connor told her to leave for the night.

I looked around the inside of the booth. "Just these few cases left."

"I'm going to let them sit overnight. I doubt anyone will be along to take them and I'm not going to pack them up just to unload them again in the morning." He stretched, arched his back and lifted his arms high over his head. "Want to grab a bite?"

"Sure, but it needs to be here. Antonia's going to give a talk on the history of winemaking in the region. I want to stay and watch."

"Hmm." Connor glanced at his watch. "Not sure how you're going to take this, but I'm going to say it anyway. I don't want you here alone after dark. I can get to the winery, pack what we need for tomorrow and come back."

"You don't need to do that. Annie's still around some- where. I can get her to stay."

"That's supposed to make me feel better?"

"Stop it. How much trouble can we get into?"

Connor raised his brows.

"Okay. Forget I said that. I just want to watch Antonia's presentation and then Annie and I will pack it in for the night. There'll still be lots of people around when it's over. It isn't like we'll be the only ones here."

"I'm not crazy about the idea. If you don't want me coming back, you two need to stay together." Connor walked away and I followed. "Let's get something to eat. I still have to load the truck with what I want to bring back tomorrow, and I sent Hayley home . . ."

"I'm just staying here at the festival and not going any- where else. It'll be fine."

He turned to me and tension tightened the lines in his face. "How long have I known you? I can remember when you were a teenager, and even then things were never 'fine' around you. There was always a ripple effect. Even then."

"What are you talking about? You remember me?"

"You're a hard girl to forget."

I was hard to forget. I sort of missed everything else he said after that. "I didn't know you'd even noticed me."

"Sure I did. Not that I would have said anything. You couldn't wait to get out of here, and back then I was the boy who wanted to stick around and run a winery. Now you're back. This place has changed. I've changed. Not you, though. You're still the girl playing in the vines, even after Antonia scared everyone else off. You never worried about the consequences of speaking your mind, even when it got you in trouble." Connor took a breath. "I bet that's what you're doing back here. Did you upset the wrong person at the paper and get fired? Did you lose your job because you didn't know when to keep quiet, when to compromise?"

He'd accused me of speaking my mind, and I wouldn't disappoint. "Look, my editor wanted me to exaggerate on a piece. Make it appear that the turnout at a riot was larger than it actually was. I didn't think it was right and I wouldn't do it." My voice cracked with emotion.

Connor stopped and looked at me. "You should have told me the reason. For what it's worth, you did the right thing."

"Thanks. Not that it changes the position I'm in." I put my hands on my hips. "And for the record, I'm not staying here because I don't have anywhere else to go. I'm here because this is where I want to be."

"Fine. And if we're going on record, I still wish you'd stayed out of the mess over at Martinelli."

"We talked about this. Antonia asked for my help and I owe her."

"You don't owe her enough to risk your life."

"Hey, I didn't ask for all of this to happen."

"No, but you put yourself in danger when you agreed to help her. I tried to tell you."

"But I didn't think anyone was going to get *killed*."

"That's right. You didn't think. You just dove right in, and now there's someone out there that wants to hurt you." He threw up his hands and turned away. "Let's just eat."

He walked away from me and my focus shifted from him to the crowd. There were a lot of waves, mostly from the women. Conversations stopped and there were a fair number of over-the-shoulder glances. I knew he was attractive, but their reactions left me confused and irritated, perhaps even a little jealous, if I was being honest with myself.

We waited in line at the Sterling booth without talking. As the silence lengthened, I looked over at Connor. "Truce?"

"I suppose. You're as stubborn as your aunt."

"Knowing how fond you were of her, I'll take that as a compliment."

I spotted Annie, waved her over and explained that I wanted to stay.

"Perfect. You can give me a ride home. I came with friends, but there's another joust, and they're giving free fencing lessons afterward."

"That's just what we need," Connor said under his breath.

"Order." I pushed him up to the counter, told Annie I'd meet her in an hour and studied the menu.

"The grilled vegetable tart is to die for," said Thomas from behind the counter, still dressed as the town fool.

"Done."

"Two tarts," Thomas said to Ross, who nodded from behind the grill.

"Tart all right," Ross said. "Just like that one you were dancing with earlier."

"Oh, please," Thomas shooed away the comment. He leaned toward us over the counter. "He's upset because I was dancing with Chantal. I can't believe he still gets so jealous after all this time. And over a woman. Can you imagine?"

"Who'd be jealous over Chantal?" Connor slipped a look at me.

"Hmm."

We took the tarts and two glasses of Cabernet and found a bench still warm from the setting sun. From somewhere on the grounds a flute and harp played, and the soft music drifted through the air. A few bites into the tart, the fatigue I'd been fighting all day rolled over me. I put down the remaining tart and brought my legs up, hugging my shins as I rested my head on my knees. I stayed that way until Connor tapped my shoulder.

"I needed to close my eyes for a minute."

"You must be tired. Look, about earlier. I don't have any business asking, but I'm going to anyway. Promise me you'll stay with Annie. I wish we got cell coverage in the valley. I'd feel better if you could call me from here."

The concern in his eyes was real, and I nodded. "I promise I'll be careful and stay with Annie."

Annie stood where we'd agreed to meet, at the bottom of the low presentation stage. Antonia was there, directing where the podium should go.

I grabbed Annie's hand and pulled her away before Antonia saw me. It wasn't the place to talk, and I didn't want her asking for an update.

Antonia's presentation was interesting but uneventful. I used the time to scan the crowd. Stephen and Veronica sat right in front. Veronica leaned forward in rapt attention, while Stephen slouched and tapped his foot with nervous energy. In spite of Veronica's claims, I wondered if he could handle the responsibility of running a large winery, even with Antonia's continued input. At that moment, Veronica whispered something in his ear. He pulled himself up in the chair.

Antonia continued to expound on the virtues of the region as a wine growers' paradise. From the sidelines Ross waved me over with a chocolate éclair as an incentive. I whispered to Annie I'd be back and made my way to the edge of the audience.

"I saved the last one for you," he said.

"Glad I was good at dinner. I just had one of the vegetable tarts."

"Interested in knowing how much butter I use in those tarts?"

"Not remotely." I took a big bite of the éclair.

"It doesn't matter. Haven't you heard? Chocolate is good for the soul."

"Hmm." I rolled my eyes in agreement as the warm fusion of cocoa and cream invaded my senses.

I stood with Ross through the end of the lecture, then we gathered up Annie and made our way to the center area. The dancing was over and the fencing instructors glided through the space as they pursued imaginary opponents.

"Going to give it a try?" Annie asked Ross.

"Only if I get to wear Thomas's suit of armor."

"They pad you up. I promise not to hurt you."

"Tempting, but no. I need to get back to the booth and help Thomas put things away for the night. Come by before you leave."

I nodded and watched as Annie mimicked the instructor. She was getting the hang of it, heaven help us all. When she was in range, I told her I'd be back and wandered over to the silent auction. The items ranged from bottles of wine to week-ends skiing in the mountains of British Columbia. There was even a mystery dinner hosted by our resident mystery writer. I wrote down bids for the skiing and dinner. Maybe tomorrow I'd be betting against myself, but it was for charity. The children's home and hospital did a tremendous amount of good. Scrape back the surface of affluent communities and you found the same cracks and the same people falling through those cracks that you find everywhere else.

I walked back to find Annie. The lesson was over and she leaned against the fence, wiping her face.

"I didn't know it would be such a good workout."

I looked around the grounds, surprised at how quickly the booths had emptied out. "I'd get you something to drink, but everything is closed."

"You're right. Let's go say good night to Ross and Thomas."

The booth was completely stripped down and tucked away. Ross and Thomas were locking the last of the portable storage bins.

Ross looked up. "Too late, my dears. Nothing left."

"Not a problem," Annie said.

"Wait a minute." Thomas reached into the cooler. "Ross spoke too soon. We have just enough raspberry sorbet left for one serving. After that workout, I think maybe you deserve it."

Annie reached for the dish. "I think maybe you're right."

"No willpower." The voice came from over my shoulder, where Antonia watched Annie.

"Nope." Annie licked the sorbet off the spoon. We said good-bye to Ross and Thomas and walked down the center of the festival grounds with Antonia.

"If you have a moment, I'd like to speak with you." Antonia glanced at Annie. "Am I correct in assuming you didn't keep quiet and your cousin knows what's happened at my winery?"

"Todd's death was in the papers, Antonia. Same with Marvin's. That's the nasty thing about murder, isn't it? It's just so hard to hide away."

Twenty-nine

"YOUR sarcasm isn't necessary, Penelope. I'd like you to drive me home and give me an update of what you've found today."

I looked at the sky. While the sun had set and the grounds security lights were coming on, there was plenty of natural light. "I have my car, and it's a two-seater. I don't want Annie waiting here alone . . ."

"So then we can walk up the path, and the two of you can walk back down."

"Are you up for that, Antonia?" A mistake.

"I suggest you worry about keeping up. I only proposed driving to make it easy on the two of you."

I looked over at Annie, who shrugged her shoulders. "Sure, we can do that, but I don't want to walk back down the hill after dark. We need to start now."

The three of us started up the path. Annie, still caught up

in the fencing lessons, trailed behind us. I repeated the judges' comments about Martinelli, and Antonia stopped me several times to repeat portions.

A frown settled on her face as we continued up the hill. "I just can't understand it. If someone is tainting the barrels, as you say, then that explains the poor showing with the judges. Other times, the wines have never been better."

"That's what's funny, Antonia. I'm telling you, the Merlot I tasted at your booth was fabulous."

We reached the house and could see out over the valley as the evening settled in.

"Annie, do you mind if I have a few moments with Penelope?"

Annie nodded and sat on the bottom step as I walked Antonia up the stairs. When we reached the door, Antonia took my hand in hers, and I looked down in surprise. She'd just walked up the steep path with hardly a pause, and yet her hand felt frail in mine. She was such a combination of strength and weakness. As though she could read my mind, she squeezed my hand.

"Never doubt I will find the fortitude to see this through. I know you're frustrated, and I realize you're trying. You didn't have to help me with this, but I'm grateful you did." Her hand swept across the vineyards that surrounded her home. "This was my life, you know. Still is. But when I look at my children, when I think of what someone did to Todd, here, at my home, I realize I could have done things differently. I don't know, maybe I would have chosen differently. Maybe I would have decided to keep love near me." Antonia continued to gaze at the night sky. "I gave up so much to keep this . . ." She stopped and gave my hand a little squeeze.

"That's enough. Don't let me become maudlin. I just wanted to thank you for all your help, and I'm quite confident we'll figure this out. Now"—she turned toward the front door—"go get some sleep. We'll put an end to this soon."

She walked into the house.

I joined Annie and we began the walk down the hill.

Annie glanced back at the house. "She sure is a tough old bird."

"I've always thought so, but this has taken a lot out of her. She hates the thought of bad publicity for the winery. Hates airing her dirty laundry in public. Old-school. I also think that for the first time she's feeling her age."

We walked in silence. The night had darkened faster than I'd expected. It always did this time of year. The moon was a sliver in the sky, but the security lights from the grounds were enough to see along the path. The air was still and carried the sound of the crickets.

Below, the festival was empty. The last of the cars left the lot and my car sat alone.

We reached the bottom of the path and the first row of booths. The curtains were down on every tent and the central area was empty. Leftover wine bottles sat stacked outside the winery tents.

We entered the main aisle and the lights went out. All of them.

I stopped short and Annie grabbed my arm. She inhaled and I turned and pushed my hand against her mouth. She nodded. The silence was as thick as the darkness. Even the crickets had stopped.

Annie moved my hand and whispered in my ear. "What

are the chances of the lights going out right at this point having nothing to do with us and just being a coincidence?"

"Not good. Not good at all."

The lights were supposed to be on all night. If they were turned off there was a reason, and likely we were it. I had no idea where the main breakers were, but someone did. Just as they knew where we were. They'd hit the switch the moment we reached the main aisle. We had to move.

I struggled to get my bearings and grabbed Annie's hand. "We can't stay here."

POP! The noise whistled above us. Wood splintered as a bullet lodged in the booth nearest us.

"They have a gun." Annie stating the obvious.

"Quiet."

Our booth was at the center of this row. The parking lot started three rows to the left and my car was in the front, maybe twenty yards behind our booth. Still holding Annie's hand, I kept low. We moved from the center of the aisle to the edge of the row, where the booths gave us protection. We'd be exposed in the parking lot. To get to the car was another story. Where were my keys?

We were at the Martinelli booth. Four booths to go.

"I thought this wasn't supposed to happen if I stayed with you," Annie whispered.

"They're getting desperate."

"*They're* getting desperate? What are we?"

"Shush."

I counted the tents until we reached our booth. I pulled Annie along and pushed her head under the railing.

"Now what?" Annie asked in a hushed tone.

"Look for a weapon."

I felt along the ledge under the counter but found only the pomegranate jam and two Christmas ornaments. Cardboard ripped as Annie tried to get into a case of wine.

I grabbed her arm. "Too much noise. Forget it."

"I could smash the person over the head, like they did to you." Her arm swung through the air right next to my head.

"Stop it. It's better if they don't know where we are. Then maybe we won't need a weapon at all. I just want to find my key. Then we're making a run for my car."

"Fine."

A clatter came from somewhere nearby. It sounded like someone tripping over empty wine bottles.

Annie stiffened.

"Keys get your keys find your keys gotta have keys." I searched through my bag. "I can't find them." I rifled my pockets. No keys.

I took a deep breath and tried to think. I had jam, two Christmas ornaments, and Annie.

They had a gun.

I started to hyperventilate.

Annie squeezed my arm.

"I'm okay. Let me think."

"Okay, but do it fast."

The jam was in one hand and the glass ornaments in the other. We needed some way to know where the person was. Then we needed to slow them down.

"Hold this."

"What is it?"

"Jam."

I crawled toward the back counter. Annie crept along beside me. I pulled a sheet of wrapping paper down to the ground.

"Have you lost your mind?"

"Give me the jam." I put the jar down and placed the ornaments on the sheet of paper. I picked up the jam and used it to slowly crush each of the ornaments.

"What are you breaking?"

"Your Christmas presents."

Thirty

I N the dark I folded over the paper and whispered in Annie's ear. "They must realize we'd try for the car. It's our only way out of here. We need to know where they are, which aisle they'll come down. Stay here."

I pushed away from her, turned and ducked under the railing. I scattered the broken glass in the aisle on both sides of the booth and returned to where Annie waited in the dark.

"Now what?"

"Now we wait."

"You don't have your keys."

"The spare is under the fender. Where's the jam?"

Annie handed me the jar.

"Don't move until I tell you. Then run as fast as you can to the car." We crouched in silence, the longest Annie had ever managed. We stayed there for so long I began to think I was wrong. Maybe the person didn't think of the car. Annie was making little hiccup noises, like she couldn't breathe, and I tried to keep my heart from banging around in my chest. My hands were slick with sweat and the jam felt heavy in my hand.

We waited until I'd begun to suspect the person had left. I was sure Annie was thinking along the same lines by the way she'd started to squirm. Then, from the left of the booth, the unmistakable crunch of glass, six feet away.

I moved to the right of the tent, pushed back the corner and threw the jam as hard as I could away from us. The jam broke as it hit something the next row over.

Someone rushed toward the sound, passing the front of the booth inches from me. I waited for the steps to fade, pushed Annie though the opening, ducked out behind her and shoved her in the opposite direction. We ran toward the parking lot and reached the car. I went to the trunk and felt under the fender. No key. *No key.* Perfect.

I grabbed Annie by the arm and pushed her ahead of me, across the parking lot and into the trees. To her credit, she knew it wasn't the time to ask questions. I concentrated on reaching the slope.

"Are we going down it?" Annie asked at the edge.

The decision was made when steps sounded behind us.

Tumbling rock and dry leaves made a crescendo of sound as we slid down the hill. My toe caught and I pitched forward. Another *POP!* and the leaves on the tree ahead of me exploded. Right where my head had been. I landed on one knee, my hands spread out in front of me. A rock tore into the skin of my palm. I scrambled to my feet and threw myself toward Annie.

"Run!" I grabbed her by the arm. Another sound above us and we turned and crashed into each other. I fell backward down the hill and Annie tripped over my legs. She fell and rolled into the brush below. I hit a tree and bit back a scream as the bark tore into my raw and bleeding palm. I brushed the hair out of my face and peered into the dark. I could just make out Annie. I stumbled down to her and grabbed the back of her shirt.

"Shh. Listen."

Annie paused then leaned over. "I don't think they're coming."

My heartbeat hammered in my ears, but it was quiet in the forest behind me. My eyes had adjusted to the darkness. The road to Martinelli Winery glimmered ahead like a band of silver carpet through the darkened landscape. Right back up the hill, the last place I wanted to go. The main road was half a mile in the opposite direction.

We heard the steps at the same time.

Annie groaned and started to move.

I stopped her. "They're ahead of us. Somehow they've circled around."

We froze as the beam of a flashlight swung through the trees.

"Penny, stop."

The flashlight shone into my face for a moment then swung up to outline Lucas.

"Someone shot at us."

"Stay down." He grabbed his radio and told someone to check out the festival grounds. While we waited, he scanned the woods with the flashlight and retraced our steps down the hill.

"Nobody out there now."

"How did you know we were here?"

Lucas pointed to the light down the road, to the welcome sight of his patrol car.

"Antonia saw the security lights go out from the house and was worried about you. Hayley wouldn't have forgiven me if I didn't come out to check on you myself. It's unlikely the person is still on the grounds, but we're taking a look. Right now, though, I want to get you two home."

We dropped Annie off first. When Lucas pulled up to my house we could see Connor and Hayley as they paced in the living room.

"Oh man, I'm really going to hear about this."

Lucas threw up his hands. "Don't look at me. I was talking to Hayley when I got the call from Antonia. Hayley must have told Connor. You know, if you didn't get yourself into these things . . ."

"Yeah, yeah." I opened the door. "You coming in?"

Lucas leaned forward and looked past me into the living room, where Hayley and Connor both stared out into the night. "I got you home. Now you're on your own."

"Chicken." I slammed the door and made my way to the house. I was prepared to argue with Hayley and to cajole and defend myself to Connor.

I stepped inside.

Hayley spoke first. "We've talked about it, and we aren't going to batter you with questions. So the lights went out. Maybe it was a coincidence. We're just glad nothing happened."

They didn't know we'd been shot at. I'd tell them. Later. Maybe. "Okay, then."

Connor raised a hand. "One more thing. There's not a chance in hell I'm letting you go alone next time, so don't even ask."

Fair enough.

Thirty-one

⚜

ANOTHER early morning. I might have slept in, but at some point in the night Nanook had climbed up, something he rarely did, and was sprawled across my legs. Syrah had added her considerable weight to the mix. I threw them both off and reached for my sweats.

"I'm fine, you two, really. Just need coffee." On the off chance I'd get more than coffee, they followed me to the kitchen. I started the pot and stared out at the empty space where my car should be. I'd need to ride back to the festival with Connor.

The morning wore a silver cloak of fog. With no harsh shadows, the light on days like this was perfect for shooting prints. I needed to concentrate on something besides the events of the night before, so I grabbed my camera and slipped through the French doors.

Nanook followed me, and I snapped close-ups of a grape

cluster, each grape dotted with opal beads of mist. The vines by the back deck were heavy with Cabernet grapes, dark purple and lightly covered with dew. They looked like they'd been dipped in sugar. The fresh air felt good on my skin. Calmness came over me, as it always did when I reduced the world to what I could see through the camera lens. I couldn't control everything, but I could control bits of it, one frame at a time.

I returned to the kitchen and, in order of importance, got breakfast for Syrah, a biscuit for Nanook and coffee for me.

The events of the past week were a jumble, heavy on my shoulders. I poured some coffee, sat down at the counter, and reached for the list of suspects written two days before. It seemed so long ago. Looking at the list, I grabbed a pencil and drew a line through *Marvin.*

I sat and looked at the names. Suddenly, the reality of last night's experience settled around my neck. Black spots appeared and my hands were sweaty. Someone had tried to kill me. Annie too. Last night the whole thing had been surreal and adrenaline had seen me through. In the soft glow of the new day, the realization Annie or I could have been killed seemed much more ominous.

I knew the person was on this list. I knew it, but I just couldn't see it. Again the answer darted just outside my conscious thought, creeping like fog through the vines. I stared until the names began to dance before my eyes:

Chantal, Francesca, Brice, Veronica, Stephen.
Chantal, Francesca, Brice, Veronica, Stephen.
Chantal, Francesca, Brice, Veronica, Stephen.

Chilly fingers of fear grabbed at my heart. I jumped up and moved about the kitchen, hugging my arms, suddenly cold.

Startled by my quick movements, Nanook was instantly

at my side. I sank down and buried my face in the soft, thick fur of his neck. Hiding felt good, if only for a moment.

Someone had taken an enormous risk to try to keep me quiet. Even if I wanted to stop now, they wouldn't. I sat, rubbing the soft velvet of Nanook's ear. The certainty of this settled into my core. They weren't going to stop. Fear was the only emotion I felt. They'd shot at me. They'd shot at us.

I pushed my fingers deeper into Nanook's coat, searching for his warmth, and hugged him close. Still on the floor, with Nanook in my arms, I felt Hayley walk up behind me. She put her hand on my shoulder and waited until I'd relaxed my grip on Nanook's fur.

"Come sit. Lucas called me this morning and told me what happened last night."

"Big mouth. I would have told you. Probably. I suppose you felt a need to tell Connor."

She shrugged and nodded. I released Nanook, grabbed Hayley's arm and she pulled me up.

I gave her a weak smile. "I don't blame you. You needed to know and your timing's good. I really need the company. Want coffee?"

"I'll get it."

"Then come back. I need your opinion."

"Opinion on what?" Connor stepped in through the open glass door.

I handed him the list. "Well, what do you think?"

"I think you've listed a lot of decent reasons to stay away from these people. The problem is I don't think one of them is going to let you."

"That's what I think. So my best defense is to go on offense, right?"

Hayley and Connor looked at me.

"Offense? After what happened last night? What exactly do you have in mind?" Connor asked me.

"At the moment, I can't think of a single thing, but I'm working on it."

CONNOR drove to the festival while I dug the list out of my bag. Any one of them could be capable of murder, if pushed.

After a couple of minutes, I put the list back down. I wasn't going to find the answer between here and the festival grounds.

"How can some people read and drive? Now I'm carsick."

Connor slowed and rolled down the front windows. Putting the list back into my bag, I looked up just as a beige Cadillac entered the intersection right in our path. As I braced myself against the dash, the driver swerved to the right, just missing us.

Thirty-two

"THAT'S Stephen! If we hadn't slowed down, he would have run right into us. Is he crazy?"

"Haven't you seen him behind the wheel before? Everyone in town knows you need to be careful when he's around. He always drives like he doesn't know what traffic signals mean," Connor said.

"Why doesn't someone do something?"

Connor shrugged. "We've learned to live with it. He caught me off guard this time. Good thing you got carsick and I had to slow down."

"Yeah. Good thing."

"All a part of small-town living. Local color."

"What did you say?"

"Small-town living. Get used to it. Why?"

I looked out the window. "Nothing, I guess. Just a feeling

I've had for most of the last three days. Like I'm missing something. I wish I knew what it was."

Connor pulled onto the grounds, found a space up front near my car and turned off the engine. I gathered my bag and started to open the door. Connor put his hand on my arm and waited until I turned to him.

"What?"

"No being alone with anyone from the Martinelli family."

"I won't."

"No being alone at all, for that matter."

"Got it."

"If anything unusual happens, I want you to find me. Lucas is going to be here today too. Watch for him."

"No problem."

He looked at me. "You're being too agreeable."

"Connor, I really get it. Someone's trying to kill me. Dead. I get it."

"So, nothing stupid."

"GOT IT."

Connor muttered something about why hadn't I followed this same advice five days ago, and we made our way into the festival. Hayley was in the booth, stacking cases of Cabernet. As I ducked under the counter, she pointed to the ground around the booth.

"Trouble with the Christmas ornaments?"

I shrugged, but she held my gaze.

"Be careful."

"Got it."

Hayley looked at Connor. "She's being too agreeable."

Geez. It was a wonder I'd avoided death this long. "Listen,

you two. I promise I'll be careful. Now let's concentrate on getting through the rest of the festival."

We worked for a while in silence, stopping to take a break when Thomas, again dressed as the town fool, brought us steaming espressos.

"Glad to see you're still with us. Just don't do anything stupid."

"GOT IT."

Thomas did the big eye-roll thing. "Ouch. Someone's a tad testy."

I gulped the coffee and grabbed his arm. "Let's go get me a refill on the java and I'll feel better."

"Stay with Thomas," Connor said.

I looked over at Thomas, complete in jingle bells and tights. "Right. I feel much safer."

Leaning close, Connor whispered, "What's that saying? God protects babies and fools?"

I wasn't quite sure how to respond to that, so we walked down the row of tents, now filling up with exhibitors. As on the previous day the coffee was the big draw at the Sterling booth.

Ross read my mind as we walked up. "Nothing like a fabulous cup of coffee and a fruit pastry to draw a crowd."

Thomas patted his shoulder. Sighs of the single women sounded in the crowd as Thomas and Ross smiled at each other in obvious affection. Just not fair.

I took the coffee and scanned the crowd. The tone was more relaxed this morning. The judges finished tasting everything yesterday, and today was focused on donations for the hospital and having fun. Tonight at seven, an hour before the close of the festival, the winners of the competition would be announced.

Lady Godiva was handing out chocolates and a list of the day's activities. I grabbed one of each as she went past. At nine the center ring was again open for fencing. I walked over to the railing where the participants warmed up.

"How you feeling this morning?" Annie stood at my side. Her usually smiling face was void of emotion and she was pale, a grim reminder last night was real, and very close to home.

"I've been better. Sorry to get you into this."

"Stop. You couldn't have known. We were careful and it still happened. Don't forget, you also got us out of it. Besides"—she took my arm—"what are favorite cousins for?"

I gave her a smile. "Buy you a cup of coffee?"

"I can't. I've got to get to the clinic. I have a Pomeranian that needs surgery. I just stopped by to see how you were doing. Don't go having any more fun like last night without me."

"Believe me, I'll try. I just keep thinking fun's going to come looking for me."

"I'm getting that feeling too. It wouldn't hurt you to stick close to Connor today. Come to think of it, it might hurt you if you don't."

"I know. I just hate feeling scared. And if someone is determined, sooner or later I'll be alone, and that someone will get their chance."

Annie opened her mouth, and I raised my hand to stop her next words. "Don't get me wrong. I'll be careful. I won't make it easy on anyone. Now go."

I gave her a quick hug and headed back to Sterling for a refill. As I walked away, Antonia was ahead in the crowd.

I didn't want a repeat of the same discussion regarding my safety.

The moment she stopped in front of me, I began speaking. "I'm fine, Antonia, and if it's all the same to you, I'd really rather not talk about it."

Antonia looked me up and down and stamped her cane. "What nonsense. Of course you're fine. Anyone can see that."

"I thought you might want to talk about last night."

"What for? If you'd seen the person, you would have told the police, and we'd be standing here having a much different conversation. As it is, nothing was accomplished."

"There's only one thing that could have happened last night. Someone watched us walk you back up the hill. They knew we'd return and be alone on the festival grounds."

"When I saw the lights were out, I immediately called the police." Antonia paused. "I don't know exactly when they were turned off. At that point, of course, I tried to find out where everyone was, but it wasn't easy. Francesca and Brice weren't planning on coming back to the house, so I don't know where they were."

"What about everyone else?"

"Veronica said she was in her car driving back from town, and Stephen said he'd already returned and was working in the fermentation building." Antonia looked away. "Chantal is unfortunately still sleeping in. I have no idea where she was last night. Believe me, I've thought about it. Nothing I can tell you about last night will help."

"Do you think you might be too close to everyone involved to be objective?"

Antonia shook her head. "I've understood from the

beginning, since Todd was killed, not to mention what happened to Marvin, that someone under my roof was responsible. Nothing is that random in life. Nothing."

"I'm close to finding the answer. I know I'm close, otherwise last night wouldn't have happened."

Antonia patted my arm stiffly. "I know you are, and so does someone else, but I wouldn't think of joining the hordes and telling you to be careful. Surely you know that. Just find them, before they find you."

I wished she'd just settled for telling me to be careful. "Right. I'll try and do that."

Thirty-three

I SPENT the rest of the morning with Connor and Hayley in the booth.

Lucas stopped by and asked how I was, but anyone could tell he was there to see Hayley. He gave her a hug and smiled. "I'm allowed. Off duty."

"Did your guys find anything to help figure out who was shooting at us last night?"

Lucas started to shake his head.

I grabbed his arm and held his gaze. "The thing is, I'm a little spooked. Anything you can tell me would be nice to know."

Lucas started to rub his eyes, something the men in my life seem to do a lot. "Penny, even if we were going to have that conversation, do you think this is the place?"

I looked around. Pretty much every suspect was within two hundred yards of where we stood. "Yeah, okay. I get it. I could come down to the station . . ."

"You're fine here. It wouldn't hurt you to stay put for a change. For now, mind if I borrow your assistant manager for a while?"

"Sure. Go enjoy yourselves. Don't mind me. I'll just try to stay alive in the meantime."

Connor raised his eyebrows. "Go ahead, Hayley. Penny can stay here and help me. We've got enough out for the rest of the afternoon, if you want to take longer."

"Thanks, Connor." Hayley looked at Lucas. "I know he's got the afternoon shift, so either way, I'll be back."

They looked so happy together and Hayley deserved the time off. My irritation passed. "Go have some fun." Lucas was doing what he could.

Lucas leaned toward me as he passed by and whispered, "Red high heels are hell to wear through the woods at night."

"Maybe they weren't being worn. Maybe they were just dropped."

"Maybe."

"Thanks."

"You've earned the right to know. Anyway"—he smiled at Hayley—"I almost feel like you're sort of family . . . more than Hayley's aunt, sort of an older . . ."

The smile froze on my face.

"Not that you look old . . ."

"Skip it."

Lucas, with wisdom beyond his years, grabbed Hayley and disappeared into the crowd.

Connor was laughing.

"I didn't want to hear the next words out of his mouth. If they included the word 'old,' then he can keep them to himself, in my opinion."

"Well, if that's your opinion, then you stick with it."

"You aren't funny. Hayley's only twelve years younger than me. That isn't all that much. I mean, we like the same music, the same designers. We even have the same hairstylist."

"The same silver streaks . . ."

"Don't even go there."

Still laughing, he turned toward the counter and a group that approached the booth.

I could still see Chantal in that red dress yesterday as she danced with Thomas, her brunette hair gleaming in the sun. She'd worn red heels.

"Penny!"

Startled, I looked over at Connor.

"You think maybe you could help me over here?"

There was a crowd of tourists surrounding our booth, all decked out in the same shorts and hats and with the same cameras. There was one guy up front waving a tall plastic sunflower around. The tour guide.

"Ah, sure. Sorry." Over the next several hours we were kept busy. Connor and I were as much an attraction as the wine. They were fascinated that we actually grew the grapes that made the wine they were buying. And drinking. With a heavy hand.

I looked around the booth. We'd brought more than we'd hoped to sell and had gone through almost all of it. A winery is never an easy business, and it's one you go into as much for love as money. The smile on Connor's face left any words unnecessary.

Things were decidedly looser than the day before. The music was loud and dancers shed outer clothing in spite of the chill in the air. The sky had darkened and clouds were rolling in. I pulled a strand of hair over my shoulder. It looked like a corkscrew. Rain was definitely on the way. Hopefully it'd hold off until after the awards ceremony this evening.

Hayley returned happy and relaxed. Lucas left the festival and Hayley's eyes followed him as he made his way through the crowd.

Connor was next to me. "Want to grab a late lunch? Hayley can handle the buyers now. Besides, we don't have much left."

"Let's go."

"Hayley, you know what to do." Connor grabbed a half bottle of last year's Chardonnay off the counter. Quiche Lorraine from Sterling completed the meal, and we moved to the same table we'd eaten at the day before. Connor took his jacket off and offered it to me as we sat.

I took a bite of the quiche. "I don't know if I'm just hungry or if this is amazingly good."

"I think it's just the company."

It caught me off guard. "Thanks."

There was a twinkle in his eyes. "I meant *my* company."

I swatted him on the shoulder and went back to watching the crowds, now separated into two groups: the ones still dancing on the center stage and those beginning to make their way to the large tent where the awards ceremony was to be held.

I glanced at my watch. "Just a couple of hours before the end of the festival."

Connor nodded. "I wonder how this will turn out, especially for Martinelli. There isn't a year I can remember that they didn't dominate. We've got three wines entered, and at the risk of sounding immodest, they're really strong vintages. Still, it's rare for a first-year entry to win." He shrugged, but I could feel his excitement. It was contagious.

"Don't count yourself short. If anyone can pull off a first-year win, it's you."

"It's *us*."

The breeze was stronger now. I pulled the jacket closer to me.

"Cold?"

"Just a bit. I think they're going to be glad they've put up the tent." I raised my glass. "I wouldn't want you to get wet while accepting the award for this."

Thirty-four

WHEN we returned to the booth, Hayley had finished packing up the few cases left. She handed me a small pile of postcards. "These sold as well as anything else at the festival."

"I need to get back into the fields and get some new shots." I looked at the pictures. Again, the shot of the Martinelli Winery was on top and again, the feeling returned that I couldn't see something that was right in front of me.

I raised my eyes to the top of the hill, toward the same view as the picture. The time of day was different. In the dusk there was a glow of lights from the windows. The weather was certainly different, the glorious blue of the sky in the print now replaced with dark, ominous clouds hovering over the winery.

The wind whipped the flags on top of the tents, bringing

me back to the present. "Come on. Let's get in and grab some good seats."

"Penny's right," Connor said. "We can wait and come back tomorrow to clean out the booth. Most people are doing that."

I looked around. The dancing had stopped and there was music from the main tent. Ross was busy in the Sterling booth, having the oven and roaster to contend with, but the remainder of the booths were completely empty. We needed to get inside. Ross was thinking along the same lines and shouted that Thomas had saved seats for all of us.

The three of us walked into the brightly lit tent, with its cheerful stripes and garlands of grapevines twirled around the supporting posts and the canopy of the center stage. The ceiling was completely hidden behind bunches of oversized grapes and leaves that draped above the crowd. The effect was that I had somehow shrunk and was out in the fields under the vines. The wind outside made the contrasting warmth all the more welcome, as did the beat of the rain, big drops that hit the ground right outside the tent.

Connor looked back over his shoulder. "Just made it."

Thomas waved at us from the fourth row and we worked our way through the crowd. It took some time, as other winery managers and owners stopped us along the way, some to talk about the festival in general and others to ask if we were finished with our harvest. It was a friendly competition, unlike some of the other awards wineries vied for, and the conversation was amicable.

We managed to get to our seats just as the lights dimmed. The judges were seated to the left of the stage, and to the right a table held numerous trophies and ribbons.

While the judges introduced themselves, I scanned the program. We were entered in three categories: Best in Cabernet, Best in Syrah and Best New Entry. The first two were long shots, and would likely go to one of the larger wineries. Best New Entry was our strongest chance to walk away with a trophy.

The judges began the presentations, going through the list of white wines first. Stephen was in the second row, with Veronica on one side and Chantal on the other. Veronica leaned forward, toward the stage, but Chantal tugged at a strand of her hair and scanned the crowd. She perked right up when she glanced over her shoulder and caught a glimpse of Connor. She tossed her hair and gave him a little finger wave. Connor nodded in her direction then studied the program.

I leaned over. "Something interesting in the program?"

"Not interesting, but certainly less trouble."

Antonia stood to the side of the stage. Her long black dress appeared blue with the stage lights. Her gaze rested on something at the back of the tent. I turned my head and looked down the row. Near the entrance Francesca stood several feet from Brice.

I watched Brice, the successful doctor, ever in control, even now. I wasn't sure how he managed to be in the same room with his wife, his mother-in-law and the sister-in-law he seduced, and still look smug and arrogant.

Francesca studied the judges and ignored him. She didn't have any wines up there yet, but her jaw was set as she watched the results and took notes.

The presence of these six people occupied my thoughts and I missed most of the program until I heard the winner called for Best New Entry—a small winery also here on a first-year invite. Not as new as us and, in my opinion, not as good. I looked at Hayley. She wore the disappointment on her face and I grabbed her hand.

"I feel like I've let you down," she said.

"Nonsense. Some of this is purely personal opinion, and it just wasn't our day." I hoped this was true and looked at Connor for support.

"Penny's right. We'll get them next time."

I listened to their gracious acceptance and watched as they made their way to the edge of the stage. As the final award of Best in Show was collected by another winery of long standing, I realized Martinelli Winery hadn't picked up a single recognition.

The slump in Stephen's shoulders was visible, but even more obvious was the change in Veronica. She was tense before; now she was rigid. As she turned away from Stephen, anger was evident in the set of her jaw and clamped lips.

There was anger in Antonia's face as well, but the greater emotion was disappointment. She was pale and leaned heavily on her cane. A man in the front row stood to offer her his seat, and she waved him away with her cane. The only Martinelli who seemed happy with the outcome was Francesca. She smiled at Antonia, but it was a sour smile and her eyes were hard. Granted, leaving Stephen the winery simply because he was the eldest male was completely outdated and, in light of the winery's performance, a bad decision, but Francesca seemed to relish the pain of her family. She deserved to be married to Brice.

Antonia moved toward us as we made our way to the aisle. Stephen, Veronica and Chantal pushed their way through the crowds as well and all of us met at the same spot. The seven of us stood for a moment before Connor and Stephen spoke at once.

"Tough to win the first year in . . ."

"Don't let it get to you; next year's around the corner . . ."

I studied Stephen and actually, he didn't look bad. He looked almost happy. Relieved. I guess it was better, even with disappointing results, to have the competition behind him. In contrast, Veronica looked pale and still. She moved to the edge of the group and didn't seem to follow the conversation. Chantal looked unconcerned and, as usual, beautiful in a red pashmina cape.

"Come back to the house with us," Antonia said.

"Yes, you must." Chantal pushed past me to stand near Connor. She managed to step on my foot and the heel of her stiletto dug into me. I looked down. Red.

"Ouch!"

"Oh, sorry. Was that your foot?"

"No. Just my last nerve."

Chantal looked back at me. "Huh?"

I shook my head. "Never mind." Connor's eyes twinkled. Laugh it up, funny boy.

"Antonia, I'm sure they're anxious to get home. We're all tired." Veronica tugged at her pearls.

Antonia looked at her. "If you're tired, feel free to go to bed once we're home. I'm not tired, and stop speaking for them." She looked at the three of us. "Come for a glass, although"— she glanced at Stephen—"with results like this, maybe you should bring the wine."

Stephen froze at the remark, the relaxed look of a moment earlier now gone.

Veronica gasped. "It was a tough day for all of us. I'm sure now is not the time to be pointing fingers."

Antonia waved her away with a pale hand. "I've heard enough. We'll pull out an earlier vintage, one fitting the occasion, and toast the success of Joyeux Winery."

"But we didn't win anything," I said.

"You competed well. Your time will come."

Hayley declined the invitation, choosing to stay with several managers still at the festival, and the rest of us made our way to the entrance of the tent. The rain was light at the moment, and we stood watching it fall on the empty fairgrounds.

"We can't walk up the path. Connor and I both have cars here, but I can only fit one more," I said.

"My car is here as well," Veronica said.

Chantal still held on to Connor's arm. "I'll ride in the truck with you, though it may be a tight squeeze."

I'd like to give her a tight squeeze. Around the throat.

"I'll ride with Connor. Chantal, you ride with Veronica." Antonia glanced over at me, and I smiled.

"Stephen, how about riding with me?" I asked.

Stephen mumbled something that could have been "sure" and walked off toward the parking lot.

Connor walked out beside me, "I'll wait for you at the parking entrance."

I nodded and caught up to Stephen. As we left the parking lot, Connor pulled in behind me to follow us up the hill.

When we were on the main road I looked over at Stephen. He kept his eyes straight ahead, his shoulders stiff. I only had a few moments alone with him but didn't know where to begin.

The silence was punctuated by the rhythm of raindrops against the car roof.

"I'm sure Connor is right and next year will be better."

Stephen snorted.

I took this as encouragement to continue, primarily because I wanted to. "Don't you think your results will be different next year?"

"Oh, you can believe me when I say it'll be more of the same, especially now that Marvin is gone." He shrugged. "I'm already dreading it."

"So why do it? I mean it. If you really don't want to do this, you shouldn't."

He turned his face toward me. "When someone you've been wanting approval from your entire life believes you can do something, wants to give you a chance to do something, whether or not you actually want to do it doesn't come into play."

Stephen had already said more than he ever had to me. We only had a few minutes more in the car.

I waited.

"I've tried, but the reality is, I'm just not cut out for this. Never was. Mother insisted on leaving me the winery. Did she ever ask me? No."

"She must have thought you were capable. Antonia would never do anything to the detriment of the winery."

"No, she wouldn't. Only to the detriment of her children."

"Antonia wouldn't want you to run the winery if you don't want to. In her own way, she wants you to be happy."

He threw up his hands. "I get it, but it isn't that easy. She has a mental block about leaving the winery to the oldest male because of some ancient history with my grandfather, and I'm stuck with my future handed to me."

We turned in to the driveway and Connor pulled in beside me. Ahead of us, Veronica and Chantal had parked and were out of the car. Stephen grew quiet but he was agitated. We watched as Connor offered his arm to Antonia for support and Chantal quickly claimed his other side.

I got out of the car and walked to the other side, waiting for Stephen.

Connor looked over his shoulder.

I waved him ahead. "Get Antonia out of the rain."

He nodded and turned toward the house.

Stephen pulled himself from the car and began to walk away from the house, toward the fermentation building.

Veronica ran to him and pulled him to where I stood. "What were you two talking about?"

"Just the festival and the awards results." I watched Connor help Antonia up the wet steps. "Next year things will be different for the Martinellis, I'm sure."

"Of course next year will be different," Veronica said. "You can't expect Stephen's improvements to have a positive impact the first year. There are always hurdles when changes take place."

Stephen held up his hand, anger in his eyes. "Veronica, that's enough. I won't do this anymore."

Once again he turned away. Veronica grabbed him but he shrugged her off. We stood and watched as he threw open the fermentation building door and disappeared inside the building.

Veronica turned to me. "I don't know what you said, but

the least you can do is help make it right." She turned and walked after Stephen.

I looked back at the house. Connor would assume we were right behind him. I wasn't sure how this was my fault, or what I'd say to make it better, but I was determined to hear the conversation between Veronica and Stephen, clearly a long time coming.

I hurried to the entrance of the building, stepped inside and closed the door behind me. The raised voices led me to the rear of the room, dim in the soft florescent light. When I saw Stephen I stopped. His hands were in front of his chest, palms pressed together, as though he prayed, pleaded, for Veronica to understand.

Veronica's voice reverberated through the building, high and shrill. "What do you mean you don't want to do this anymore? You have a chance to run one of the largest wineries in California and you want to turn it down? What exactly do you plan on doing instead?"

Stephen reached for her. "Veronica, I've given this a lot of thought. I want to do something else with my life."

Veronica pushed at him and turned away. "What else are you trained to do? Nothing, that's what. You were born to do this." She turned again to take his hands. "*We* were born to do this."

This time it was Stephen to push away, backing toward the rear wall. "No, Veronica, I mean it. I don't want to do this anymore."

He looked up and spotted me. "Penny, I want you to hear this too."

I walked over beside Veronica.

Stephen took a deep breath. "I've tried to learn this business, to understand the art of winemaking. All of the improvements that worked were Todd's ideas. It's true," he added, cutting off any objections Veronica might have made. "I haven't had a single suggestion that's had any value since, well, ever. Then I figured a couple of bad years would make Mother come to her senses and remove me. I've insured, in my own way, that this year's vintages wouldn't meet with Martinelli standards."

My thoughts went back to the last time I was in this building, back to the footsteps, the yeast and the broken bottle on the floor.

"You. You're the one sabotaging the wines. You're the one who ran from me that day."

Stephen looked at the both of us. "I want out."

"No," Veronica said. "Don't say anything else."

"Veronica, please."

"I mean it, Stephen. I don't want to hear another word." Veronica ran to the rear doors of the building and pulled them open. Lightning flashed, showing her outline as she disappeared into the wind and rain.

"We can't leave her alone out there." I moved across the floor, Stephen behind me.

"I'm sorry she's disappointed in me, but I mean it, Penny. I don't want this. I won't pay the rest of my life just because I was born first."

There, in the darkness, what I'd struggled to piece together was suddenly clear. Why hadn't I seen it before? Seen it in Stephen's clothing, in his driving. Heard it in Antonia's comments in the attic about children, birth certificates and the promise to her father for the firstborn to inherit.

I reached the door ahead of Stephen and stepped into the storm. The wind howled now and whipped rain across my face and into my eyes. I strained to see Veronica in the night. The wind slammed the door and I turned. Veronica stood behind me. The door had an open padlock and as I watched her push it in place and lock it, the last pieces fell into place.

"It was you. You killed Todd. You killed Marvin too."

She watched me through the rain. "You're just guessing."

"No guess. It was Stephen's clothes and his driving that really gave it away."

"What are you talking about? He can't drive or dress, but he doesn't do anything right. What does it matter?"

"Stephen can't match his clothes and he mixes up traffic signal colors."

Veronica moved closer.

I backed away, not feeling land beneath my heels.

"Yeah, so?"

"Did you know Stephen is color-blind?"

Veronica clapped her hands. "Good guess, but who cares? What does that have to do with anything?"

"Joanne told me Todd's father was adopted. She also said he was killed in a car accident, probably because he had the same problem with the signals Stephen does. They can't distinguish between certain colors. Also, Todd said on the night you killed him that Joanne wasn't letting him help with the wedding plans because he was color-blind. It runs in families. Stephen and Todd were related." I took a step toward her.

Veronica pulled a gun from her bag. "Keep going. Really, I must insist. What else gave it away?"

"The missing gun from the attic?"

She nodded. "Now talk."

I eyed the gun. "I should have guessed before now. Antonia

said something the other day in the attic, looking at birth certificates. She said there were three of them. Why would she say that if she only had three children? Who else was she thinking of? Then last night, she said she gave something up, something to keep the winery." I looked at Veronica. "Todd's father was Antonia's son, wasn't he?"

Veronica moved closer.

The ground shifted under my feet.

"Too bad you didn't figure it out earlier."

I tried to not to stare at the gun. "Does Stephen know?"

Veronica pushed the hair from her face. There wasn't a hint of indecision as she laughed. "Stephen? I haven't told him anything, not for twenty-two years."

She moved closer and, with the gun in my ribs, pushed me farther down the slope. I stumbled and risked a quick look. Fifty feet down, at least.

"You've been planning this for twenty-two years?"

"Of course not. I wouldn't have done anything if Todd hadn't come to work here, but he was with Antonia every day. There was too much risk she'd see something, hear something. What if Todd told her his father was given up for adoption? What if the dates came up? I didn't care how unlikely it was. You think I was going to take that chance?"

"How did you find out about Todd's father?" I glanced to the side. The path down to the festival grounds was somewhere to my left.

"I worked at the hospital, remember? A nurse, invisible, cleaning up after people. Little more than a servant. Then as a volunteer in the office. Much nicer. The records are all there, if you know where to look."

The wind had calmed a bit and the rain had lessened. Connor must have realized we weren't behind him. Surely he'd come. "How did you get a copy of the birth certificate? I thought those things were kept locked."

Veronica raised her voice. "I *said* I worked at the hospital. I made myself indispensable and had keys to the records and documents rooms. I showed a copy to Todd the night I killed him. At the crusher. I dropped it in. When he reached for it, well, then it was easy."

"The torn paper that Lucas found. That's how you got Todd out there?"

Veronica nodded. "I said I needed to tell him something personal. Imagine"—she smiled—"just moments before he died, Todd found out Antonia was his grandmother."

"How did you know Antonia had a child?"

Veronica shrugged. "When I started dating Stephen, I went through the family records. I wanted to know more about this family than anyone, and I do. I found the birth certificate and made a copy. It's nice to know things about people, isn't it? Imagine Antonia having a baby out of wedlock. My perfect, perfect mother-in-law with an illegitimate child. How do you think she'd feel, knowing she had her grandson right here and didn't even realize it?"

"Stephen was her legitimate heir. She might have decided to leave things as they are."

Veronica laughed, holding the gun with both hands. "Do you think I've put up with Antonia all these years to take that chance? It's my destiny to run this winery."

"Think, Veronica. Everyone knows we're out here, just the three of us."

"Well, there are only two right now, and your falling

wouldn't be hard to believe. Accidents happen, and you're known for being impetuous. Besides, you haven't had a chance to tell anyone your theory, so why would anyone suspect I wanted to kill you?"

Damn. Good point.

"So what do we do now?"

"I need to run to get help for you."

"I don't need help."

"You will after you hit the bottom." She swung the gun toward my shoulder. I turned away and heard a snap as the gun landed on my collarbone. The pain was blinding and brought my feet out from under me, but instead of falling backward off the hill, I twisted to the side. I landed in the mud on my knees and clung to the side of the slope.

Veronica moved above me, raised her foot and dug her heel into the back of my hand.

"I see you hurt your hand, Penny. Cut it in the woods last night?" She then raised her foot and kicked at my shoulder. The pain exploded in my head when she made contact with the broken bone, but I kept my grip on the jagged slope. Dirt and mud got under my nails. A rock sliced into my knee.

When she raised her leg to kick me again I ducked, and this time her foot glanced off my shoulder. I grabbed her leg and pulled her forward. Veronica screamed, dropped the gun and began to slide down the hill. She reached into the dark and grabbed my arm. We both slipped farther down the ledge. With my other hand, I searched the slope. Tree roots. I clung to them as Veronica pulled at my arm.

"Veronica!" I heard Stephen before I could see him. He was flat on the ground above me, his arm out over the ledge above my head.

My fingers slipped down the muddy roots.

Stephen looked at me. "Take my hands."

"Get away from us," Veronica said.

"Give it up. It's over." I raised my eyes toward Stephen. "I can't hold the both of us."

He pushed himself farther over the ledge and grasped my arm.

"You kicked her," he watched his wife. "I saw you kick her. Why would you do such a thing and what's she talking about? What's over?"

Veronica dug her nails into my skin. "Everything. I'm losing everything, but I won't go back to what I had before."

"Whatever you're afraid of losing, it isn't worth this," Stephen said.

"That's because you've always had it. You don't know what's it's like to do without."

Stephen tightened his grip on me. His jaw was set and he held my eyes. "I'm not letting go."

I nodded, and he turned toward Veronica.

"It was you, wasn't it? For what? The winery? Is that all I'm good for?" He nodded at the field below. "Some lousy grapes? You've hurt people. Marvin and Todd didn't deserve to die. How could you do something so terrible?" He shook his head, a puzzled look on his face. "The worst part is you didn't need to, Veronica. All you had to do was ask. After it was mine, I would have given it to you if you wanted it that much. Just given it."

Stephen faced me and, with determination I'd not suspected him capable of, he pulled at my arm.

I moaned as my shoulder strained and Veronica's nails dug into my skin. Stephen didn't let go and Veronica's grip tightened.

"I'm not letting go of her," Veronica said. "If I go over the side, I'll take her with me. I swear."

Stephen shook his head. "Don't add anything else to your list of regrets. You're still the woman I married. I think you loved me at one point. I know I loved you and I don't want anything to happen to you."

"Look at what I've done. I could have had everything. We could have had it together."

Stephen reached toward Veronica with his other arm. "I thought we did. Here, take my hand. You need help. We can find someone to help you."

"It wasn't just for the winery. You've always been good to me and, in my own way, I really did love you."

"I know. Take my hand."

Veronica paused, then reached for Stephen just as he cried out. The world seemed to tilt before the slope slipped under our weight. Stephen grabbed for her, but the rain-soaked hill shifted and pulled her away. She raised her hands above her head to reach for him and appeared to hang, suspended, before she plunged into the darkness. I looked at Stephen through the rain, at what he clutched in his fingers. Pearls.

Thirty-five

L UCAS didn't seem surprised when I turned up with my third body of the week, which worried me a bit. I didn't want this to become a habit. A medic wrapped my arm in a sling and cleaned and bandaged the scratches. As he worked, I told Lucas about Veronica. I asked if I could be the one to tell Antonia, and he nodded.

"We need to speak with Stephen, but I'll leave Antonia to you."

I got the chance the next day with a knock on the front door.

She followed me into the sunroom, walked to the French doors and looked out at the vineyards. "We didn't get a chance to talk last night."

"This can wait if you aren't ready."

She raised her hand. "I wouldn't be here if I weren't ready

to talk about it." She paused. "Before we talk, though, how are you?"

"I'm a little bruised and I've got a broken collarbone. Thanks for asking." I couldn't help it; even I heard the surprise in my voice.

"What? I'm perfectly aware of the norms of social etiquette. I just don't choose to follow them often." She paused. "I'm going to try to remedy that in the future."

"That would be nice, Antonia."

She nodded. "Now then, since we've established you're going to be fine, I will continue. I saw Stephen and know he doesn't want the winery. Also, I know he was the one responsible for the sabotage." She shifted. "I suppose it could be said I didn't actually ask if he wanted to be in charge. It's something I've wanted for so long, sacrificed so much for, it didn't even occur to me that my largesse would be rebuffed."

"Stephen loves you and wants you to be proud of him. He just needs to do something different with his life."

Antonia nodded. "I understand that now. He's moving into the city. Wants a job in advertising. Maybe he can handle the advertising for the winery—"

"And maybe you should let him decide."

She stopped and nodded. "I haven't had to change my ways in a long while. It's going to take some time. Now, Stephen said you knew Veronica killed Todd and Marvin. He didn't know how you knew. I want you to tell me."

I thought back. "It was the picture. It was right in front of me in the picture."

Antonia waved her hand and some of the old Antonia was visible. "Explain yourself."

"It was the picture I took the day before the murder. Remember when you said the bushes were all overgrown and I should have waited?"

"You should have. The gardeners came two days later."

"Exactly. Then it would have been too late. Don't you see? The shrubs were high above the winery office window. I watched the gardeners cut them away without putting it together. Veronica had an alibi because Marvin said he saw her from that window, when he couldn't possibly have seen into the kitchen because of the shrubs."

Antonia looked at me and nodded. "That meant he saw her somewhere else."

"I'm guessing when he brought his dinner tray back to the house, he saw her outside the fermenting building on her way to meet Todd. He knew she was lying when she said she was in the kitchen making tea. He'd just been in the kitchen. He knew she wasn't there."

"So he gave her an alibi by saying he saw her there from the winery office, but it was impossible because the shrubs blocked the view."

I nodded. "Then he had a chance to blackmail her."

Antonia turned from the window. "Why? Why would Veronica murder Todd?"

I wasn't going to tell her Todd was her grandson. Maybe someday, but not now, so soon after she'd lost him and didn't even realize it. "Veronica didn't tell me. I'm not sure she had a plan. She was just afraid of anyone who threatened Stephen's position." Antonia watched me for a moment then nodded.

I joined her at the window and spotted Chantal talking with Connor in the field. "Chantal came with you?"

"We're on our way to the clinic. She wants to try again.

For the first time, it's her idea." Antonia smiled at me. "I have hope."

I nodded. "It's a good first step." I thought of Martinelli Winery and the loss of Todd, Marvin and even Veronica. "What will you do?"

She turned to me and there was a spark in her eyes. "To be honest, I wasn't ready to give up the reins just yet. Now I need to rebuild the brand name of Martinelli. The challenge will be invigorating. I'll need to decide on a new heir, one who will run it the way I want it run, but I don't need to decide that now."

I thought of Francesca and what her conniving had cost Marilyn. I'd promised Francesca I wouldn't tell Antonia the story, and I'd keep that promise. On the other hand . . .

"At some point, ask Marilyn how Francesca purchased her land. Tell her I said for you to come. Tell her you want to hear the entire story."

Antonia watched me for a moment. "I'll be sure to do that. And believe me, if I don't like the way it was handled, I'll make it right, even if I need to use Francesca's inheritance to do it."

"I know you will." She smiled and shrugged.

"Let's leave that for the time being. The only problem I have right now is that I don't have a winery manager."

"The only manager I know who's really exceptional is Connor."

"No doubt." Antonia's eyes gazed out on the fields. She didn't turn to me and the silence lengthened. I knew she had an idea on how to solve her dilemma and I didn't think I was going to like it.

"I'm not giving him up without a fight, Antonia." The thought of the winery without Connor was unthinkable.

Hayley wasn't ready but, beyond that, Connor was the heart of Joyeux. What the loss would mean to me was something I couldn't imagine.

Antonia's next words alleviated my worst fears. "I was thinking we could work something out. Our land is adjacent, which is a big plus. I realize we grow the same varietals but I have my own style of winemaking, as does Connor. Hayley needs Connor's guidance, but she's ready for more responsibility. And after this past week, I think we've proven we can work together. Besides"—she turned to look at me—"you're family."

"We certainly have a lot of shared history." I paused. "I never got a chance to thank you for helping Aunt Monique at the end."

She didn't move. "You never need to. Now"—she turned toward the door—"I need to go."

She walked down the path.

So many things had changed in just a week. The truth had been captured in a single photo, something I would never underestimate again. I thought about what Antonia wanted. There was probably a way for Connor to manage both wineries. Antonia would continue to make most of the decisions on Martinelli, while Connor would remain in charge of Joyeux Winery, with Hayley's help.

Antonia waved to Chantal and turned toward the car. Chantal wore a subdued, for her, black suit, the collar of a red blouse at the neckline. She walked with Connor and tucked her arm in his. Some things might have changed, but other things remained constant.

A twinge of annoyance went through me, as usual, and I opened the French doors to join them.

WELL-CRAFTED MYSTERIES
FROM BERKLEY PRIME CRIME

- **Earlene Fowler** Don't miss these Agatha Award–winning quilting mysteries featuring Benni Harper.

- **Monica Ferris** These *USA Today* bestselling Needlecraft Mysteries include free knitting patterns.

- **Laura Childs** Her Scrapbooking Mysteries offer tips to satisfy the most die-hard crafters.

- **Maggie Sefton** These popular Knitting Mysteries come with knitting patterns and recipes.

- **Lucy Lawrence** These brilliant Decoupage Mysteries involve cutouts, glue, and varnish.

- **Elizabeth Lynn Casey** The Southern Sewing Circle Mysteries are filled with friends, southern charm—and murder.

M5G0610